In the Dead of Summer

In the Dead
of Summer

AN AMANDA PEPPER MYSTERY

Gillian Roberts

BALLANTINE BOOKS · New York

Library of Congress Cataloging-in-Publication Data
Roberts, Gillian.
  In the dead of summer / by Gillian Roberts.
    p.   cm.
  ISBN 0-345-39136-5
  I. Title.
PS3557.R356I5   1995
813′.54—dc20   95-7627
                                                                   CIP

Manufactured in the United States of America

First Edition: September 1995

10 9 8 7 6 5 4 3 2 1

For Jane Walsh and Howard Pearlstein,
with Sisterly Love

Special thanks and gratitude to Susan Dunlap and Marilyn Wallace for sharing their considerable talents with me, and to the Emergency Muse Cooperative—Freddie Greene, Maggie Mascow, and Helen Preston—for riding to the rescue when needed.

In the Dead of Summer

One

REETINGS from the Big Lemon, formerly known as the City of Brotherly Love.

The good news: a Duke University study officially declared Philadelphia number one in the nation.

The bad news: the study had tested which American city had the highest level of hostility. We outmeaned the Big Apple.

The researchers hadn't polled me, but truth is, if they'd questioned me the day of my summer school faculty orientation meeting, I wouldn't have skewed their findings. Ten minutes into our prep session, I was skyrocketing off the hostility meter. My principal and his verbose inanities had that effect on me. So did

3

the prospect of trying to teach in an under-air-conditioned building through the hottest weeks of the year.

My face hardened into what from the inside felt distinctly like a glower.

I have done my share of scowling, frowning, grimacing, and pouting, but this was my first glower. This was big-time, the face you made when the school doors clanged shut and you realized that while the lucky portion of humanity roasted weenies, you yourself would roast in the company of pubescents with whom you had nothing in common except a species designation.

This was the glower of being unable to remember why it was I had chosen to be a teacher. I was never naïve enough to be attracted by the pay, so what had it been? Had I really thought I'd make a difference? That I could single-handedly turn the tide of the twentieth century and make old-fashioned, nonelectronic, nondigitalized objects like books and ideas and written and spoken language valuable commodities again?

I had signed up for summer school teaching for economic reasons. But I'd also been excited by this particular program, working with teachers from all over the Delaware Valley and with students from all sorts of backgrounds. The exchange of ideas, the possibilities of the two months, were invigorating.

But ten minutes into our prep session it was obvious that Maurice Havermeyer, Ph.D., principal of Philly Prep, who had, as he pointed out, written the grant application that funded this program, was going to make sure nothing innovative or creative took place.

I submit to the bench example A: the memo in my hand from my leader. "Miss Pepper, in the light of our mandate to integrate cultural diversity sensitivity throughout the curriculum this summer, please be advised that a sufficient number of copies of *Romeo and Juliet* are in the book room. Also, we have access to a tape of *West Side Story*, if you requisition it three days in advance."

There isn't much in life I can control. But surely viewing *West Side Story* again, hearing Richard Beymer pretend to sing "Maria" again, was one of those few things.

4

English departments are always the designated carriers of culture. That's okay with me. But nowadays they've also been appointed society's repairpeople. When attitudes, values, discipline, job-application skills, etiquette, and sensitivity training are required, the English teacher is the appointed handyperson. Other instructors teach their subjects. We are supposed to teach Life, and if only we taught a little harder or better, all would be well with the world.

Havermeyer's memo implied that he had extended the multicultural mandate to other departments as well, although I knew that was a pose. What variety of diversity could he dream up for the math teacher? To use both Arabic and Roman numbers, perhaps? And were foreign language teachers required to teach languages other than their subject, to maintain the PC quotient?

My leader had avidly pursued this lucrative summer gig, during which we became something akin to a magnet school. Instead of classrooms filled only with our usual population of overprivileged underachievers, this summer we also had *under*privileged underachievers. Scholarship kids. Recent immigrants. Experimental kids, or, more accurately, adolescents who were part of a public-private educational experiment.

Be careful what you ask for. Having gotten what he wanted, Maurice Havermeyer, whose Ph.D. is probably in Euphemisms, was panicked. He apparently had just now realized that diversity implied differences, and he seemed terrified by the concept. He stood on the auditorium stage and mopped his broad forehead. "We anticipate a most unique session for this venerable establishment," he said.

Redline that sentence, Maurice, beginning with the royal *we* and crossing out the redundant *most* before unique. I wanted to tape his mouth shut until he learned to speak. I entertained myself by wondering what would happen if I rushed onto the stage next to Havermeyer and did a simultaneous translation into comprehensible English.

"It is heartwarming to discern so many old and for-the-moment new visages," he said. I controlled the urge to gag. About thirty visages sat sprinkled around the auditorium. We

5

didn't know each other well enough to clump or huddle, because most of the summer staff was imported and Havermeyer had not seen fit to introduce us before he began his Ode to Diversity. We would have comfortably fit into a classroom. But that would have encouraged intimacy, or a sense of equality, concepts that appealed to Havermeyer only when applied to others. So he spoke down from above and kept us feeling like marooned survivors on an archipelago.

"It is a pleasure," he intoned, "to experience the fresh air of change as it wafts into Philly Prep."

This produced a ripple of rueful laughter. Any fresh air would have been welcome, but virtually nothing wafted from the ancient air conditioner except exhausted, endlessly recycled gasps.

Havermeyer frowned. His script hadn't included a pause for snickers. And then he got it. "Ahhh," he said, "as you are obviously aware, we are experiencing temporary difficulties with our climate control apparatus. Remember, this building was constructed long before man knew how to manipulate his environment, temperaturewise. Please bear with us, particularly during this unseasonable heat which in any case, I trust, will ebb forthwith."

Forthwith, indeed. And unseasonable? What calendar, what climate, had he been studying? This was summer, the infamous season of get-out-of-here, when anyone who could afford to do so escaped.

Even two hundred years ago, when one-tenth of the population died in four months of yellow fever, the disease was blamed on the summer climate. Philadelphia was always a low, level town, perhaps the hottest and dampest of all the seaports—hotter even than Charleston, Savannah, or the West Indies, people said. I know this because my semisignificant other, C. K. Mackenzie, was recuperating from a shell-shocked leg that itched beneath its cast in the summer heat, and was making sure he stayed depressed by reading and sharing more than I ever wanted to know about the 1793 Great Yellow Fever Epidemic. "Now that was a *really* bad summer," he was fond of saying.

That was supposed to make us feel better about his leg and my teaching obligations.

In any case, Havermeyer's "unseasonable" tag was a lie, an excuse for not having had the air-conditioning system fixed in time. "But in any case and any clime—" he now said, pausing to give us time to admire his ability to create an archaic, annoying segue from the wretched air-conditioning to the work ahead of us. We all, from what I could see, managed to contain our awe. "—we must all keep a cool head this summer."

I wondered if he'd let us vote as to whose cool head we could collectively keep.

Havermeyer waved the list of summer students' names and their schools of origin. We all had copies of it, so that nobody had to say words like *poor* or *black* or *Asian* or *Latino* out loud. Despite the fact that motivated young adults—or people who loved and believed in them—were paying good money so they might sweat through physics, geometry, French II, and writing skills, their odd names, their *diversity*, Havermeyer implied, translated into a dire potential for civil uprising. He made everything that had intrigued me sound inflammatory and to be avoided.

Eventually he completed a meaningless spiel about how the staff as well as the students came from a mix of backgrounds ("a heterogeneous commingling of variegated prior experiential modes," I believe he said)—and our need to work in harmony for the greater good ("... the potential for synthesizing differentiated pedagogical philosophies and styles ..."). I wondered if anyone else questioned the man's right to guide instruction, given his inability to speak the Mother Tongue ("... producing a synergistic fusion of ..."). It's an odd world in which a Rodney King is a better communicator than the idiotic and incomprehensible Ph.D.'d headmaster of a private school. "Can we all get along?" is exquisite and to the point and would have been a waft and a half of fresh air in the stuffy auditorium.

It doesn't look good for a teacher to fidget, or fall asleep, or throw paper airplanes or spitballs, so I tried to clear my brain, to find an un-Philadelphian wellspring of serenity deep inside me.

I searched, but failed to find it.

Havermeyer continued his multisyllabic mutilation of any possible meaning.

"What is *wrong* with that man?" a stern-faced woman three seats over muttered. She rolled brown eyes in disgust, then looked at me as if she expected an answer.

Why me? Was I stamped PROPERTY OF PHILLY PREP? "Far as I know, pretty much everything," I whispered.

She shook her head and put her hands into a position of prayer.

Havermeyer concluded his gibberish. Now, when we'd all been stupefied, he had us introduce ourselves, one by one, and, he said, "explain what brings you to us this summer," as if he were a cruise ship's activities director.

I felt instead as if I were at a meeting of Educators Anonymous. "I'm Mandy P.," I'd say. "And I have a problem with surviving. I've been sinking economically for a long while, but I hit bottom when my landlord threatened another rent increase. So, well, I realized I needed help, and so I'm here." And everyone would applaud and be supportive.

The rest of the staff was either less resentful or less frivolous than I, and one by one they stood and duly said their names, their schools of origin, and what they would be teaching this summer. I tried to memorize them—employing all the build-a-better-memory games I'd read in magazines. But no sparkling personality called herself Diamond the way they always do in those articles, and Mrs. Hart, who should have taught biology or at least phys ed or health, if she'd wanted to be helpful, was instead an algebra teacher. Phyllis Something-Sibilant taught Biology I. I couldn't figure out how to make that connect, or how to remember Walt Smith, whose looks were as nondescript as his last name.

He was one of several new men being scoped out by the female faculty. The pickings looked dismal. Of course we hadn't had time to find out what really counts—personality, brains, sensitivity . . . but Walt Smith's stubble and sweat-stained beer belly didn't exactly catch the eye.

Nor did the next fellow, a twerpish sort named Lowell Diggs. I thought I might be able to remember that one. Low Diggs—Diggs Low. Something molelike about his features. Of course, I had the option of not remembering him at all. He was less than prepossessing. Scrawny and stoop-shouldered, he had a sharp nose and very little face below that, as if nature had made her point with the nose and then lost interest, so that his face dribbled back into his neck. He also had a piece of toilet paper clinging to a bloody spot on his cheek.

The eye-roller who'd wondered what was wrong with Havermeyer turned out to be a history teacher with the exotic name of Aldis Fellows. All Dese Fellas, I said to myself, superimposing an image of a lot of *his*tory—dead male kings and warriors—over her name. As long as I didn't call her Genghis—she was really forbidding-looking—she might justify the six thousand memory articles I'd read and forgotten.

There were familiar faces, too, permanent members of the home team, and as they introduced themselves, I focused on a lost, long-winged flying insect making the rounds of the auditorium and barely heard the rest of the string of names.

Except for one. First of all, and maybe second and third of all, he was the best-looking male in the room—not a great feat, perhaps, given the competition, but all the same, noticeable. The uncontested faculty centerfold. He cleared his throat. "I'm Bartholomew Dennison," he said. "I've taught government and social studies out West for a long time, but as an American history buff, I defied Horace Greeley and went East. I've been subbing for a time, and I'll be in King of Prussia starting in September."

Before he sat down, he held up one hand. "By the way, I'm actually Bartholomew Dennison the Fifth. A long family tradition, although not, perhaps, a wise one. Anyway, the other tradition, for which I am grateful, is that we're called by our number. My father was Mr. Four and I've been Five—or sometimes even Mr. Five, if you want to be formal. I get confused if you use my impossible given name." He sat down.

Five. Even I could remember that.

Every woman in the room smiled at him. He had that effect. Even on Moira DeLong, one of the regular Philly Prep staff, a French and Spanish teacher in her sixties who wore a lorgnette and had hitherto exhibited passion only for Romance languages and her white Persian cat. Moira stretched burgundy-painted lips into a smile for Mr. Five.

And Edie Friedman, who had been stocking a hope chest since third grade and was high on supplies but running out of hope, looked near fainting with renewed optimism. Or maybe it was just the heat.

My turn. I stood up and said, "I'm Amanda Pepper. I teach English, all grades, at Philly Prep regularly, and I'll be teaching Communication Skills Workshops this summer." I sat down. Mr. Five smiled at me in a way that suggested we had just met someplace much nicer and more intimate than here, the two of us and nobody else. I returned the smile. It was the least I could do.

If it were not for C. K. Mackenzie, with whom I was tiptoeing toward an understanding, Five's smile might have made for a charged summer.

I sighed and returned to glowering.

Two

I WAS sorting file folders, deciding which were recyclable for the summer students and trying to forget Havermeyer's pompous and patronizing talk, when the fellow with the pointy nose tapped on the frame of my open door. Damn—what was his name? It was the one I'd been sure I could remember. Something ground-level. Rodentlike. Mr. Weasel? Bottom? Hole? Pitt?

"I'm glad you're alone," he said. The patch of toilet paper with its red-brown bull's-eye was still stuck to his cheek. "Didn't mean to be rude, but it seemed awkward to go through the formalities down there with all the others."

He whined even when presumably trying to be endearing, but his pleasantries struck me as decidedly weird. What others? And *what* was his name? Little? Could that be it? He wasn't exactly a giant, about five-eight, my height. But insignificant. Mr. Down? Downs?

I must remember to never read another article on improving my memory.

"Don't take this the wrong way," he said, "but it's been my experience that the older generation exaggerates when trying to make a match."

Although the idea made the pit of my stomach contract, mention of the words *older generation* and *match* put me on red alert and gave the situation an imprint like guilty fingerprints at a crime scene. *Ma*, I mentally whined, *not again*. I refused to accept the idea.

"But this time," he continued, "every word was true." He was a head shaker, too, nodding agreement with himself. Nod, nod. "I hope you feel the same. Do you?"

"Excuse me," I said, "but there seems to be some misunderstanding. Do I know you? Have we met before?"

"Not in person. I would never have forgotten."

Was he implying we had met in a past life, or via astral projection?

"But your picture didn't do you justice. Did mine?"

"Your what?"

"Photo. Did it do me justice?"

I didn't know how to answer. First of all, what would be justice as far as his likeness was concerned? His features, what there were of them, crumpled into worried insecurity. Pathetic. We were going to work in the same building for the next two months. I tried to be gentle and discreet. "Before we get to that—I was just wondering exactly when was it you saw my photo. I mean, which photo was it again?"

She wouldn't give a total stranger a picture of me, would she?

"You were wearing a big straw hat. It hid your hair, which is, I might say, a lovely hue. Chestnut, is that what they'd call it?"

I remembered the snapshot. It had been taken when I was in college, ten years ago, and the straw hat completely shadowed my face. The only thing clear in that picture was that I was either female or a guy with severe hormone problems. How desperate was this man? How desperate was she?

"Aunt Melba showed it to me three weeks ago, when I was visiting her. Melba Diggs." He nodded and paused, waiting for my happy shout of recognition.

I had never heard of the woman, but Diggs was the name I had heard in the auditorium. Something Diggs. Shovel? "Is Aunt Melba still"—time to reveal the horrible truth—"enjoying Florida?" I asked.

He nodded extravigorously.

Damn. I knew only one woman in Florida, and she wasn't Melba Diggs, but it didn't matter, because the woman I knew knew everyone else. Particularly anyone in contact with single males.

"Well," he said, "I mean, it wasn't Aunt Melba's photo, of course, it was your mother's. It's nice how close you are with her. She couldn't stop talking about you and your interests and accomplishments and your desire to settle down and about what a coincidence it was that we were both teachers. And she was really, really excited when she found out we'd be at the same school this summer, too!" He flashed a smile that emphasized his lack of a chin. "And," he added, lowering his high voice to a near-normal pitch and wrinkling his brows with solemnity, "hope this doesn't seem out of line, but she mentioned that you also were recuperating from a disastrous . . . relationship. I know how it is, believe me. I share your pain."

My mother would do anything, invent a soap-opera history for me if she thought her improvisations would land me a man—any man.

But this poor fellow's romantic disaster had been real, as was his delusion that I expected, even wanted, to meet him. Mother Nature had been mean-spirited in allocating him features, Mother Pepper had lied to him, even if he didn't know it, and a third female had broken his heart. I didn't have to mend him, but I didn't need to inflict further damage, either. "Well," I said, "it's good to meet you at last."

He glowed with relief. I could almost see through his skull to his brain, which was flashing in neon letters that I had just agreed to be his reentry gal. "Me, too," he said. "Mandy Pepper, Mandy Pepper. Nice name. I just wanted to touch base."

He looked as if maybe he expected to touch more than base. "Glad you did," I said.

"Me, too." Still more nods. "And even gladder that we'll be seeing a lot more of each other! A *lot* more," he added with a wink, a pivot, and a slouched, but mildly jaunty, retreat.

I still didn't know what name to call him, but I didn't have that problem when I thought about my mother.

The second time someone tapped my door frame, I yelped, terrified by images of more suitors sent compliments of Bea Pepper.

"Have a minute?" a decidedly nonwhiny masculine voice asked. "Am I interrupting?"

Of course he was, but I waved him in and felt the corners of my mouth tilt up.

"My room's down the hall," he said. "Nice old building, this. I think my side of the hallway is a little shadier and cooler."

"It's the trade-off for having no view." My sunny and therefore hot room overlooked the square, a green city oasis populated by an interesting parade of locals.

He stood at the window and considered the scene below. "There it is," he said. "Penn's Greene Countrie Towne."

His history was good. William Penn was the first city planner in the new world, and a believer in open space. He designed a series of pocket parks way before there were streets to ring them. One of the five original squares lay across the street from the school.

"Where out West are you from?" I asked. Had he said? Had I forgotten? Was I being rude?

"Idaho. Ever been?"

I shook my head. Nobody I knew had ever been there, and I

had no empirical evidence to believe Idaho existed. I stacked my file folders.

"People here think it's nothing but potato fields, but it can be spectacularly beautiful. I miss it. However, it was time to find out what else there was. Expand my horizons. See where the history I'd studied happened. But you, of course, are a native Philadelphian."

"How did you know?" Had I said *yo* even once? Asked *Wassup?* when he entered the room? Addressed him as *youse?* Was I eating a soft pretzel with mustard or practicing my mummer's strut? What? "My accent?"

"Your name."

"Amanda?"

"Very funny. Pepper!" When he smiled, the skin around his eyes crinkled in a wonderful, Idaho kind of way. "A prestigious Philadelphia name if ever there was one. By coincidence, I visited Pepper House this weekend. A handsome place, and such a good example of the Philadelphia style."

The only Pepper House I knew about was the one I'd grown up in outside the city, a standard-issue two-story brick colonial. The floor plan you knew even before you opened the front door. Little center hall. Living room on one side, dining on the other, kitchen behind dining. Three bedrooms upstairs. We'd been part of a postwar development. There were probably a few thousand similar homes around the city and a goodly proportion of those in my neighborhood. I didn't think that was what Five meant by the Pepper House.

"And there's George Wharton Pepper, of course," he continued.

At what point was I required to break his enchantment with me and tell him that I was not a part of any illustrious Pepper lineage? I decided I was supposed to tell him that when he asked.

"*The* Philadelphia lawyer," he went on. " 'Old Philadelphia's Grandest Old Man,' he was called, and how does that *Life* magazine poem about him go?"

Luckily, that was a rhetorical question I wasn't expected to answer, because I was fully occupied by trying not to gape. The man was a master of Pepperabilia—a subject field I'd never known existed. He recited:

"G. Pepper of Penn. is a model for men;
 A bulwark in peace or in war,
With character rounded and solidly founded
 On learning and logic and law.
When Senators bicker of tariff and liquor,
 As Senators will now and then,
The speediest stepper is certainly Pepper,
 George Wharton Pepper of Penn."

"Not precisely poetry," he said. "What would you call it? A jingle?"

I would call it amazing. Incredible. Where on earth had he heard that, and why on earth would he want to know it?

Perhaps he noticed my dangling lower jaw. "I've been reading as much local history as I can," he said, "especially about the movers and shakers who shaped this country."

Wait till I told the detective that there was a history besides that of the yellow fever plague to be read. Even a poem—okay, a piece of doggerel—about a Pepper, and he hadn't known about it. But did I also have to tell the history teacher that my family wasn't known for shaping anything, except maybe cousin Lou who'd been a doughnut maker?

"Original family name Pfeffer. German. Anglicized it. Any Pfeffer cousins left?"

"I really wouldn't—" I began, but a cloud of scent and a long flowered skirt interrupted my weak stab at honesty.

"It looked like you two were having just too good a time," she said, "so I thought I'd join you. I'm Phyllis Esther Estes-Sessions." The name emerged as one long hiss. "This is going to be fun, don't you think? Nice old building, an interesting mix of students, nice location. And how are you liking our fair city?" Phyllis asked Five. "The Cradle of Liberty and all that. What have you seen and do you need any suggestions, or guides?"

A little obvious, Phyllis, I thought. Ease up. And what were those last names about? Didn't they imply a Mr. Sessions? Or a Mr. Estes?

"I've been in the area a few years," Five said kindly.

"I suspect this man knows more about local history than any of us," I added. "Definitely more than I do."

"And do you like it here?" Phyllis continued, looking only at him.

"Very much so."

"And Mrs. Dennison? Or do we call her Mrs. Five?" Phyllis-the-unsubtle inquired.

"My mother died when I was a child," he said. "And she was Mrs. Four."

"I meant—"

"Actually, since we seem to have reverted to talk of our ancestors, the fact is, we were just discussing Amanda's, not mine," Five said. "Her forefathers were much more illustrious."

Phyllis tried to look delighted by the swerve in attention and topic, but she succeeded only in looking queasy.

I hated disappointing this man, particularly in front of the snaky Phyllis. Still . . . "The Senator wasn't related to me," I said. "I don't think we're a branch of that particular Pepper family tree." I *knew* we weren't. My mother was chronicler of the Delaware Valley's web of human connections, and never had she mentioned anybody of historical significance with our name. In fact, most of her energy was devoted to getting me to give up that last name and take on somebody else's, so she couldn't have considered it wildly renowned.

"Really?" Five sounded unwilling to believe in my ordinariness.

Phyllis smiled. One small step for her sibilant, nonacclaimed last names.

"Different Peppers," Five mused, almost to himself.

"Maybe even different Pfeffers," I added.

"Your family's German, then? Like his?"

"I didn't mean that. My family is a hodgepodge that would give a genealogist the shakes. Kind of the prototype for the melting pot concept."

"Have you been to Valley Forge yet?" Phyllis asked over-brightly. Asked him. I had slipped over the horizon again where she was concerned. "We always think of it in winter—Washington's soldiers in the snow and all. But it's gorgeous in the summertime. A great place for a picnic."

"You know your Philadelphia history," Five said.

"I'm a buff. People think because I'm a biology teacher that I'd be narrowly focused, but—"

"You'll have to tell me more of your ideas as soon as I have time to do them justice," he said. "Right now, I'm afraid I . . ."

And without saying what he was doing right now, he demonstrated it. Right now, he was gone. Phyllis-the-S-woman had no use for me whatsoever, and I was pretty convinced she wasn't about to become my new best friend. People say women's goodbyes take forever, but it surely wasn't true in our case. We were not off to a good start. But maybe that's S.O.P. in the city of maximum hostility.

Three

DESPITE my having claimed to be something scraped out of the melting pot, I never was overfond of the term. It raised hellish images of folks boiling in an iron cauldron, liquefying into shapeless, indistinct lumps. So I had no impulse to apply the tag to my class, which was lucky, since despite my hopes, they showed no desire to become anything except what they were, very separate ingredients that'd be damned before they'd combine.

This was apparent on day one. On minute one, actually, despite the high hopes I'd had for the potential in this combination.

19

One more high hope lowered. One class down. One half day closer to the end of summer school, I comforted myself. But each step would be a long one, because classes were bloated four-hour sessions. That's how an entire semester is theoretically condensed into eight weeks.

My A.M. Communications class—that sounded less politically incorrect and offensive than Remedial English or Primitive Skills with Paper and Pen—had fifteen teens. Three were Philly Prep hardcores. It's damned difficult to fail a course at our school if your tuition payments are up to date, because parents seldom are glad to shell out for a second dose of what we did not impart the first go-round. Any failure is taken to be ours.

But this trio had forced the issue. One had missed an entire semester—the rumor was a drug rehabilitation program. I wasn't sure at first glance whether the rehabilitation had taken. A second, "Toy" Drebbin, actually could communicate quite well. I knew that because last autumn he had clearly explained that his allowance was larger than my paycheck, so why should he "break his back over dead writers"? What had they ever done for him, or for his family's tow-away business? And the last of the homegrown musketeers, Rina, had spent her sophomore year drowning in hormones, unable to spell anything except M-A-L-E. I had little hope that summer's heat would help her adjust to the idea that there were two sexes, and until such time as she did, all concepts that made it through her brain were X-rated.

The semischolars from other private schools looked suspicious and hostile. This was not how they'd planned to spend their summer vacations, although it was probable that planning was not their forte, and that they had fiddled while a school year burned.

And then we had the students who gave my principal dyspepsia. They came from the public schools on special grants, and they had names like April Truong and Miguel Hernandez and Jhabal Muhammed. Or they were like Tony "Model T" Ford, who had a skull tattooed on his cheek and two gold hoops in his right nostril. Or his pals: Woody Marshall, who may have provided the swing vote in the All-City Hostility Sweeps, and pale, silent Guy Lawson. The three were a sullen but constant trio.

Or Carmen Gabel, an "Oh, yeah?" girl whose sneer was on automatic pilot and who had obviously never met a cosmetic she didn't like. And Miles Nye, a gangly Norman Rockwell–freckled redhead who managed, even on this first day, to challenge—in a cockeyed, good-humored way—every idea I put forth. Could he *please* be a little creative with assignments? he asked. He couldn't define that any more closely, because he was talking about *creativity*. Did he really have to use *words*? Why shouldn't "Communications" include nonverbal techniques? Wasn't it true that sixty-five percent of all human communication was, in fact, nonverbal? But if he did use words, did it matter if they were prose? He liked poetry better, I was made to understand. I wished I remembered the Pepper of Philadelphia jingle. It might have impressed him. Nothing else I did was able to. He seemed a nice enough kid, and probably bright, but that didn't mean he wasn't a prime incentive for a nervous breakdown.

Don't despair, I told myself as they filed out. It was only the first day. With time, maybe there'd be a miracle, and the little collection of separate people would chemically reinvent itself into a class, with its own personality and dynamics. A class that put out as much energy as it received. That's when teaching justified itself, became exciting.

And maybe not. Maybe they'd stay hostile and barricaded, fifteen black holes in classroom space.

And my reward for completing class and walking outside would be Lowell Diggs, lurking somewhere even as I thought about him. I now knew his first name because my mother's note about a perfectly *lovely* young man she'd met had been in my mail the night before. She'd enclosed a studio portrait that was so flattering, the photographer must have served a long apprenticeship with aging movie stars. Vaseline on the lens, soft focus, magnificently hazy lighting all made Lowell Diggs seem almost attractive.

The letter and photo had arrived weeks late because the envelope had the wrong zip code. I wondered what Freudian repression or sense of underlying guilt or remorse had caused my mother to suddenly forget my full address.

I sketched a calendar in my head and ticked off the first half day of it as I watched a slender, long-haired student go to the window and look out, as if checking the weather. Two of the toughs—the Model T Ford and the scowler, Woody—stopped en route to watch her from across the room. So did tall, gangly Miles of the nonverbal expressions. And he'd been correct about body language conveying a great deal. His said that he, too, was watching the girl—but watching the two boys observing her as well. And while he wasn't exactly on the outs with them, *they* were buddies, and he wasn't one of them.

The girl turned from the window. She was quite lovely despite her worried expression. She glanced at the two toughs and, I thought, half nodded. It was a subtle gesture, if it was at all intended, and I couldn't be sure. Then she came to my desk.

"Miss Pepper?" Her voice was not much more than a whisper. I glanced at her almond eyes and down at the roll sheet.

"Truong," she said softly. "April. I introduce myself because I have five years here in the U.S., and my English writing is weak. I wish to learn that, also the history. And to go to college. I am older than my classmates. I need to learn fast. I hope I will not be a problem, Miss Pepper, because of my slowness."

A problem would never say anything like that. A *student* would say something like that. The summer now had possibilities, all contained in the slender form of April Truong. I reassured her. "And if you need additional help, we can arrange that," I heard myself say. I decided I meant it. "An hour after school as needed, maybe?"

"Yo, April," Miles said from where he stood. "Want lunch?"

She froze for a moment, then shook her head and waved him on. Model T Ford and Woody the sulker stayed put, looking quizzically at both Miles and April.

"But I keep you from your lunchtime," April said to me. "I should not do that. I will see you tomorrow." She glanced at the two young men at the doorway. "Perhaps we could . . . if you mean that offer—after school? Tomorrow? Would you help me with how I talk?"

I nodded, and she seemed so pleased and relieved that I allowed an actual frisson of teaching-excitement to fizz through my system.

As she left the classroom along with the two hulking young men, Five himself appeared outside my door, eyebrows raised. "With that grin on your face, you look like one of those ads for . . ." he said when I came out of my room.

"For what?"

"I don't know what to call it nowadays. For an old-fashioned kind of teacher. An old-fashioned kind of school."

I wasn't sure if that was a compliment or a put-down. Nostalgia for the good old days—which, if you really study them, weren't, except for a handful of the privileged—makes me nervous. I must have looked wary.

He chuckled. "I'm jealous! You obviously had a great morning, and I felt as if I were pushing at Mount Everest for four hours. It's a good thing U.S. history is required, or nobody would take it. If it's going to be history, they want knights in armor, assassinations in togas, or the little boys locked in the tower."

"Maybe you'll get lucky. I felt just as frustrated, except for that young woman, right at the end. Sounded like her other course would be history. She's so enthusiastic. Been here from Vietnam for five years and her English is amazingly good."

He looked dubious, then sighed. His every expression and gesture had an athletic grace and attractiveness. I wondered how aware of it he was. "Lunch?" he asked, and I nodded.

"Oh, good, because I can't remember where the faculty room is," he said. "I'm having one of those first-day-of-school nightmares."

I guided him to our makeshift lunchroom. The heat was even more oppressive in its undersized, crowded quarters. After today, I was sure we'd split forces and dine al fresco in the square across from the school, or in air-conditioned and student-free restaurants. But today it was important that we, along with the students, attempt to bond and become a unit.

"Mandy Pepper!" Lowell said with a whiny sort of surprised joy. He was sitting at a long table with a vacant chair next to him, and he patted it meaningfully. Then he glanced at Five and scowled, as if I'd betrayed him.

"Hey, Lowell." I shrugged, and kind of rolled my eyes toward Five, intimating, I hoped, that etiquette forbade my dumping this man who had entered with me.

Lowell's face flushed. He picked up his sandwich and gave it all his attention.

This was going to be a long hot summer. It looked as if the heat or student stress—and there should surely be an index of those combined factors—had already gotten to some of our more fragile peers. Phyllis-the-sibilant had angry crimson splotches on her cheeks and her hands on her hips as she faced Flora Jones, the wizard woman who taught computer courses at Philly Prep while working on her MBA at Wharton and running in marathons.

Flora was capable of sounding calm and furious at the same time, a talent she now demonstrated.

"I said the girl was handicapped, and she is," she told Phyllis in a low, resolute tone. "She needs extra time at the computer because her arm is in a brace. Cerebral palsy, I think it is."

"She's physically challenged," Phyllis said. "Handicapped is *negative*. What will it do to her sense of self? What does it do to the others who hear it?"

"What's wrong with the word? Are golfers given a physical challenge nowadays instead of a handicap?" Flora snapped. "Words aren't loaded unless you make them be, and after you do, then the new euphemism becomes loaded, and then the—"

"Oh, you!" Phyllis said. "You'd think you of all people would show a little sensitivity to the power of language. If we stopped stigmatizing exceptional people through the violence of our syntax, if we—"

"For Christ's sake, why me of all people? Were you trying to say that I'm black? Well, hey, I'm aware of that," Flora said. "And I feel sufficiently sensitive to issues of that sort, thank you. I'm not talking about insults or slurs or epithets or ugly slang. I'm talking about factual, reasonable language. Or, excuse me—did I identify myself correctly? Is black still acceptable, or should I be saying that I'm really white-challenged? Or you are differently melanined?"

"A PC face-off," I murmured. I directed Five to the two empty chairs at the end of a scarred table filled with munching teachers, all of whom seemed to be trying to ignore the battling women.

"God, that stuff is tiring. And tongue-tying," Five said, unwrapping a fragrant sandwich. "You can't say anything anymore without somebody jumping down your throat."

The bland man whose name I had known I wouldn't remember—Smith? White? Jones? Adams?—spoke up. "It's out there, too, in Utah, is it?"

"Idaho," Five said.

"All you Western states look alike," I said. "We have been geographically insensitive."

Moira, the Romance language teacher, raised her lorgnette and looked meaningfully in our direction. "Oh, please," she simpered, "forgive us, Mr. Five." She pursed her lips and fluttered her eyelashes and might even have blushed, were it visible beneath her artificially rosied cheeks. "We're being so *rude*," she said with a dismissive wave of her hand. "Acting as if civilization hasn't moved west of the Mississippi when"—and now she gazed at the history teacher—"it so *obviously* has."

"You're *right*," Edie Friedman said. "We must sound like such boobs to you." She smiled at him with terrifying neediness. I could envision her adding riding boots to her hope chest, and hoping for the eventual pitter-patter of little Sixes.

It had taken no more than a nanosecond to move from political correctness, students, curriculum, anti-intellectualism west of the Mississippi, summer school, or any of the many other topics that might have been of concern to a group of professionals meeting a new challenge, to sex, or lust, or the power of great looks and charm on female teachers. Business as usual, summer or winter. Nothing was going to be any different.

I was wrong on that last point. And naïve to yearn for change, any sort of change, as if different automatically meant better.

But I was only a half day into summer school. I had a whole lot left to learn.

Four

APRIL Truong looked at the classroom clock and gasped. Five-fifteen. Our after-school session had run late. As of the second week of summer school, we'd decided on an extra hour of tutoring three times a week. I was disappointed by what wasn't happening in the classroom, but April was the exception. She was so motivated and bright that the after-school hours had become my favorite part of the week. I would never have believed I could feel this way about additional, unpaid teaching.

We always stopped promptly at five so that she could get to her after-school job, but we'd forgotten today. April had been talking about Juliet's options—as good a topic as any on which to practice tense and syntax, and interesting, because her view of the world was very different from mine and from most of her classmates. Family obligation was extremely important, and April worried at length about the morality of Juliet's refusal to bow to her family's wishes. We had both ignored the clock.

"Sorry," I said. "Are you going to be late? I can drive you there if that would help." I was on my way to dinner at Mackenzie's. A detour wouldn't be any trouble—Star's Café, where April worked, was in Chinatown, en route to Mackenzie's place in Old City. Besides, even if it had been out of my way, April Truong brought out whatever residual altruism I had left. I didn't think that was a bad thing.

"No, thank you. I am fine," she said, but she rapidly pushed papers into a backpack, looking concerned. I, too, gathered my things and flicked off the lights as we made our exit.

I always felt hulking next to her. She was tiny, barely five feet tall and made of reeds, not bones, and she dressed simply, a study in black and white. She wore black jeans that had to be sized in the minus range, and a white T-shirt floated over her slight body, as did a fall of gleaming black hair that reached almost to her waist.

Halfway down the marble staircase, she dropped her backpack, and stopped to retrieve papers. I looked back. "It's fine," she said. "I have everything." I continued down—and gasped. She was behind me, but now I saw her in front of me as well, standing by the front door of the school. A double, except that she had short hair.

April laughed softly—behind me. "You're frightened?" she asked.

"For a second I thought—do you have a twin sister?"

"That is Thomas, my older brother."

A brother. Had I just been grossly insensitive? As in the all-Oriental-folk-look-alike school of jerkiness?

"Many people think there is a resemblance," she said, "although I cannot see it."

I was sure she'd said that to let me save face, but even at second look, the figure by the door seemed her double. It wasn't until we were close that his harder features were apparent, their masculinity unmistakable.

"My teacher, Miss Pepper," April said, introducing us. "My brother, Thomas Truong. He drive—drives—me to work on these late days. And he picks me up, too, when I am finished at eleven."

"How nice!" I said.

He nodded brusquely at me. "You're late," he told his sister in an annoyed voice. "I been here long. Everybody else gone. I thought maybe you don't want me to see you, that you were with—"

"No!" she said.

"She was with me," I said. "We were working hard. My fault, sorry." His powerful effect on his sister worried me. Her normal calm self-possession seemed to have dissolved the moment she saw him, or before, when she'd seen the clock and realized we were running late. All I could assume was that her job was of enormous importance to the family, and that tardiness was a potential disaster. I would have to make certain that we completed our sessions on time from now on.

Thomas Truong scanned his surroundings, like a bodyguard might, and then, with another curt nod in my direction, he took his sister's elbow and ushered her away. It was a brotherly, helpful deed, this chauffeuring her to work, so I couldn't figure out why it bothered me so much, why his gallant gesture seemed so much like that of a warden, or a guard.

I DIPPED a chip in salsa and munched on it as I downloaded—I love sounding high tech, and it's such a reach, given my field—the day's grievances onto the chef. "The class is like a jigsaw puzzle nobody wants to put together," I said. "They obviously arrived with old alliances—and old angers, too, I think—and there's a tension, a fragmentation, that has nothing to do with academics."

Mackenzie made a polite noise that meant, I hoped, *Go on*. "One of the kids," I said. "Woody Marshall. All he does is glare, four hours straight."

"At you?" Mackenzie carefully peeled a shallot.

"Not exclusively. At his classmates—except his good buddies, who do their own separate glaring. At his hands. At the textbook. This morning, while we were having the most innocuous class discussion—we're staggering through *Romeo and Juliet*, how much less urgent can you get?—the glare became nuclear-force. I didn't know what to think. He's like those traumatized vets. Something waiting to explode just behind the eyes, and anything could set him off."

"He do anything besides glare?"

"Not really. Not yet. Besides, he's only one piece of the problem. That whole morning class . . . Like a miasma. I could handle it if it were them versus me. I'm used to that. There's a point at which a class becomes a unit and acquires a personality, even if it's a rotten one. But the only personality this one has is of a paranoid schizophrenic."

"Prob'ly 'cause they aren't a class. They aren't an anythin' except an assemblage. Short-timers, together for five more weeks, then they'll go their separate ways again."

"Six. Six more weeks." My time already served felt interminable, but in truth, only two of the eight weeks were partially completed, a fact that horrified me. I mentally shook the calendar the way I would a watch, to make sure it was moving at all. "And it isn't because of their 'ethnic diversity,' to use a Havermeyer. It isn't because they are strangers—some of them know each other from before, are even from the same high school."

"You had a bad day," Mackenzie said, "and you're only seein' the worst of them. You've told me good moments already. Lots of them. The funny kid?"

"Miles. Miles Nye."

"He the one makes up songs?"

I had to smile, despite my fervent desire to stay sour. But during the first week, Miles had burst into class in top hat and tap shoes and performed a routine based on grammar exercises. I wish I had taped it. Even seeing was barely believing, but maybe Mackenzie could get some sense of his performance if he could see a tape of Miles's curly carroty hair as he performed, his comic body language, his hands raised, feet tapping double-time as he belted out, "And maaaake . . ." (shuffle, shuffle) "your syntax—" (shuffle, shuffle/tap, tap) "cleeeeear!"

I didn't know how he'd do academically, but I hoped Miles wanted to be an entertainer, in which case he had a brilliant future. Meantime, he treated my course—and every other course he'd ever had, I gathered—as an independent study in a performing arts school. He wasn't fond of assignments, except the ones he gave himself, which tended to take twice the time and four times the creativity.

Most of his audience didn't get it. Still, they cheered him on and applauded because he was a diversion from the assignment, and that seemed enough to power Miles's batteries.

"An' that little girl who wants to learn everything," Mackenzie continued, "April?"

I hate it when this happens, when Mackenzie pays closer attention to my life than I do. And of course, this focus was more intense than ever lately, while he was on medical leave and his own active life was virtually nil.

"Okay," I agreed. "But even with her . . . her brother was at school today, picking her up, and she was fifteen minutes late and there was something wrong there. Something's going on with her. Some kind of tension . . ."

"I din' think that was our topic," Mackenzie said in a mild, infuriating voice.

"She really is quick," I said. "I enjoy those extra sessions with her." She absorbed whatever was presented as if she were porous, but still she worried that she wasn't moving quickly enough, that she wasn't "learning to be an American," as she put it, speedily enough. "So it's April Truong versus the entire rest of them. If, for example, you saw how X—"

"Who?"

"His name is Robby, but he insists on X, and he hangs out with Peewee Smith and Abdul from my afternoon class, and they—"

" 'Spect you'll live through it. It's about attitude, not reality."

"Huh?"

"You know, like what Epictetus said?"

I controlled an urge to kick him. His leg had already been done sufficient damage. "No," I said, "I don't know, but I bet you do. And why *do* you, anyway?"

"Because despite Yankee prejudice, some of us Southerners received truly fine educations."

"*Fahn* educations?" I mimicked. The man couldn't even speak properly.

"And since you din' ask, I'll tell you. Epictetus said, 'Men are tormented with the opinions they have of things, not by the things themselves.' "

"Men!" I said idiotically, as if it were some kind of considered response. "What is it with you people, always quoting other people to me?"

He raised an eyebrow. He didn't have to speak. Even I knew how stupid I sounded. If only I had a better memory, I'd have quoted people whose ideas I liked. "His observation is so *obvious*," I said—just in case I didn't sound bullheaded and stupid enough yet. "It's like apparent temperature. Not the heat but the humidity, too."

He stopped sautéing and looked at me with genuine concern.

"You know what I mean. What we make of the weather, how it feels, not just what some thermometer says."

I'd lost the man's sympathy. I'd had it for a few seconds there, but now it was gone. In the most elegant of ways, via Eppa-whatsis, he'd told me I had an attitude problem. Obviously, he couldn't cook and be sympathetic at the same time. Or at least not cook, be sympathetic, and recuperate from a maiming. I almost felt sorry for him as he added chopped vegetables and ground herbs to the saucepan and sipped at a drink, a set of crutches propped against the nearby wall.

But I was too busy feeling sorry for myself. Besides, providing dinner had been his idea, and he'd declined my offer of assistance. "I'm stir crazy," he'd explained. "No pun intended. I've degenerated to readin' the food section of the paper, an' this orange-sauced pork sounded good. Willin' to be part of an experiment?"

So I was doing my part, and offering, in return for dinner, my miseries. He was not impressed.

"Two classes," he murmured, bending over the saucepan and inhaling with histrionic admiration. "Thirty kids total, you said. Two weeks gone, almost. A little more time and it'll be over."

"Think about it. Thirty kids times eight hours. Four hours a session. That's two hundred and forty kid hours a day. That's worse than the normal year, when there are five one-hour classes with twenty kids each, which totals only one hundred kid hours."

He turned, favoring the leg that was mending from a bone-crushing gunshot wound. "Kid hours?"

"As based on the KHI, an important index I just made up. Like Apparent Temperature or the Windchill Factor. A way of measuring precisely how miserable you feel and explaining why you feel so rotten."

I sipped the incredibly good margarita he had offered me at the front door. "Great drink," I said. "The fresh-squeezed limes really make a difference."

"Thanks." He didn't sound as if fresh limes were enough to make his life worthwhile. Frankly, I didn't think he was taking his enforced hiatus with good grace. Life was really unfair. I would have been jolly about accepting a pin or two in the leg in exchange for a large bottle of painkillers and an honest-to-God release from work. A summer of ease, reading without guilt or deadlines and no adolescents or Lowell Diggs waiting around every corridor turn, ready to say, "*Hi!* Mandy Pepper." Sounding mildly aggrieved. "Haven't seen much of you today. Where've you been?"

"Teaching," I'd say. And he'd chortle as if we'd just exchanged brilliant repartee. His laugh was explosive and deadening, producing an irresistible urge to squelch it, make him miserable and silent and certainly never to encourage it.

"Is this to be the noon we dine together?" he'd ask every noon. Luckily, he never dared ask in advance, so it was easy to express regrets over plans already made.

So I'd love to be an invalid for a while, to discover the joys of peeling shallots and squeezing limes. I wondered if I could arrange for a mugging of my own. I might not even have to exert myself much, given my current students.

But getting hurt was the easy part. Maurice Havermeyer and Philly Prep were not going to be as generous with time off for battle wounds as the Homicide Division was being with Mackenzie.

Mackenzie swigged his margarita, smiled at the skillet and hummed. His kitchen was the only part of the apartment he'd personalized. His pots and pans were carefully chosen and maintained. He ate at home perhaps once a month, but when he did, he did it right. This was doubly amazing given the rest of his abode, a large loft that had been a warehouse for Oriental rugs before Old City became semiyuppified. It had a skylight, one interior door leading to the bathroom, a half divider symbolically marking a sleeping area, and a permanent FOR SALE sign outside.

Mackenzie's digs were living testimony to buyer's remorse, a generic habitat with no personality, no visible preferences, no evidence of ideas. Indeed, it had been "decorated" by a rent-a-room firm that furnished your space in sixty minutes or your first month was free.

The first time I'd seen his mostly mauve Santa-Fe-Meets-Philly decor, heavy on cockamamie fake-Navajo motifs, I'd reconsidered our relationship.

"I refused the howling coyote accent piece that came with the suite," he said in his defense. "They had four choices. This was brighter than the Colonial Homestead and better than the Marie Antoinette or the Spanish Inquisition. I meant to replace it.

But why get things for here? Maybe they won't fit wherever I wind up."

The only signs that a breathing and sentient person was in residence were on the walls. First, in an enormous Howard Schatz photograph of an orangutan, arms flung to the sky. "It makes me happy to come home and see him," Mackenzie said. "He's got somethin' figured out."

Then there were the renta-shelves holding twelve billion CDs, heavy on Cajun and jazz, and zillions of books. Poetry in dog-eared paperbacks, scripts of plays, sociology, criminology, and psych texts. Classics, books about computers and the Internet, and anything that had to do with his home turf of southern Louisiana. Plus his current interest, Colonial U.S. history. There was also audio equipment with sufficient dials and gears to launch a space shuttle. I would call it a tape deck and disk player. People with lots of testosterone refer to it as a sound system.

When he first moved north, Mackenzie had thought that owning property would represent commitment to change. It had turned out to represent only a commitment to change housing. Fixing up the large loft required too much effort, work, and money.

But nobody else wanted the place I called the Waiting Room. The real estate market had fallen into the toilet, and though Mackenzie lamented it, I secretly appreciated the shelter impasse. It provided a guilt-free impediment to our combining households, a topic we now and then sashayed around. To my surprise, on our last dosey-do, I'd discovered that I was the more terrified of the two of us about such a move, but as long as Mackenzie thought he was in transit, and as long as my place, which was rented, was too small and cramped for both of us, I didn't have to deal with my ambivalence.

I settled down on Mackenzie's silly sofa and dared to look at the day's essays.

I pulled one out at random and felt a bone-marrow weariness that had nothing to do with physical fatigue. It's easy to call a course Communications, but impossible to teach such a subject.

The real material of the course was learning how to think logically, then getting those thoughts onto paper in the same fashion. However, saying that out loud would make it too clear that what we had here was not an eight-week kind of learning task.

I had asked them to write an editorial, their opinion on any topic of the day. Why something should or shouldn't be or happen, why something was good or bad. The assignment was supposed to build skills in how to develop an argument without using semiautomatic weapons.

Predictably, I suppose, the paper I now held argued that there should be no such thing as summer school. The second essay passionately, if quasiliterately, argued against the writing of essays.

I did not want to read a third. I didn't want to face teens tomorrow in the muggy schoolroom, and didn't want to stay up half the night marking their insincere attempts to communicate. Most of all, I didn't want to be this kind of disillusioned, cynical teacher.

"Tomorrow, I'm buying a copy of *What Color Is Your Parachute?*" I announced. "I'm going to find a happier, easier way to make a living."

"How about a career in design?" Mackenzie suggested from his home near the range. "Startin' here. Then you can write *What Color Is Your Living Room?*"

"Just because you're lame doesn't mean your sense of humor has to be, too."

"At least I have one. You're spendin' entirely too much time grousin' about nothin'."

"It isn't nothing."

"A double negative?"

"There's something creepy there, bad chemistry. The kids seem to be waiting for something to happen, something wrong. And the tension's contagious. You know what I feel like? A fleck in a sink near a drain. I have nothing to do with the work of the drain, but I'm getting sucked in nonetheless."

"They're kids, Mandy. Kids confined to a creaky old building and—face it—boring lessons when they most want to be outside.

Kids who must feel out of place at your expensive private school. Gettin' their short fix, then bein' shipped back to wherever while other kids get to stay in the posh halls of learnin'. Relax. Give 'em an inch. You're bein' overly dramatic. Nothing bad or unusual is going to happen, an' dinner is ready."

He wasn't completely wrong about everything. Dinner was, indeed, ready. Score him one out of three.

Five

FLORA Jones manages to live with both precision and speed. She's in graduate school, getting her MBA, teaching computer science, whatever that is, at Philly Prep, and living a life, and she never seems overwhelmed. I'd like to think it's because she hadn't opted to be an English teacher. A computer, odd life form though it may be, operates on a logical system, unlike our language. A computer does not produce semi-intelligible essays to grade. A computer knows how to spell and how to process words. My students do not.

And Flora's long-term, if low-wattage, relationship is with a copyright lawyer, and surely it's less troublesome and time-consuming to deal with somebody interpreting the law than it is to cope with someone enforcing it. Do copyright lawyers ever have to break dates because an offender has brutally violated a brand name?

Or was all of this a rationalization of my inferior capabilities? Mackenzie's lack of empathy for my teaching woes echoed through my system, so the next day, as Flora and I sat on a sunny bench in the square across from the school, having lunch—and avoiding Lowell—I decided to ask her.

In typically overachieving, easygoing, but distinctive style, Flora usually brought a clever Japanese lacquer box instead of a paper or Ziploc bag. Today the box was filled with cold salmon, grilled and marinated vegetables, and a chunk of crusty bread. She also had a marketing textbook, in case she wound up eating alone.

I'd brought a flip-top can of tuna and a fork, and I'd been proud of remembering the fork. I'd forgotten a napkin. My pitiable lunch seemed symbolic of an inability to handle my life, Flora's stunning repast equally telling of her expertise with everything. "What's wrong with me?" I asked.

"Is that some kind of rhetorical question? Or are you saying you feel sick?"

I shook my head. "Not sick."

"Then your question is a setup, girl, and I'm not touching it with a ten-foot pole."

"I feel like I'm not really living my own life. I'm going through the motions, but I can't get into it. Or I'm in it, but it doesn't fit anymore."

"What happened? You outgrow it? It shrunk, or what?"

"Don't push my imagery too far," I said. "The truth is, I don't know what's happened or what I'm saying. The other thing I don't know is if I want to be here, doing this, anymore."

She looked at me with a curious absence of expression, as if it wasn't exactly my voice she was hearing. The lacquer box sat open on her lap, its contents untouched. When a fat fly started drooling over the salmon, I was the one who waved it away.

"What made you think you don't belong anymore?" she finally asked. "Somebody say something? Something happen?"

I shook my head yet again, like one of those wobbly-neck dolls. "It's only a feeling. It isn't about anybody else."

She squinted at me, as if I might have been lying, then exhaled audibly, shook her head, and lifted a fork full of salmon. "Why make up troubles you haven't been given?" she said.

One nice thing about Philly Prep was its location across from the leafy-green square. And another nice thing was that our students, many of whom were also having picnic lunches, were not the sort to spend free time cozying up to teachers. They flirted with each other, munched, and smoked in apparent obliviousness to us. We were given privacy by default.

"I don't think I'm making it up," I said. "There's something wrong about this summer session."

"There's something wrong about this summer," Flora said. "Half the kids in the city have shot the other half within the last two weeks, for starters."

"How else could we have won our infamous hostility title?" I asked. "What a claim to fame. But maybe I'm a part of the problem. Maybe I'm the whole problem."

"For the city?" she asked. "For gangs? For drive-by shootings? For hate mongers on radio and TV? For—"

I put my hand up. "For my own problems. I can't get in synch with most of these kids, and I keep wondering what I'm doing there, aside from needing a paycheck. And then I see you, and you're always self-possessed, elegant, on track . . ."

She put down her fork before it reached her mouth. Flaky pink salmon was still attached to the prongs. She looked at me as if I were insane, and then she looked overwhelmingly sad.

"What?" I asked. "I only said . . . What is it?"

Her hair was close-cropped, her only ornamentation amber hoop earrings and dark coral lipstick that contrasted with her café au lait skin. She was starkly chic in the way only beautiful women can manage.

"Nothing," she said. "I didn't know whether to laugh or cry. I was stunned, how you could think I'm cool and collected." It was her turn to shake her head, slowly, with wonder. Her ear-rings swung back and forth like double metronomes. "I'm going through a . . . I can't believe it doesn't show. I try not to let it, but I was sure it was obvious. But no point to talking about it. It has nothing to do with your teaching problems. Nothing to do with school. I think."

She thought? There was an invitation to further probing if ever I'd heard one. "What's wrong?" I asked. "I didn't mean to imply you're incapable of having problems. I apologize if some-how I've hurt your feelings."

She shrugged. "It's nothing you did. It's reality. Look, even in the City of Brotherly Love, not all brothers are equally loved. Things happen. To sisters, too. It's not like I've lived my life without being aware that some people have problems, and they think their problems have to do with my skin's color."

For a moment all the air disappeared. We had suddenly hit something way beyond my capacities for assistance. Something so deep in the fabric of our society, I wanted to pretend it was dead and buried, the way it should be.

The way it looked to be in the square today. On every side people were enjoying the day and the site. I wanted to deny Flo-ra's obvious statement of fact. I wanted to say "Don't be silly—look. Right here." An old-fashioned Norman Rockwell cover for the *Saturday Evening Post*. Only the outfits had changed.

Elderly women, wrapped up despite the heat, slowly made their way on the walkways. Summer students, including April and Model T and Miles and X and Manuel, sat on the lip of the fish fountain, talking and laughing, their feet immersed in its cool waters. Nearby, three younger boys spun a Frisbee across a corner of the square as a young child and his uniformed nanny watched. One of the Frisbee players had freckled milky skin and white-gold hair, a second was olive-skinned and heavy-featured; the third had skin the color of smoke and wore dreadlocks. The little boy was Asian, with gleaming black bangs above chubby cheeks, and the small uniformed woman caring for him had the broad, strong features of a sunny Latin country.

Reader's Digest would make a cunning anecdote out of this

41

sliver of Americana. Except the reason the sight had so impressed me was because it was rare. It was how it was supposed to be, more or less, but not how it was. And next to me I could feel Flora struggle for words to suggest that this was illusion and not the picture at all.

"That's horrible and true," I said. "And unfortunately not news. But you seem shaken up by something less abstract—something more personal. Did somebody say something? Did something happen to you?"

"More or less." She looked at me. "I'm not trying to be oblique or coy. It's just that I don't know what's going on. It could be a fluke, a crazy kid prank, even. I remember all those crank calls asking if your refrigerator was running, then saying to go catch it. Maybe this is somebody with a really bad sense of humor."

"Somebody phoned you?"

"Somebody has been leaving messages on my answer machine the last few days. *Several* bodies. Male voices, all of them, although maybe not full adults—one voice broke in the middle of his big macho putdown—and I didn't recognize any of them. Pretty similar messages. They all used my name. As in, 'Go back to Africa, Flora,' to quote one of the milder ones." She said her own name with contempt, imitating the voice, spitting it out as if it were a curse. "Obviously, they didn't know I was born in Cincinnati," she said dryly. But she blinked several times and bit at her bottom lip.

Across from us, the group around the fountain abruptly fractured. X pointed and shouted at a thin figure partially obliterated from my sightline by a tree. April immediately swung her legs over the edge, picked up her shoes and ran barefoot across the street and into the school. I thought of how, every day before lunch and after each tutoring session, she looked out the classroom window. I'd thought she was checking the weather, but perhaps that wasn't it at all.

I leaned forward, to try and see who was behind the tree, but the figure was already in motion, running away from our side of the square.

Miles loped after April, and Model T ran—with shoes on—in the direction of the man who'd been behind the tree. So much for the tranquil tableau of a moment ago.

So much for Flora's peace of mind. I pictured her forcing herself to listen, over and over, to foul words and malevolent messages, needing to learn whatever she could from the tape.

"My machine message doesn't say my name, only the number. My first name isn't in the book, only my initial. *Jones* isn't necessarily any one race, and I live around the corner—definitely a mixed neighborhood. So it wasn't some random crank. My caller knew me, named me, targeted me. I feel . . . tagged, like those animals they use the stun guns on." She paused and studied her hands. Her fingers were long and tapering, and her nails matched the dark coral of her lipstick.

She put her lacquered box, its contents untouched, beside her on the bench. "Maybe it started when I was so upset about that Jewish cemetery. Remember?"

I couldn't follow her until I realized she was talking about the cemetery of Mikveh Israel, a Colonial synagogue, that had been defaced with graffiti the week before.

"Some people have such big hates that even when people have been dead and gone for hundreds of years, they still have to go after them."

The vandals had desecrated four gravestones, one of which was that of Rebecca Gratz, the model for Sir Walter Scott's Rebecca in *Ivanhoe*. They'd spray-painted a jagged, sloppy, sideways bolt of lightning on it. I had tried to find some literary connection, but couldn't.

All the graffiti was meaningless. Haym Solomon, who financed the American Revolution, had something akin to a scarlet A on his stone. Two other markers had also been defaced with initials, and several stones tipped over. Random rage. Senseless destructiveness.

"I wrote a letter to the editor about it," Flora said. "They printed it in Monday's *Inquirer*. The day before the calls started."

"Except how would they have gotten your phone number?" I asked.

She shook her head and sighed again. "Talk about not feeling like you belong here. That's why I said you shouldn't make up problems that aren't given to you."

"That's awful," I whispered, knowing my words were pathetically inadequate.

"It feels like hell to be hated," she said. "Particularly by somebody who doesn't know you. That makes you an object, a symbol, not a person." She shook her head so that her earrings bounced. "And to have them be faceless, nameless, anonymous, so all you're getting is the hate itself, like bad breath blowing on you. There's always a certain level of this stuff, but I feel something in my bones. Something worse and growing."

Around us the square was semideserted. Most of the students were gone, scattered. The nanny had whisked her charge away from the running students, and the Frisbee game had ended. Isolated people made their way from one corner to another, or sat quietly on benches. I wondered at the change. It seemed connected to the chase of the person behind the tree, although nothing had come of that, either. I wondered who he'd been and what was so provocative about him. And I wondered at the learned skittishness of everyone who'd taken for cover as soon as anything out of the ordinary began.

"It's like how they say we always carry viruses in us," Flora said. "We don't even notice them. We fight them off. Only sometimes, when our resistance is down, they take over. Well, if hate's a virus, and why shouldn't it be, then that's what it feels is happening now. Something in us has gotten weak, and the virus is running rampant. There's an epidemic going on. A plague."

The midday weather stayed hot, the pavement still reflected glaring bits of light, and the pattern of leaves on the grass didn't change. But all the same, I could have sworn that an enormous cloud had obliterated the sun, and that we were suddenly shivering and in the dark.

FRIDAY was not one of April's tutoring afternoons, and I was glad to leave for home an hour earlier. I was exhausted and increasingly disheartened, still thinking about Flora. Phone calls were small potatoes by today's violent standards, yet their purpose remained mean-spirited, and their effects were painful and profound.

I scanned the room for left-behind valuables and erased the board. And then I went to lower the shades against the sun and heat, and that made me think about April's habit of looking out, and about the mystifying scene around the fountain this noon.

The square was almost empty now, except for the through traffic of our rapidly exiting students and some postnap children out with their mothers or au pairs. The little park was a touchstone for me, an oasis against dehumanization and ugliness. And I loved my vantage point, from what was the second story of the school, but which, given the high ceilings of the ground floor, would be almost the third story elsewhere. I saw the tops of people's heads and very few features, but the perspective made the goings-on seem like an impressionistic painting from another era.

I watched, feeling a measure of peace return, then shatter when a bark of noise cut through and above the traffic. A backfire, my mind registered—at the corner across from the school, where people waited for the light to change.

But one of those people, a slender dark-haired boy, levitated. Rose from the ground, as if jerked from above, arced, then landed on the pavement, on his back.

I had seen that violent leap before, in films, on TV, but it was the stuff of stunt men and illusion. It didn't belong in real life. Except in headlines that had nothing to do with my life. It did not compute. It didn't belong here.

Not at my school, near children, near students and babies and nurses. At the square. No matter what was in the headlines every day. A plague on all our houses—except mine. Reality belonged elsewhere.

A woman standing near the boy waved her arms at the figure on the sidewalk, then at nothing while she screamed and screamed.

The dark-haired boy didn't move. A crowd cautiously gathered around him—Philly Prep students, mostly. They looked at

45

the ground, and then turned in semicircles, looking for the assailant. When I saw them tilt up my way, I realized both my hands were at my mouth, muffling a scream I was too terrified to utter. The eyes moved on beyond me, to the roof, back to earth. The nannies scooped up their charges and backed off from the corner where the boy lay.

I shuddered, and ran down to the office. "Call for help!" I shouted.

Helga didn't question me or protest or tell me to do it myself.

"A shooting. A drive-by." I hated that there was a word for it, that it was common enough to have been named, to have become a category of killing. "There's a boy on the sidewalk on the corner."

Helga had the receiver in one hand, but she kept her eyes on me as she dialed. With her free hand she offered me a box of tissues.

Only then did I realize I was crying and must have been for some time.

Six

YOU adapt. The world becomes more frightening, but it doesn't stop, so you become more cautious, more twitchy, which means you lose a little bit of your perceived freedom, but that's how it is.

The dead boy turned out to have been named Vo Van Tran. He was twenty years old and a member of a Vietnamese gang. That didn't help anything make sense, it merely labeled it. They thought he'd been killed instantly by a shot from a passing car. By whom, nobody knew. A rival gang, it was assumed. Nobody seemed overly concerned about why he'd been murdered. It happened all the time.

And nobody, including me, had seen anything helpful. I hadn't been watching the traffic flow, and try though I did, I couldn't remember any specific car, anything that had caught my attention while I lowered the shades. The police could barely believe that an eyewitness could have such a poor eye. All I could establish was that I, along with every other person who'd been there, hadn't seen anybody on foot running away. Which left it classified as a drive-by. One more unsolved murder.

But life, as they are always insisting, does go on, as does time. The weekend passed, and by Monday, via some strange chemistry, Vo Van's meaningless urban death seemed to have settled all of us down. Now, in the third week of summer school, I finally stopped physically bucking and rearing, and my morning class also seemed to have resigned itself to its hot-weather fate.

We finished *Romeo and Juliet*.

April Truong burst into tears at the ending. "Why?" she said, "Why must such things happen? I don't understand people." The class glared at her, but she seemed oblivious. She was pure intensity, giving off energy like the filament burning in the center of a lightbulb.

"There's nothing harder to understand," I answered. "All our plays and novels are attempts to comprehend a little piece of the puzzle. That's why they were written; that's why we read them. And this one," I said, still seeing the hideous ballet of the young man across the street arcing backward in his last leap, "this one touches on issues that are certainly still relevant, like the hatred that led somebody to shoot that boy Friday afternoon. Or, like the hatred that I was told about last week as well. Against an African-American woman whose only offense seems to be the color of her skin."

They switched off all visible emotion and watched me impassively. I was lecturing, hectoring, but I couldn't help myself. What else was there to do except go on record against the viciousness?

"The Montagues and Capulets had it easier," I said. "At least murder had to be done by hand back then. Shakespeare wrote this play a long time ago, about a time even longer ago—and what has changed? Three days ago, in front of our eyes, a young man was murdered, and for what?"

Expressions grew stony, and I realized, with a mixture of nausea and shame, that what was news to me was not to them. That they'd seen other people blown away in their neighborhoods, that Vo Van was one more statistic on a long list to them, and they were not impressed that, unlike them, I had been spared until now. They watched me from a great distance.

April was still absorbed by Shakespeare. "I was thinking that it was a good plan of Juliet's," she said. "She could not openly defy her parents. But if Juliet did not lie and pretend, Romeo wouldn't kill himself. So everything is her fault."

"Maybe she was given bad advice," I said. "And they both were young and unlucky. And Romeo was impetuous—he acted before he thought things through."

"I thought they would be *happy*," she said.

"What *is* this," Model T asked. "Carrying on about *Shakespeare*?" His pale clone, Guy, echoed him. "Yeah, what is this?"

"But it is so sad," April said. "So scary."

For her, raised in a completely different tradition, the play was filled with tension and mystery. She had been in suspense straight through, hoping for a happy ending, wishing the young couple well and becoming heartsick when fate worked against them.

The rest of the class was less affected. Rina was still up to her nostrils in hormones. Toy Drebbin was still convinced that a future devoted to towing cars need not include poetry or plays. Woody Marshall glared on, but I took that to be his unfortunate natural expression and not a manifestation of any personal hostility. Miles Nye had burst into class that morning with another installment of his improvised curriculum, presenting the "R and J hand puppets." Romeo was a frog and Juliet an antelope, for reasons that escaped me, and instead of dying ("too passive, too *then*," Miles had insisted), they killed their parents and anyone else who got in their way.

So the day lumbered on, and the boy who'd been shot receded from the center of our attention. By lunchtime the crimes we were examining were Verona's ancient ones.

Flora claimed to be cramming for an exam, and ate lunch alone in her classroom, with food, a highlighter, and a book as her only company.

Maybe she really did have a test coming up, but I was afraid that instead she regretted telling me about the phone calls and somehow had come to see me as part of the enemy camp. I didn't know what to do about either my fears or hers.

At the end of the day I sat waiting for April, looking at the morning paper. I'm not sure why I ever look at it, except as an antidote to any possible pleasure I might be getting out of life. You'd think we'd learn from the past. I remember that Thomas Jefferson said he did not take a single newspaper, nor read one a month, and he felt infinitely happier for it. I used to sneer at the idea, but no longer. No news was good news.

Once again, the rule held. Global self-destruction, ethnic cleansing, tribal wars, and terrorist bombings. Everybody part of an in-group that furiously wanted the "outsiders" dead and gone.

Locally, there'd been two more shootings on Sunday night, and a Baptist church vandalized, with three smashed stained-glass windows and red-paint graffiti on the front doors.

"Miss Pepper, I am here now." April was intense about everything—Romeo and Juliet, her history project, and the less dramatic subject matter of crisping her diction and smoothing the kinks in her grammar.

"My paper for Mr. *Dennison*," she said, trilling out his name. One of our earliest exercises was the pronunciation of his name, because she referred to him so often, and not by his nickname. "Mr. *Dennison*," she said, her syllables only slightly thickened, "he is instructing us about the Boston Tea Party. About the patriots."

She wasn't the only female constantly referring to him. Not by a long shot. Phyllis-the-politically-correct-and-sibilant-hyphenate, whose marital status was still murky—she referred to one man as her "erstwhile husband" and another as her "so-called husband"—remained in hot pursuit, as did Edie Friedman. The two women's competition for the prize had been the first week's entertainment. They'd bared their teeth in false smiles as each of them, almost on a daily basis, appeared with home-baked "surprises" they'd had sudden urges to create. Never had the Philly Prep lunchroom contained such elegant cuisine.

Phyllis and Edie upped the ante, day by day, producing more and more esoteric delights. Figs wrapped in filo, and fruit tarts the size of one's thumbnail, and meringues swirled into swan shapes.

Five drove them crazy by seeming bent on a democratic appreciation of every offering. No favorites, and a decided lack of a sweet tooth. With one of his charismatic smiles, he most often declined their baked goods. The rest of us snarfed his rejects.

The Phyllis and Edie show ended its run after ten performances when Five absented himself from the lunchroom altogether. He decided to use the hour as conference time—he said my work with April had inspired him—and he seemed as popular with his students as he was with the female staff. I'd squelch a surge of jealousy when, on my way back to my room after lunch, I'd see half a dozen students crumpling sandwich wrappers as they concluded an hour with Five. I'd seen it and squelched it again today.

I hoped the attraction was that his side of the building was cooler than mine.

"I thought to study psychology," April now said, "but I am writing this paper and I am wanting to study politics as well."

I hated interrupting her flow of ideas with usage corrections, but that was my job. "I want to," I said. "I want to study politics in the future—in college, perhaps? And I want to study politics now, too."

"I *am* study politics now!" she said. "Mr. *Dennison* is instructing."

In my next life I am going to teach something simpler than English, a language as complicated as all the different people and tongues that put it together. "I am study*ing* politics now," I said weakly. "I'm glad you're enjoying your history class. And how's the paper coming along?"

She turned a sheet toward me. On it was typed *The Wretched Refuse*. "From the poem on the Statue of Liberty," she said.

51

I've never appreciated that line of the Lazarus poem, or even the sentiment. I looked at the lovely and earnest young woman across from me and could not bear to think of her as "wretched refuse." Even more, I didn't want her to think of herself that way. "How about 'Give Me Your Tired, Your Poor' as a title, instead?" I suggested.

"Somebody else has that."

Pushing the issue would be insensitive. I began a chart on past, present, and future tenses. It was good to busy ourselves, good not to keep one ear cocked for the sound of another gun going off across the way. *Yesterday, I—* I wrote in the first column. *Today, I—* and *Tomorrow, I—* in the next two.

"Yesterday, I want*ed*—what did you want yesterday?" I asked.

She flushed, looked at her hands and shook her head.

"This is an exercise," I said. "Say anything. It doesn't have to be true. I hope this will help you understand how to use the verb *to want.*"

Whatever her discomfort or shyness, she was too obedient a scholar to refuse. "I—yesterday, I was want—"

"Yesterday, I wanted," I said gently.

"I wanted to see my friend."

"Good!" I wrote *I wanted* in the first column. "And if it had been your friend's idea, you could say to her, 'You want*ed* to see me.' And if you were talking about still another friend, you would say, 'She wanted to see me,' but if we were talking about now, today, this minute, the present, do you remember what you would say?"

"I want to see my friend." It was a lament, not a usage exercise.

"You're right, but you sound so sad," I said softly.

"I think that maybe to want in the past is better than to want now. It is sad to want what cannot be. Look what happens to Juliet and Romeo."

Look what happened, I thought, but I didn't say it out loud. Instead, "Do you want to talk about what's troubling you?" I asked, but as the word *want* came out of my mouth, I felt suspended between the lesson we should be doing and her obvious agitation.

Through bits and pieces offered during other after-school sessions, I knew her family was large and hard-pressed. Her older brother Thomas had dropped out of school and didn't really help the general finances, and there were younger siblings. Her parents were both employed, but America was expensive. Her own job, every night till eleven, was at a nice café, but the manager bothered her and made her uncomfortable. Still, she said, it was a job.

She sighed. "I thought here it would be . . ."

"Here? At Philly Prep?"

"Yes, that. But more, in the United States . . ."

Her power slowly failed. The April Truong lightbulb was dimming.

"I thought . . ." She shook her head.

She was young and bright and beautiful, but her fine bones, delicate features, and shining fall of jet hair now added together to make the very portrait of loss and desolation.

"April," I said, "I'm concerned. Can I help you in any way?"

"It is too late," she said softly. "He is dead. The boy on the street."

"You knew him?"

She nodded. "Vo Van is—was—my brother's friend. Is . . . very scary."

"Who shot him?"

She set her jaw as if to keep it from moving. For a moment her eyes widened and she seemed on the verge of saying something more, but then she shook her head, as if chastising herself. "Vanny had enemies," she said. "His group, they do such things."

For the first time in our brief acquaintance, I didn't believe April, didn't think she was telling me the truth. Her truth, that is.

She pushed the "Wretched Refuse" paper toward me. "My work," she said, reminding me of what we were supposed to be doing.

Her family had given and received one combined gift the previous Christmas—a computer for all to share, because her father believed, with some validity, that full Americanization and success could come only to those who knew how to use the machine.

"Mr. *Dennison*," she said with a sudden burst of her usual enthusiastic energy, "he is not yet to the immigrants. He is telling us about the Founding Fathers."

Founding Fathers are not considered immigrants, for appallingly ethnocentric reasons. What the language is saying is that obviously, before them, there was no *here* to which they could emigrate. They presumably created the *here*, and native populations be damned.

"I am trying to—is this said right?"

I nodded.

"—to write about then and now. Differences. Reactions to people coming here. Laws. I am interested mostly in immigrants now. People like me, my family. Or," she said with a touch of wryness, "like them."

Her head gracefully tilted toward the newspaper on the edge of my desk. She wasn't looking at the headlines about ethnic cleansing. She pointed, instead, at a senatorial candidate's call to "Close Our Borders." If she'd looked a little longer, she would also have spotted a story about another illegal boatload of Chinese indentured servants trying for the Golden Mountain. One day, one page, two don't-give-me-your-tired-and-poor stories.

The current unwillingness to be sent any wretched refuse, including April Truong, would have to sting. She had come so far, was learning a whole new life and culture and language—the better to understand the hostility in those stories.

Her special summer was providing a harsh curriculum. Heartbreak compliments of Romeo, Juliet, gang wars, immigration policies, and a city that ranked number one in hostility. And something else, too. Something about the friend she wanted to see, something she didn't want to or couldn't talk about.

We worked on her project. My role was to help her organize ideas and polish written language skills. All the same, I had to stifle an urge to ask her why she had chosen this depressing topic.

"Do you think . . ." she said haltingly. Her paper, heavy with numbers and dismal projections, seemed like a weight pulling her under. She looked at me, her head tilted, a worry line between her brows. "If it is accepted that some people hate each other . . ."

I felt a nervous thrill. She was looking for guidance, for American wisdom. What could I say that offered comfort and wasn't an outright lie? Everything from the Declaration of Independence, my own great-great-grandparents' flights from poverty and oppression in Europe, to nightmare photos of Vietnamese boat people and massacres in El Salvador pushed for attention in my mind.

But when April spoke again, her words and worries were a surprise and my speech-making died unborn. "Juliet should have listened to her nurse, do you think?" she asked.

"Excuse me?" Juliet again? "Why?"

"Our elders know better. They have the wisdom of time." April Truong, former human dynamo, spoke with almost no emotion.

"Sometimes differences are too great for young people to overcome," she continued. "We are children who do not think ahead enough. Cannot." I could almost hear a stern father or resolute mother imprinting those words on her brain.

"What are we really talking about here?"

"Look at the sorrow Juliet caused." Her eyes were on her tightly clasped hands. I thought I saw a tear on one eyelash. "She should not have involved Romeo."

"How could she not?"

"She could leave sooner. Right after they met."

"But Romeo was also responsible for his reaction, for what he did. You can't blame Juliet for everything."

"If she tried more to make peace first. Tried harder," she whispered. "If not, then what should she have done? Every choice sounds sad. Is there no good choice?"

"April, what is this about?"

She looked as if she'd just been brought back, as if the alien that had possessed her for a while had retreated. "Forgive me," she said. "Many things confuse me."

That clarified precisely nothing.

"And I am going to be late for work!" She stood up, curling her lips into an exaggerated downturn. "The café will fire me, and then I will have even more things confuse me."

I glanced at my watch. "But it's only . . ." The hour wasn't up. April had always been hungry to use every possible minute, and had never left this early before. "Did they change your hours?"

She looked flustered. "This time, I forgot to say, I have to leave early."

"Is your brother waiting?" He seemed a strict taskmaster. Maybe that was it.

"Not today."

Perhaps she had to take the bus, and that was why she had to leave early. Further discussion didn't seem possible, and I wasn't particularly eager to stay in the stuffy, quiet school any longer. Mackenzie and I were going to the Mann Center that evening, and it would be wonderful to be unrushed for once. "I'll see you tomorrow, then," I said.

She solemnly gathered up her notebook and papers.

"Remember," I said as she left the room, "*Romeo and Juliet* is a story Shakespeare adapted. A *story*, not a how-to book."

She looked at me as if checking whether I was mocking her, then she bit at her bottom lip, nodded, and waved farewell.

I halfheartedly tidied my room, packing a set of grammar exercises into my briefcase even though the odds against marking them tonight were astronomical.

I nervously lowered the shades, unable to stop constant glances toward the corner, where the pavement remained stained. I kept reminding myself that the square was back to being its normal busy but peaceable self.

I had covered two windows before my heat-saturated synapses connected and what was going on near the corner registered. April Truong, who had bustled away prematurely to her after-school job, was sitting on a bench next to a young man with a signature scowl.

April, her face a mask of misery, looked skyward, then directly at Woody Marshall, her mouth moving in an unending stream of words, all the while shaking her head in a long, emphatic no as he gesticulated and looked both angry and frightened.

I couldn't imagine what he wanted of her, what the unlikely pair could have in common, or what could have upset both of them so quickly and thoroughly, but it didn't take much imagination to understand that this meeting had been prearranged and was the explanation for April's quick exit.

Woody Marshall and April Truong? She was quicksilver and determination and ambition. He was muscle and pout and resentments. And where were his eternal sidekicks, Tony and Guy?

Was April that naïve that she didn't see trouble a mile off?

Or that romantic that she looked at his angry face and saw, instead, Romeo?

Dear Lord. *That* was what—that was who—she'd been worrying about?

I watched awhile. April bent forward and put her head in her hands. Her back shook. Woody lifted a hand as if to reach over and console her, but ultimately he did precisely nothing. His hand dropped to his side.

I pulled down the rest of the shades. I was supposed to help with English language skills, not meddle in affairs of the heart. After all, Juliet's nurse and the priest were also culpable, for being older people enchanted with the dumb romantic desperation of kids. Besides, on a less lofty level, I knew how receptive I'd have been to a high school teacher's decision to edit my love life. I backed away from the window.

They'll work whatever it is out, I told myself. Everything will be all right.

I was not succeeding in fooling myself. Nothing so far had been all right, April bent over crying continued the not-all-rightness, so why should the trend suddenly reverse itself?

Seven

WE hadn't planned far enough in advance to request bench seats. I prefer the romantic blanket-under-the-stars approach to al fresco concerts, but I quickly understood that the blanket-under-the-broken-leg has quite a different ambience.

We were enveloped by bugs and heat. Mackenzie sat with his cast straight ahead of him, like a log awaiting a bonfire. He made his discomfort acutely clear by incessantly denying it, over-reassuring me that although he might look like a torture victim, he was actually quite comfortable. All of that was uttered in a tone that said: *I'm lying for your benefit. Aren't I noble?*

I passed him the insect repellent and pretended to believe that he was having the perfectly marvelous time he insisted he was.

During his endless convalescence, there weren't all that many adventures we could easily share. He was not a man used to confinement or limits, so he was continually surprised and annoyed. I had thought, however, that music and stars and hot summer nights would soothe his soul.

I had thought wrong.

No sooner were we sticky with repellent than he began his oratorio. "I cannot tell you how boring it is to do nothing worthwhile, day after day," he said.

Not only *could* he tell me, and not only *would* he tell me, but he had *already* told me. Countless times. Secondhand boredom is much harder to endure than problems are. Not that he asked, but at least my woes were variegated, different from day to day. His were the same—and that very sameness was their cause. The fact that this condition was finite and would soon end didn't console him. I tuned him out and concentrated on the hums around me—distant traffic and very close mosquitoes.

"Not a single real buyer in the lot," he grumbled. There'd been an open house, or open loft, the past Sunday, and only lookie-loos had shown up.

"They don't have any idea who did the drive-by shooting," I said.

"Damn, but the heat makes my leg itch." I handed him the chopsticks we carried for under-cast scratching. They didn't reach the afflicted spot.

"I wondered how much attention the police give to incidents like that drive-by."

"You implyin' we don't care?"

"No, but—"

"We care. Thing is to try an' find the guilty party before his gang does. It's not easy, and then you have another killin' to solve, and so on. I sometimes wonder who'll be left eventually."

"I can't stop replaying that moment in my head."

"Air-conditionin's feebin' out at my place."

I gave up. His litany, even told in a lilting good ol' boy from

Louisiana voice as it was, and even sprinkled with glints of humor and self-awareness, as it now and then was, made me want to hold up a great silver cross and run for the hills. I again reminded myself that the morose man sharing my blanket wasn't really Mackenzie, but Mackenzie's doppelgänger who, I trusted, would disappear when the cast and reduced mobility were gone.

"What were those wise words by Epicurious?" I asked. "Weren't they about attitude?" Philosopher, know thyself.

A violinist walked on stage, generating scattered applause. Slowly, the violinist's fellow orchestra members straggled on and arranged themselves, their music, and their instruments, which, as usual, needed tuning. I never understood why they didn't take care of this backstage.

"Who's Epicurious?" Mackenzie asked. "Sounds like a clown."

My compassion reservoir was drained, its last droplets drying in the hot sunset. "Epi-whatever, damn it! He who said something about men being tormented with the *opinions* they have of things, not the things themselves, that's who. Don't you listen to your own wise quotations? Life isn't that bad if you'll look at it differently. You have all the time in the world to catch up on everything you always wished you had all the time in the world for, including memorizing Greek quotations."

"*Epictetus,*" he said. "The Stoic philosopher."

Which only proves that you can lead a man to stoicism, but you can't make it stick.

"He believed that there is only one thing which is fully our own—our will, or purpose. We aren't responsible for the ideas that come our way, only for how we respond to them. As for me, I *am* puttin' my downtime to use. I'm studyin'."

Studying how to pontificate, and getting really good at it. "Greek lit, by any chance?"

"Why'd you say that?"

"Elementary, my dear Watson, given that Epictetus comes to mind so readily."

He raised one eyebrow and said nothing. I got the message. A well-educated human being already knew who Epictetus was.

My ignorance was so humiliating he spared any mention of it. "Studyin' Philadelphia history," he said. "I told you."

"You did. What are you up to now?"

"The yellow fever epidemic."

Still? The actual epidemic had lasted a shorter time than Mackenzie was giving over to the study of it.

"Real depressin'. Not only what happened, but also 'cause it's eerie, lots of parallels to today, to our plague. Nobody knew where it came from, what to do, so they blamed it on refugees from Santo Domingo. That's today's Haiti. Sound familiar?"

"Why in God's name are you still reading about it?" I asked. "Lighten up! It's summer. You're supposed to read fluff. Beach books."

"I got shot at the beach. And I like history."

"Then read happy history." Except I couldn't think of any. "You've got a few hundred years' worth to pick from—why that? Why not sanitized, whitewashed textbook history where anything our side did was for the greater good, out of pure motives and for the best?"

"I want to read *history*," he said, as if that were an answer. "What I'm reading *is* history."

"Speaking of which," I said, "April's paper on immigration is called 'Wretched Refuse.' Don't you think that's a negative—"

"They thought tobacco prevented it."

"Immigration?"

"Yellow fever."

I took a deep breath. He wasn't himself. "I didn't know that," I said. "But I'm worried about April. She overreacted to *Romeo and Juliet*, and seems really troubled." A mote that had seemed peripheral and had been resting in a side pocket of my brain floated into center field. "She ran away from the fountain Friday. Barefoot. Right at the time the others chased a boy. She knew Vo Van, the young man who was shot a few hours later in that same park. And she always checked before she went outside. Do you suppose all of those things are connected? Maybe she was afraid of Vo Van?"

"Don' badmouth history," Mackenzie said. "You should give it more of a try."

I bit at my upper lip. He was injured, petulant, not himself. Not himself.

Please God, let this not be himself!

"This drive-by thing," I tried again. "If April—"

"Shhh." He looked shocked that I was making any sound, and he waved toward the stage where, indeed, Dutoit had entered and was tapping his baton on the podium, then lifting and holding it aloft.

I looked at the conductor and then at Mackenzie. Sometimes, for all my long-suffering tolerance of his pain and inconvenience, the man just plain got on my nerves. I should read history, indeed.

I wondered whether Mackenzie would get out of that cast before I read about us—when we, too, became history.

NORMALLY, when I can't find something, I keep looking. My organizational powers are peccable, which is to say, things are often out of place.

But sometimes I instantly know that the object is not only not where it should be, but that it's lost forever. I get a specific, sick feeling in the vicinity of my belly button. It is a nearly infallible predictor. Once I've had that queasy presentiment, I just about never have found the lost item. Gone is gone.

That's how it was with April Truong. As soon as the morning section entered the room and didn't include her, I felt a nauseating, dread sureness in my stomach.

Lost. She's gone, my belly button said. *Something terrible has happened to her.* Even as another part of my brain started the counterrefrain: *Nonsense! She's late, she's ill, she had an appointment. You're becoming an hysteric.*

But the feeling in the pit of my stomach persisted, and April never showed up.

I stopped Woody as he was leaving the room. It wasn't easy. He was built like a Doberman and moved quickly, and he pretended not to see me at all. "Could I have a second?"

He grimaced, then sulked his way over to my desk. His pals stayed outside the classroom, watching, their arms crossed like mob bodyguards. I wondered what they expected me to do. I was tempted to close the door, but this wasn't top secret, only a question.

"Do you know where April is?" I asked.

"Me? Why would I?"

"She isn't here. I thought maybe she might have told you where she'd be."

"Why would I know anything about that? Why'd I know anything at all about her? I'm not like a truant officer." His T-shirt looked as if it had been custom-fitted to highlight his pecs, and, like his friends at the door, he now crossed his arms, accentuating their every muscle. The official thug pose.

"But ... I ... I thought the two of you ..."

"Me and a gook?" he demanded loudly.

"Really, Woody—please don't use words like that."

"Are you crazy? Me and her?"

Outside the doorway, Tony elbowed Guy in glee, then licked his forefinger and chalked one up in the air for their team. Woody wasn't taking flak from the teacher. Woody was giving back in kind.

"Didn't I see the two of you ... yester—"

"I don't know what you saw ever," he said, "but it wasn't me and her. Not me and her."

I gave it up. What was the point? I wished I could close the door, wondered if it would make any difference. I felt as if he were performing for his pals, but on the other hand, maybe I had misinterpreted the scene outside yesterday afternoon. Maybe their encounter had been accidental. Maybe April had cried because he'd called her names.

"My mistake," I said. "I'm sorry to have bothered you. Hope I didn't delay your lunch too long."

"No problem," he said, already loping toward the door. But just at it, he turned his back to his friends and gave me a small salute. "Thanks," he whispered, so softly that it was more a shaping of his lips than sound.

As soon as my shock ebbed, I understood just how grateful he must have been that I hadn't persisted with questions. But why?

Meanwhile, he'd turned with almost military briskness and, surrounded by back-slapping allies, the smile, the friends, and Woody were gone.

But, of course, so was April Truong.

PHILLY PREP was originally built as a turn-of-the-century beer baron's statement of his net worth, which made for quirky, not always logical school architecture. This included anachronistic, politically incorrect conceits like a narrow back staircase that was off-limits to students, for reasons of liability. However, nobody worried about the odds of servants or teachers—if anyone distinguished between the two—tripping on its dark and narrow treads and breaking their necks, so I used the back stairs regularly.

En route, I passed Five's room. At least half a dozen students—including, to my surprise, Woody and his pals—milled around inside, some holding soda cans, others settling in with sandwiches. At the moment I passed, Five was sitting on the edge of his desk saying something I couldn't hear. The robber baron's house had solid-core doors.

I could see the boy nearest him laugh in response, however, and I was suffused with envy. Summer in the city, and the hardcore mob suspended its contempt for school and all things related and hung out with their teacher. How did Five inspire such devotion, and why couldn't I manage even a shadow of its intensity? Was it a guy thing? Or a gender-free failing on my part?

Farther down the hallway, I passed Flora Jones's room. She was reading at her desk again, oversized tortoiseshell glasses perched on her nose.

I walked on, then doubled back. Her reading matter had looked unbusinesslike. Aura of mass-market paperback.

I knocked on her door. She looked up, smiled—a little tensely, I thought—waved me in with one hand and opened a desk drawer with the other and dropped the paperback into it. My suspicions had been correct, and I wasn't interrupting a serious study session.

"I hope I'm not—" I began.

"Not at all."

"Just that I miss you. Can I tempt you outside?"

"Sorry. Not today. So busy. Besides, it's cooler in my room than anywhere else."

"How come you get special treatment?" An enormous unit blocked one entire window.

"Don't get jealous," she said dryly. "The climate control's for their computers, not me."

"Listen," I asked. "Are you . . . I mean last time we talked . . . is everything okay? You aren't staying up here because you're angry, are you?"

"About what?"

I shrugged. "I don't know. Maybe something I said? Or didn't say?"

Flora shook her head. "Don't take it personally just because I prefer a quiet lunch hour. Besides, I never thought it was you."

"You can't think that anybody here, that somebody at Philly Prep, a teacher, made those calls. That's the only thing that happened, right?"

It's interesting how a whole passel of needs can shape a sentence. Instead of asking Flora whether anything else had happened, which was my real question, I virtually answered myself with what I wanted to hear. Nothing more had happened. Flora had suffered a one-shot of ugliness. Over and done. A fluke.

"No," she said softly.

Unfortunately, juggling syntax does not alter reality.

"It's still going on. I just didn't want to talk about it."

"With me?"

"With anybody except the police. And they said not to. But two days ago, there was a letter, like a ransom note—words and letters cut out of newspapers and magazines. It said: 'Stay where you belong or else, Nigger.' " She took a deep breath and was silent, then she spoke again with her normal, brisk delivery.

"Or else what? And where is it I belong? What makes me not there now?"

"Flora, I don't know what to say."

She stood up and stretched. "And then, yesterday, last night, painting, graffiti. All over the brickwork in front. Letters, zeroes, swastika. It's making me crazy."

"It'd make anybody crazy. But maybe you'd feel better if you didn't isolate yourself. Maybe if you'd be with other people at lunchtime—or take a walk. Want to?"

"I don't want to be with the other people here," she said softly. "There's one thing I didn't mention," she said. "I'll tell you, but you're not to tell anybody else, understand?"

I nodded.

"That note made out of clippings? The word *belong* was made up of a few words, and the second half, the *long* part, was set in type so that it *was* long, all stretched out. It looked familiar. Not like the daily newspaper or any magazine I read in particular. And then I figured it out. Those words were cut out of this school's paper. A headline from the last edition in spring. Remember the 'So Long, See You in September!' banner? How the word *long* was stretched out? It was a perfect match."

I am the faculty sponsor of the paper. The journalists are *my* kids. I felt irrationally responsible for whatever became of our words.

"Maybe terrorism is the way Philly Preppers fill those lazy days of summer," Flora said. "When they're too old for summer camp."

"Somebody could have picked the paper out of the trash, or found it." It sounded unlikely—a terrorist who collected and saved high school newspapers just in case he needed that typeface? "Or," I said, being more honest, "a person who knew the school could go downstairs to the files and help himself. But I hate thinking that."

"Until I know for sure," she said, "I seem to have lost my appetite—both for lunch and socializing. At least around this place." She sat back down. I wondered when she'd had her last good night's sleep. "Present company excepted, of course," she said. "I didn't mean to include you."

"What do the police think?"

"Not much. There's been a rise in hate crimes, and they're concerned, but this is considered something less than a crime. Harassment, I guess. Low priority in today's world. The police are overworked, busy folk. They're sympathetic, want to be kept informed, but aren't overly involved. Of course," she said drolly, "if I'm killed, that'd be a different story. That'd be an authentic hate crime. They're interested in the sticks and stones that can break my bones, not in the names they think can never hurt me."

Eight

As I entered Mackenzie's loft, a delightfully Mediterranean fragrance greeted me: essence of peppers, olives, and tomatoes that still seemed hot from the sun.

I could get used to coming home to a lovingly prepared repast. I could get used to having a good old-fashioned wife.

I'd spent a few hours taking care of scut work—retrieving a silk blouse from the cleaners, drudge shopping for kitty litter and lightbulbs, restocking Macavity's bowl so that the oval kitty didn't starve to death in my absence, and returning a phone message from my mother. Normally, I'd have let that last item slide, particularly since I was still miffed about her tossing Lowell at me. But her message was too bizarre to ignore, even considering the source.

"This is your mother," she'd said although I'm such a quick study that I can, at age thirty-one, recognize my mom's voice. "With *such* a good idea! Mandy—join AA." End of message.

I was sufficiently worried to dial her back. "Mom," I said when I reached her, "I must have misunderstood. It sounded like you wanted me to join Alcoholics Anonymous."

"Yes!"

"But I don't have a drinking problem. And although Lowell Diggs has not turned out to be Prince Charming, that isn't going to drive me to drink, either."

"Do they check? Is there some kind of secret password or salute? Does somebody have to verify that you drank too much?"

"I . . . well, from what I know, of course not. But what—"

"If they don't check, then who's going to know whether or not you belong there?"

"I will. What is this about?"

"Now listen, Amanda, Mrs. Farber's niece?"

I hated it when she inventoried strangers' genealogies. It almost always led to a Lowell Diggs. I didn't know who Mrs. Farber was, let alone her niece. But if I dared to ask, my mother would insist that I *did* know by default, because I knew ten other people with connections to the Farbers, a delusion she would work to prove by chopping at more and more family trees. To my mother, the fabled six degrees of separation is nothing. She's willing to go seven, ten, fifty degrees of separation—to find the missing links between all mankind.

I remained silent.

"The girl—Claudette, I think is her name—the blonde with the ankle bracelet, remember?"

I waited.

"She had a problem with liquor, caused her family a lot of grief."

"Mom, I'm on my way out. I have a *date*." That generally stops her, and in fact it worked now, too, but only for a second.

"With the cop? The . . . Chuck person?"

I admitted that I was, indeed, seeing C. K. Mackenzie again. Déjà Mackenzie. I'd never told her I didn't know his first or middle names. Actually, she was fond of the man she called Chuck. She used to slow down significantly in her matchmaking when I mentioned him. But she refused to come to a full stop. Her bumper sticker read: I BRAKE ONLY FOR SERIOUS MARITAL CONTENDERS. After a year and more of our dithering, she was beginning to fear there was no future with him.

"Chuck can wait," she said. "The point is, Claudette went to AA and met the most wonderful man. He was drying out, too. They were married last week."

"Give the Farbers my congratulations."

"You're missing the point." She sounded almost testy. "They're *there*."

"What's where?"

"Men! *Eligible* men. Eligible again, but only for a short window of opportunity. While they were drinking, most of their marriages have been wrecked, they're—"

"You're telling me to use AA as a dating service? Scope out the drying out at their meetings?"

"Why wait until they're all better and set loose to scatter over the face of the earth? Then, who knows where to find them? Then, when they're all fresh and dried out—"

She made them sound like they'd been to the cleaners for One Hour Martinizing.

"—they're scooped up by other women!"

Why I continue to be amazed by her skewed approach to love, I don't know.

"Think about it," she said.

I thought about the time, instead. Maybe Mackenzie wasn't as prime a candidate as a semidrunk, otherwise-unwanted stranger attempting recovery—but he was what I had, and he cooked, and I didn't want to keep him waiting. "Sure," I said. Why not? I would definitely think about what she'd said. In fact, it seemed unforgettable. My dark mood lightened. Not everything was about hate and division. Some things—albeit dizzy and wrongheaded—were about love. Or at least about Bea Pepper's tireless attempts to fill in for a goof-off Cupid.

"One more thing," she said as I was hanging up. "Only meetings in good neighborhoods, you understand? Meet a better class."

"So," I asked Mackenzie, after I had shared my mother's latest aberrant scheme, "I got to wondering what you'd do at an AA meeting. They don't use last names and you don't use a first or second. Who would you be? C.K.M.?"

He grinned. "Have some more wine. Then we'll go to meetings together and figure out what to call ourselves."

The ratatouille and sea bass were delicious and the company just about its equal. Mackenzie was becoming a better end of day destination because he finally understood that he was on the mend. He was sloughing the pessimism that had weighed him down like so much dead skin.

"Welcome back." I lifted my wineglass. I wasn't sure either of us understood where he'd been, but I didn't care. I was trying to treasure these moments when I had the best of Mackenzie—he had regained his personality, but not his profession.

"A few more days," he answered. "*Then* I'm back."

More or less. The cast would come off and he'd be on crutches or a cane and would require lots of therapy to restore his muscles and agility. But it was nonetheless a major step forward. Flesh was always preferable to plaster as leg casing.

We were becoming giddy with the possibilities ahead. I decided to keep his mind busy in the meantime. "Tell me," I said, "how'd the great detective like to do a little consultation for the next few days?" Beneath my mother's foolishness and Mackenzie's new buoyancy, I still saw the dejected image of Flora Jones.

"I don' like the words *detective* and *consultin'* to be in the same sentence, when that sentence is spoken by you."

"Okay, I'll split them up. How'd you like to do some detection while you're recuperating? But not firsthand—or firstfoot. Only as an adviser, or consultant."

71

"What I was tryin' to say, in plain English, is: Are you getting yourself involved again?"

"Me? I'm trying to get *you* involved again."

He sighed. "You can be straight with me. I've been wonderin' how long it'd take you to bring her up, is all. I actually thought, for a while, that you were goin' to let this one lie. Let the police handle it."

I pushed a dollop of eggplant around my plate as if food rearranging might cure murky thinking. Then I put down my fork. "How do you know about Flora?"

"Who is Flora?"

"I've told you about her. She's that supercompetent computer whiz at school. Can handle anything, I thought, a dynamo, but she's going through . . . wait a minute—if you didn't mean her, then what were we talking about?"

"I know what I was talking about, but I don't know what you—"

"Who?"

"Shouldn't it be *whom*? I'm talking about whom?"

"You're talking about death if you don't answer me soon!"

"The girl on the six o'clock news. The Vietnamese girl."

"Oh, God. Do you remember her name?"

"Not Flora."

"Not April?" Please not on the six o'clock news. None of their news is good. April had been *absent*, that was all.

"That was it. April. They said she went to your school, but hadn't shown up today."

"And that made the news? Jeez, it used to be the truant officer got upset, but not the media! And they say we've gotten lax."

He looked at me oddly.

"I'm sorry. You're making me so nervous . . ."

"If you'd get that car radio fixed, you, too, could know what's goin' on all on your own."

"But still and all—she missed a day of school. Big deal. Why broadcast it?" My vital signs accelerated until they broke the speed laws. That damnable belly squish had been on the mark again. Something terrible had happened to April Truong, and I didn't want to know what. Had to know, but didn't want to.

He poured himself more red wine. "I'm sorry. Sounds like a whole lot more than truancy. More like abducted."

"April?"

"Last seen about eleven last night in Chinatown. In front of a massage parlor. As soon as her brother couldn't find her, he called the police, but April's eighteen, old enough to decide to cut out, and it wasn't even twenty-four hours that she was gone yet. Then somebody found her backpack. It had all her ID, plus books and notes. No money, assuming she carried some. They called the number on her ID. Thought there might be a reward. That's when the parents called the police again. Since then, they've found a witness who says he saw a girl being dragged into a white van in the area where they found the backpack."

"Somebody saw and didn't do anything?"

"It's not the best neighborhood, and he said kinky things happen around the massage parlor. He wasn't about to interfere."

I stood up, just to have something forward-moving to do, and I cleared our plates. I scraped and rinsed and put the dishes in the dishwasher, then I leaned against the sink and waited for Mackenzie to tell me what to do from now on.

"I thought you knew already," he said. "I wouldn't have said anything if . . . as it was, I waited until you brought it up—or I thought you had. What *were* you talkin' about if it wasn't that girl? What about Flora?"

I shook my head. "She's being harassed, but it has nothing to do with—this is awful! What was April doing at a massage parlor? She had a job at a restaurant."

Mackenzie managed to make his shrug exceptionally cynical.

"She didn't work in a massage parlor!" I snapped.

"They showed a photo. Pretty."

"Extremely," I said softly.

He stood up as best as he could. "Isn't much consolation, but I made you dessert."

I couldn't stop picturing April. Stop realizing that last night, while I was sitting on that blanket listening to Brahms and thinking the worst problem in town was being with a grumpy Mackenzie, April was terrified and in danger, grappling, perhaps, for her life.

"Peaches and toasted almonds," Mackenzie continued. "Sit yourself down while I whip up the cream topping. Maybe it'll make you feel a little better."

"Thanks," I said, "but I'll have to pass." My stomach was otherwise occupied, predicting disaster.

THE NEXT MORNING, as I walked into school after a troubled night, even Rina was animated. Rina normally confined herself to overwrought, sultry body language, but today I heard her as soon as I neared the building and continued to hear her until the door was shut behind me.

"So I go 'Stop the B.S., what do you mean, like snatched? I mean, like right off the street or what?' And he's all, '*Snatched, snatched.* You know, like snatched? You never watch TV or what?' He goes, 'It was on the six o'clock news'—like duh, that's what I'd do when I come home after a whole day here, watch news, right?"

Rina's sullen silences no longer seemed all that offensive. But obviously April Truong's disappearance—I refused to call it any more than that—was the morning's universal topic of conversation. Particularly in my first-period class, where her empty chair sat as mute testimony.

We had an essay exam scheduled, but everyone seemed so unnerved, I suggested postponing it. "We could talk instead," I told them. "I don't suppose anybody has answers, but saying how you feel can help."

"Help who? Not April," somebody muttered.

"Right," I heard in several low variations.

At first I was upset by the anonymous hecklers. Then, in a way, I was glad. The class had bonded, even if I hadn't noticed. There was concern. There was a Them versus a Me. On some small, irrelevant scale we'd made progress.

"Too depressing to talk about," Miles said. "What's to say about April?"

"Which one was April, anyway?" The blonde girl, Miss Lethargy, yawned after she asked the question.

The class—close to the most unacademic bunch imaginable—voted to take the exam and then to work on dangling participles and gerund phrases.

Boring, perhaps, but within their control. At least Shakespeare and grammar—unlike real life—made a rough kind of sense.

They settled into their chairs and gradually into themselves. Even Miles seemed willing to commit ideas to paper rather than sing his opinions or turn them into a cartoon panel on the blackboard.

About ten minutes later the deep quiet was broken by the squeal of the door. There'd been no knock, which violated pedagogical etiquette. I should have known my rude caller would turn out to be Helga, the office manager, She Who Is Impervious to All Rules that Apply to Peons Known as Teachers.

A woman in a blue uniform followed her in.

"She's from the police," Helga said in a stage whisper.

"Ah, duh," somebody in back said.

Everyone had stopped writing. That wasn't amazing, but the fact that they seemed sufficiently transfixed to actually watch us rather than use this test break to copy each other's papers was nothing short of historic.

Helga continued to behave as if what she was saying was for my ears only. "They think maybe one of our students might know something," she said with bellowing confidentiality. "About that little Vietnamese girl who disappeared. She wants to talk to them about it. The disappearance. The whole school, really. She's talking to everybody."

"Well, of course she can—" Silly me. I'd thought Helga had been asking permission to disrupt me, but she'd already turned away.

She clapped her hands twice, as if summoning chickens. "Children, someone wants a minute of your time and all your attention. This is Officer Deedee Klein. Now pay good attention because it is your civic duty to cooperate with her."

The class was sufficiently engrossed to not make fun of

Helga's manner of speech, which would have struck even pre-schoolers as patronizing. Eyes shifted between the secretary and the policewoman, between Helga's hennaed hair and Deedee's sandy brown curls. I expected my students to look heavenward as well, to thank the Deity that had sent in an actual, legitimate reason to interrupt their exams.

I, meanwhile, nodded at Officer Deedee, pretending that I was giving her permission to go ahead, pretending that she needed it. Pathetic, but *I* needed it.

"I'm sorry to interrupt you." Her voice matched her hair, soft and tentative. It was not the sort of voice to shout, "Halt in the name of the law!" or whatever they shouted these days. But maybe she upped the amps on the street. She wrote a two-foot-high phone number on the board, then turned back to the class. "You probably all know about the disappearance of your class-mate, April Truong. She was last seen at eleven P.M. the night be-fore last and is presumed to have been criminally abducted. We know that this summer class is made up of people from a lot of different area schools, so you don't have the usual longtime rela-tionships with everyone, and in fact some of you may not even know April. But if you do, or if you know anything at all that might be of some help—please call the number on the board. Ask for me—Officer Deedee Klein—or for anybody else on duty. Anything you say will be handled with total confidentiality. I thank you in advance for your concern for April Truong and for the help you will, I hope, give the Philadelphia Police Depart-ment. Anybody?"

Then, for what felt an eternity, she silently faced the class, as if expecting someone to leap up and present the tidbit of infor-mation that would crack this case.

No one moved. I looked at Woody as inconspicuously as I could, but he had adopted a purposely blank gaze, as if his eyes were sightless and made of glass.

Officer Klein gave up. "Thank you," she said. I wondered if a more forceful official could have generated a response. That raised esoteric questions of gender identity and style, so I squelched that concern.

I made a separate plea for cooperation after she left. "It won't help April if you play us versus them—whatever you feel about the police, get past that. Whatever you know, tell. If you don't want to deal with the police, call in anonymously or tell me and I'll pass it on. But whatever you can do—do it."

I thought that was pretty stirring, but the class looked at me with the same impassivity they'd shown Officer Deedee, then they suggested that it was time to return to their *Romeo and Juliet* exam. Eventually, after what felt like years, the morning session ended.

I walked toward the back stairs, deciding to bypass the faculty lunchroom and Lowell's greetings altogether. In fact, to bypass lunch. I thought I'd walk for the hour, despite the day's clamminess and drizzle. I needed to be alone, and I hoped a moving meditation might produce a useful idea about this abrupt, awful turn of events.

En route, I passed Five's crowded room. I'd had one devoted student, and she'd been snatched away, literally, but Five's boys' club, as I thought of the lunchtime convocation, bubbled along. *News flash*: life wasn't fair.

I peeked in. They didn't look organized. Two were talking to each other in a huddle in a corner, three were reading, and Five was talking to another. What was the allure?

I realized how pathetic I looked, the impoverished orphan at Christmas, peering through Five's window while I clutched the piece of coal that had come in my stocking. I turned and walked on. I heard his door open behind me.

"Mandy," he called, leaving his classroom and his disciples behind. "Have a minute?"

I stopped and nodded, mutely.

"Did you hear?" he asked. "I had no idea. I spent last evening reading, didn't turn on the TV, and I walk to school, so once again—my morning class told me. Who do you think could have done it, and why?"

"Maniacs don't need a *why*."

"So you think it was just another random city thing?"

"I don't know what else to think. It's not as if anybody's asking for ransom—and what could they ask for, anyway? She's poor. So I'm afraid—"

"I feel a special tie to her, don't you? You and I—we were the only teachers here who had her. That makes me feel responsible for her welfare. As if I should have been able to predict—or prevent—or solve this." But he turned his palms up, empty. He had no more solutions than I did.

I smiled in sympathy. We were two well-meaning, absolutely useless adults. I felt sorry for us, too. I changed the subject, hoping to ease his discomfort and some of mine, as well. "Five," I said, "what are you doing with those kids at noon? What goes on?"

He smiled disarmingly. "The truth?"

I nodded.

"And you won't tell your coworkers?"

I nodded again.

"Nothing much goes on. No offense, and I hope they aren't your best friends, and I don't want to sound like a complete egotist—but I couldn't stand the lunchroom scene and nothing I did seemed to stop it. Leaving the premises didn't help—I was 'accidentally' joined."

The Phyllis and Edie Bake-Off. "There hasn't been a home-made goodie since you disappeared," I said.

He nodded. "So I, ah, offered extra credit to those who wanted to be part of a noontime current events discussion."

"A bribe," I said with a smile.

He nodded. "Absolutely. But not a complete lie. Sometimes we do actually discuss government, or foreign affairs, but mostly they discuss current sports events, current women, current movies, MTV videos, things like that, and I eat my lunch in peace. Are you going to turn me in?"

"I salute your diplomacy and determination. Besides, having no break from students all day seems a terrible price to pay for your deception. You're already being punished. Of course, I could blackmail you, tell the bakers what's really going on . . ."

He grinned, as did I, but then the subject had run its course and the atmosphere changed as once again April dominated my mind. And at the same instant, it became obvious that Five had made the same transition.

"What was she doing at a massage parlor?" he asked. He didn't have to say her name. "She didn't seem the type to make her money that way, even if—"

I waited, but he didn't seem willing to finish his sentence. "Even if what?" I prompted. "Go on."

He shrugged. "Even if you never really know a person, not in the superficial way of a classroom. Besides, I was told that most of those places—the massage parlors—are run by Asian mobs."

"But April wasn't a mobster." The word sounded ridiculous. "She wanted—wants to go to college. You know her."

"That's why I didn't want to finish that sentence."

"Sorry. But I'm sure there's a logical explanation for where she was seen and why. And I'm sure she didn't work at a massage parlor."

"But I hear her parents didn't know where she worked."

"Nonsense. I know. It's in Chinatown at some café."

"The kids said the name she'd given them—Star's Café— doesn't exist."

"Her brother drove her there every day."

"Dropped her off at a street corner. Tenth and Race. Near the massage parlor he and his gang members run, the place she was last seen." He looked thoughtful. "Mystifying, makes me wonder if there might be something we know that could be helpful to the police. Through her writing, or class discussions, or the tutoring you did."

"You're assuming a logical reason for all this," I reminded him. "A plot to be untangled, deciphered."

"And you aren't? You think this has no logic? That it's irrational, unfathomable? I don't accept that idea. Everything has its own logic."

"What logical reason could there be to force a struggling wisp of a girl off the street and into a van?" I said. "Everything may have a rationale, but that isn't the same thing as logic. Or sanity."

Nine

WHEN I returned from my lunchtime walk, hot and weary, I cut across the green and leafy square, which was filled with other shade seekers, including half our students.

And Aldis Fellows, who was abruptly striding beside me. I had no idea where she'd been before she appeared. We greeted each other, then walked in awkward silence.

"I'm not comfortable with that, are you?" she said with no preface.

"I'm sorry, I must have missed—what aren't you comfortable with?"

"Them. I thought you were looking at them, too. When we just passed them."

I turned as discreetly as I could and saw an assortment of students.

"Interracial dating," Aldis said. "Or are you one of those pro-diversities?"

She must have been watching a black boy who had his arm around a blonde girl. Both were laughing. "They're talking," I said. "Horsing around."

"I don't think so. In any case, each step leads to more. And to more trouble."

"Well, since you asked, I don't really have any problem with . . ." But she zoomed on, almost speed-walking her way back to school. I took the opportunity to deliberately lag. The woman didn't belong on a summer's day.

Normally, I wouldn't have approached Woody, given his contemptuous use of the word *gook* the day before, but as I wandered toward school I saw him, looking miserable and sitting by himself on the end bench, smoking. You can hang out with Five, but you can't smoke in his room. School rules. So Woody was outside in the postdrizzle midday steam, moodily staring into space, his jaw clenched except when he dragged on his cigarette. There was something intensely alone and alien about him, as if he were outlined in black, superimposed on his environment. Maybe he was the kind who needed a crowd around him in order to have any identity at all.

He was on that same bench—the one where he denied he'd been with April. He looked like a sleepwalker, not able to withstand a sudden shock. "Woody," I said softly.

He blinked, then nodded. "Yo, Miss Pepper," he said in a dull voice. Then he looked at his cigarette as if watching it consume itself into ash were fascinating and all new.

Only minutes until we had to get back. Uninvited, I sat down beside him. "Okay?" I said when he looked mildly wild-eyed and alarmed. "Your friends going to make a civil case out of a teacher sitting on the same bench as you?"

He controlled the search for peers his eyes had been doing,

shrugged and managed a small, off-center grin. "My reputation is shot now."

"So how are you doing with this?" I was willing to bet I didn't have to explain myself any further.

"Look, Miss Pepper, like I told you, I . . . we . . . there's no reason I should be having any problem with it. Except we were in the same class and all like that."

Up close like this, with his face semirelaxed, he wasn't that menacing or homely. In fact, he looked pale and plain and exposed, as if his scowl and belligerent pose were accessories he'd forgotten to put on today.

"But I was wondering, ah . . ." He flicked the remains of the cigarette onto the paving and stepped on it. "Do you think the visit this morning from the police lady was it? You think they'll come back?" he asked in a too-casual voice.

A return visit seemed a distinct possibility. "If they found some more out, or thought we knew something specific."

"Like what?"

"Suppose she had a serious grudge match going with someone. Things like that."

"April? If anybody had a grudge, it'd be his gang, now that Vanny got killed."

"What would that have to do with her?"

"He liked her and was always bothering her, but she didn't want him and he wouldn't get it, you know? He was a little off. Bad temper. Followed her. Here, at school, too."

The window. The figure in the square. April's fear.

"How do you know all this if you and she didn't have any kind of . . . anything."

He looked at his knees. "We go to the same school wintertime, too."

"Friends?"

He shrugged. "Not enemies."

"Why are you so nervous about her? The guys you pal around with on your case?"

He shook his head. His hair was a soft brown with gunk on

it. It didn't budge in the little gusts of damp wind. "My old man," he said. "He'd kill me if he knew I hung out—ever—with a gook. He was over there, you know? He fought them."

"Not April's family. They were on the same side. We were fighting for them, at least in theory."

"Don't matter to him." Woody's jaw reset. "How he feels is they sent him to fight them and now he's supposed to let them live in our block. Doesn't make sense. They're not our kind, he says. And April's family's the same," he added. "Thomas—he's a little crazy. If he'd thought his sister was with a white guy . . ."

"He did, didn't he?" I said.

"What do you mean?"

"Is that why he picked her up on her late days? To make sure she wasn't with . . . anybody?"

He continued to find his knees engrossing, and said nothing.

"Look, Woody, if you know something, if there's something you could do that might save April, you owe it to yourself and to her to let somebody know. You could call that phone number anonymously, or tell me and I'll call, if that would work."

The whole time I spoke, he shook his head, negating me, my suggestions, and who knew what else. "Can't," he said.

"But—"

"*Can't!*" He seemed taken aback by his own explosion. "Sorry," he said more calmly, "but you really don't know what you're saying. And it doesn't matter, anyway. It's too late. April's . . . *dead*, don't you understand? You think the person who took her is going to let her come back and send him to jail? It's because of Vanny, I'm sure."

"That doesn't make sense—what did April have to do with the shooting?"

"Nothing, but they don't know that, do they?"

"But she's Vietnamese, too."

"So what? She wouldn't go with Vanny. Shamed him. And what if . . . what if she did go with somebody else? Somebody white? She was the problem, they must think. Besides, it could have been her brother, maybe, who shot Vanny, to keep him away from her. It doesn't matter, anyway, does it? She's *dead*. But ..." He clasped his hands as if they might fly away and shook his head, mumbling.

"Yes?"

"The worst thing is ..."

We were close to a revelation. Unfortunately, we were also close to the school bell. "What's the worst thing?" I prompted.

He looked full of tears. Not ready to cry, but loaded with moisture and pressure, like a storm cloud that hovered dark and low. "It's my fault," he whispered after glancing around. "It's because of me."

"Because you were close with her? More than just two people who attended the same school?"

"We—" And suddenly the urgency and the anguish disappeared and he grinned at me as he gathered up his books. "So I smoke," he said loudly. "So what? I don't do it inside school, and it's a free country out here. So I'll live a year less. Big deal. Thanks for the lecture, but I'm not askin' you to pay my health insurance, Miss Pepper."

"What on earth are you talk—" Then I got it. "Some day you'll be sorry, Woody," I said, also in an overloud voice. "Young people think they're invincible, but when you're wheezing with a respirator—"

I am amazed at how easily I can slip into the role of obnoxious, meddling elder. Like those dolls that have two heads. Turn them upside down, invert their long skirt, and you have somebody all new. My change of costume came complete with a script and a sound tape of one meaningless prefabricated admonition after another.

Woody was just as good a quick-change artist. I watched him pull on his Hostileman cloak, face mask, and dialogue. He didn't even need a phone booth for his quick-change.

It was a convincing exchange. His buddies slapped him on the back, looked at me with a bare minimum of grudging deference, then ignored me. "Gotta light?" Tony asked him just as the school bell—purposely loud enough to be heard across the street where we were—rang.

"Sure," Woody said, and they moved toward the school with all due sluggishness, lighting up and dragging deeply.

As I passed the dawdlers I shook my head at their smoke screen. Woody made no sign. Woody, who thought April was dead and that he was to blame for it.

Woody, who'd just passed some sort of test with his friends. If only I knew what it was.

ONCE INSIDE the building, I thought I heard another bell, or a warning siren. But it was Flora Jones, shrieking.

Flora, the elegant and unflappable, outside her classroom, splattered with viscous brown globs that leaked down her cream pantsuit jacket as she screamed. "Whoever did this! This is the absolute—"

A crowd of returning students and faculty formed around her. "Flora," I said, "what happened?"

She turned in my direction. Dark goo dripped onto her forehead from her hair. "I *quit*! This does it—I can't take any more of this. My civil rights are—"

"What is that gross stuff on her?" a girl behind me asked.

"*Dirt!*" Flora screamed. "Dirt all over my room—dirt in my files and wet dirt smeared on the boards. *Dirt on my computers!* Dirt in a bucket over the door so that when I walked in—*look at it in there! Go look at it!*" A dozen students accepted the invitation, as did I, for a second.

There were dribbles and splats and small mounds of wet earth everywhere, smeared on the chalkboard, clogging the computer keys. The look of the room and its purpose felt lost, and for the first time I understood what the word *defaced* really meant.

"*It says mud on the board. M-U-D! Do you know what that means?*" Flora's hands were shaking up to the elbows, the veins in her neck looked ready to pop, and tears filmed her eyes. I put my arms around her shoulders, trying to avoid as much mud as I could as I steered her away from her room, hoping we could make it to the nurse's office, to any place with a couch, better still, with sedatives. I almost asked the gathered students if they had any spare downers.

"Don't tell me it'll be all right," she said as we walked. "It won't. It hasn't been. I'm quitting, that's what. I don't know how I'll afford grad school—won't go, then, that's what. Because I'm not coming back to this—this is—nobody should have to—intolerable! My *computers*! My *files*! I was at *lunch*! The one day I go outside—it happens *here—in a school*!"

We approached the wide marble staircase to the first floor. "I hereby *quit*!" she announced to gape-mouthed students coming up from lunch. "You see why? Huh? You see? Find some other fool to try and teach you. I know you're here, whoever made those calls and sent those notes and painted my—I know you're here."

I said nothing. She wasn't ready for words yet. But neither was she necessarily right. Outsiders could and probably had done this for reasons of their own. I visually checked the doorways. We didn't have much in the way of security. Anyone could come in while the doors were wide open. Something had to be done about that, although the idea of a permanent guard further depressed me.

When we reached the bottom of the stairs, I guided her toward the office and the nurse's room, but she pulled away. "No," she said. Her voice now contained only a normal amount of decibels. "I'm out of here. Tell my class to do whatever they want to, somewhere else. The computers need to be looked at before anyone touches them, anyway."

"But—but you'll be back tomorrow?"

"I'm not dirt, Mandy. I'm not slime and slop and mud. *Mud!* You know why they wrote that on my board? Because the crazies call people like me and Asians and anybody who doesn't have their gray skin—they call us the mud people. It's more of the same, it's the letters and the phone calls and the paint on the front door, and I'm not taking it anymore."

"Flora, please. Think about what you want."

"My grandma used to say that when hell was full up, the dead would walk the earth. Hell must be full up, because we're surrounded by ghouls."

I hugged her, I wished her well, I offered to drive her home, to have somebody cover my class. I promised to call her this evening. I made her promise to call me whenever she needed me, wherever. I gave her Mackenzie's phone number, too. I told her to call the police again.

She left, and I couldn't blame her, but I felt a wave of pure terror and saw the edge of the earth, with people falling off it—good people like April and Flora. Or maybe they were being pushed.

EVEN without major miseries like disappearances and defacings, these quadruple-long sessions themselves provided heat rash. I could barely endure my afternoon section, and not because of anything its participants did or didn't do. Blame it on the clock, which insisted on creeping at its normal rate. Blame it on the D.D. Index, which estimates Deodorant Despair. There are days where the combination of heat, humidity, and adolescent hormones defeats the heavy artillery of the pharmaceutical companies. Nobody's fault, precisely, but if there's anything to aromatherapy, then eau d'afternoon is its antithesis—aromatraumatic and catastrophic for one's mental health.

But blame it more on the lasting image of Flora Jones, mud-splattered and justifiably enraged. What was going on? Should I have anticipated what felt like an unending series of ugly events as a part of growing up and being an adult? Or was the world really getting more and more mean-spirited?

The class didn't need to talk about April, because she'd been discussed in their morning sessions, and nobody had anything new or tangible or helpful to offer. I didn't feel like rehashing the attack on Flora Jones's room, so it seemed important to move on, at least imitate normality in the form of a planned lesson on writing business letters.

A schizoid afternoon. I made notes on the board as we collectively created a request for an interview. "You think there should be something in here, too, about why you want a job at this particular place?" I suggested. "A little flattery, maybe? A little selling of your special aptitudes?" Meanwhile, my brain ignored their employment futures. It kept picturing the boy being blown off the sidewalk; April being dragged into a van; Flora, splattered with mud, accusing the school population of viciously harassing her. And to balance things out with a bit of the irrelevant and ridiculous, my stomach keened, audibly, a primitive lamentation because I'd skipped lunch.

The class talked about salutations and conclusions, then switched to the actual writing of letters, answering job opportunity ads they'd clipped the night before. They uncapped pens and opened notebooks and busied themselves. Quiet time for me, a little independent thinking for them. Running a summer school class is a lot like running a nursery school. Class time is drastically longer than attention spans, and keeping the group from becoming a mob depends on changing activities at regular intervals. Make them use different muscles, feel that what they're doing is forever new. I just wish we had nap time, too.

This was an assignment they appreciated because it was pragmatic. It didn't require analysis of anything except what they themselves wanted. I watched with pleasure as they wrote away, even though their work would become my work this evening, as would the morning class's essays.

I should have taught driver's ed, or gym, or cooking. I'd leave school empty-handed, whistling, and free. Or even math, if only I were better at it, because there an answer was an answer, not something to be pondered and explained the way a sloppy sentence needs to be.

I pulled out the morning's exams and flipped through masochistically, guesstimating the degree of misery they'd provide. I was hoping that inside the fractured syntax and shattered spelling I'd find interesting ideas. They'd been asked to discuss the relative responsibility of Romeo, Juliet, and their respective families and society in creating the tragedy. We'd discussed aspects of this, such as prejudice, immaturity, hot-headedness, rigidity, grudges, and adult roles.

I saw the usual suspects—smartasses, semiliterate, unpunctuated, nonresponses: "Well of course Juliet was immature isn't it obvious she still had a *nurse* what do you think that means when a grown girl is still nursing?" We needed a lesson for the comma-challenged. Or "Romeo should have dumped her right away, get somebody who'd come down from her high balcony and party." Or "It was everybody's fault—they talked so funny how could anybody know what was going on? Why didn't they say what they meant instead of whithers and yons?" Also, there were the uninspired but well-meaning ploddings of a flat-footed mind. "Although it is my understanding that people married much younger in those days, if you ask me, thirteen is not mature enough to make major life decisions like who a girl is supposed to marry. I think you should be sixteen before you make major life decisions like that. If she had waited until she was sixteen, like I have, to make such major life decisions, maybe things would have worked out better instead of so tragical."

And always, creative spelling and expressions: "Nobody was to blame for nothing. It was there fate. They should have stuck with there own people not the enemy and not brought wrath down on there heads with all that pubic fighting." Would I tell him what he'd said?

And a surprisingly good one. "It was a setup, the way all blind prejudice is. People Romeo and Juliet didn't even know had decided for reasons nobody can even remember—probably power or money or something else completely irrelevant to this generation—to hate one another, so of course their children became forbidden fruit to one another. Nobody should have to deal with secondhand hate." That was from a small and silent boy who had never before voiced an opinion on anything. I was heartened, and I resolved to work on one of my many prejudices. I too readily dismissed the pod-people who occupied chairs and did nothing else but deplete the oxygen supply. Look what had been going on behind those vacant eyes.

I flipped through all the papers. Woody hadn't handed one in. That can be a ploy—the student insists he turned in his exam and implies that I have lost it, but I didn't think Woody was playing that game. I thought that instead, whatever had driven him outside to smoke and brood had been operating in the classroom while time passed and the paper in front of him remained blank. After all, I had asked about fault just when he believed himself responsible for a fresh tragedy.

I rifled the stack a last time and was struck by the odd look of Miles's paper. I'd been surprised when he docilely consented to a garden-variety essay exam, but I'd assumed he lacked the energy to be his usual overly creative self, because he'd been distracted and agitated at the time. He, too, had come from April's home school. She was his friend.

However, his "essay" was anything but standard.

> Who's supposed to say whether present guilt lies with
> A group? An idea? A tradition? A
> Person? Not Romeo, Juliet or that gang. They're dead.
> Assigning guilt is useless, something he wouldn't dare.
> Would he?
> Ask him.
> Perhaps he is
> Afraid.
> Probably is, because
> Reality
> Is too much like fiction and
> Life sucks.

I sat down and reread it. Who was the *him* I was supposed to ask—assuming I was supposed to ask anyone, that the question wasn't rhetorical—and about what? And what was that about present guilt? I was tempted to leave my class and, if Miles was enrolled in an afternoon class as well, find and interrogate him.

Maybe this was just a cryptopoetic outpouring, or a bluff, words on paper, any words, arranged "poetry style" as a sop for the teacher. Or maybe Miles thought poetry was supposed to be obscure, that ideas were more impressive if incomprehensible.

Or maybe it made sense and I simply wasn't getting it. Maybe it meant what it said. Life sucks.

Ten

At the end of the day, tired as I was, I didn't feel ready to leave the building, even though my classroom felt sore and empty like the gaping socket of a missing tooth.

April should have been here, working on pronunciation and writing. Learning. But the room was silent.

I couldn't bear to accept Woody's assumption that the girl was dead, although I understood the logic of it. And even if she was, miraculously, alive, I didn't want to think of her in fear, or pain.

Five was at my open door, his hand raised as if about to knock on its frame. "You in a hurry?" he asked politely, even though I was an inert lump.

"Kind of the opposite. I feel at loose ends. Normally this would be the hour I tutored April."

He sat down in one of the classroom chairs and lowered its writing arm so that he could stretch out his rangy frame. I wondered if they grew all of them like that out there. He made the rest of us seem not only pale and unathletic, but crabbed and undersized and Eastern.

"That's kind of why I hoped we could talk," he said. "Maybe I seem fixated, but let's forget the word *logic*. I won't use that anymore, but all the same, there must be a motive behind it, and if all of us who knew her pooled our data, we might get somewhere."

"Like what? You don't think anybody from here in school took her, do you?"

He shook his head. "I mean maybe we learned something relevant through her essays and class discussions, and your extra time with her. Something we don't yet recognize as useful. Reasons for her behavior and what happened. For starters, what was she doing hanging around a—let's face it—a whorehouse? What kind of family does she come from that lets their daughter—"

"She couldn't have worked at a massage parlor." Of course, I had no hard evidence, only instinct, scraps and tidbits, bits and pieces of what constituted April Truong, the kind of information you glean when you aren't in search of any. The kind that simply stuck to what you were wearing. "She said she worked in a café. I believe her."

"Then why did the news say the place didn't exist? Wouldn't you make up a cover story for your teacher if you worked in a massage parlor?"

"She didn't! I'm sure she wouldn't have. There was a—there *is* a great innocence about her. Not naïveté, but an excitement about the future, a belief in herself and the possibilities. It isn't how I'd think a girl who had to do that kind of work would sound."

"Drugs?"

"I'd be astounded."

"Maybe not using, but involved in sales—"

I shook my head.

"—or having a boyfriend who was? Sometimes revenge is carried out pretty widely by those gangs."

"What gangs?" Who had said anything about gangs?

"Gangs involved in drugs and massage parlors. Vietnamese gangs."

"No boyfriends, no drugs that I know of," I said honestly.

"Who were her friends?" he asked. "Was she a loner?"

"The other people from her home school seem as if they were friendly one to another, but I don't know how social a person she—"

"Hello there!"

It was nothing short of amazing. Phyllis the Sibilant hadn't visited me once since the day before school began, when, by incredible coincidence, Five had also been in my room. Now that he'd escaped the lunchroom, she must have been prowling the building in search of him. I wondered how often she found him.

However much it was, was too often. He flinched when he heard her warbled greetings.

"Isn't it hot, though!" She wore a flowered, filmy skirt, and high-heeled sandals with ribbons that wound around her ankles. The ensemble ached for a large-brimmed hat and a cup of tea. "I thought this day would never end. I'm not sure my stamina is up to summer sessions anymore. I must be getting old!" She put her hand to her mouth to muffle a Scarlett O'Hara titter that begged for a gentleman's denial of what she'd said.

The gentleman present failed to respond properly. "We were talking about the missing girl," Five said instead.

Phyllis adjusted her face to the solemnity of the topic. "So dreadful—the police disrupting class and all. It took me forever to get my people back in stride."

"Pretty dreadful about her being abducted, too," I said quietly.

"Of course. I didn't mean I don't care about little June."

"April," I said.

"I knew it was a month. Besides, that wasn't her real name."

Phyllis sounded triumphant, as if she were revealing something important we'd missed. "She picked it out of the blue. I was told that she's really something like Your Duck. The girl Americanized it for us, although how you get from duck to April beats me."

"Maybe that's what the Vietnamese meant." I didn't see what was noteworthy about making her name easier and less conspicuous, but Phyllis looked scandalized, as if any defection from Your Duck constituted betrayal.

"And where was that girl's common sense?" she asked. "Hanging around a neighborhood like that late at night, alone. Honestly!"

"She worked in Chinatown. At a café."

"I heard a—"

"A café," I repeated.

"I find the term Chinatown offensive," Phyllis said. "It isolates one ethnic group, and besides, shouldn't it be *Chinesetown* if that's what they meant?"

"Who are *they*?" I asked.

"Actually," Five said, "with all the different sorts of people who live there now, maybe it should be Orientaltown."

"Oh, no. Oh, my, no! That's truly offensive. Nobody says that anymore. Orient means the East, and what does that imply—that some other place west of it is the center of the universe?"

"Asiatown, then?" What in God's name were we talking about? "Pacific Basintown?"

"But don't you find it offensive to label a geographical area by the country of origin of its settlers?" She beamed a large-toothed smile at Five. "We wouldn't say Irishland, would we? We make some groups so conspicuous—denigrate them, really. I consider it *them*ism, the verbal ostracism of the perceived outsider."

"Of course you're right," he said. "That's why I never refer to New England, or Germantown, or New York, or New Jersey, or even go near them."

"If you're going to be that way," she said, but gently, flirtatiously.

I'd had it. "I'm bushed," I said. "As you can tell, my room tends to overheat, even on a dull day like this, and I find it difficult staying awake all day. But be my guests as long as you like. Just close the door behind you."

And damned if they didn't say they would. Well, more accurately, Five made moves to leave, but Phyllis implored with small, cooing sounds. She had a question about grade-averaging. Apparently, she wasn't interested in my opinions on the subject.

Five checked his watch and agreed to stay a few minutes.

"Thanks," Phyllis said, as if she'd been given the world's most valuable gift.

What the hell—at least she was having a grand day. It's only right that somebody in the known universe should.

IT BOTHERED me that I didn't like Lowell Diggs. It felt prejudiced and narrow. Another example of us-against-themism, as Phyllis might have put it.

I told myself that it wasn't his fault that his features had been put together the wrong way, or that his sweat glands were hyperactive. The absence of a chin is not a sign of unworthiness, a thin and whiny voice doesn't necessarily reflect a worldview, and the fact that he was shaving-impaired should have provoked pity, not contempt. But I couldn't squelch my annoyance at the inevitable missed clump of hair and the tissue-covered specks where he'd cut too deeply.

And yet once again, as I left school, he called my name and hurried to walk beside me, and I fixated not on Lowell's hidden potential but on the scraggly patch below his left nostril. I disliked it—and him, by default. And me, for my pettiness.

"Need a ride, Mandy Pepper?"

I shook my head. "Thanks anyway. I'm walking to school and back these days. Easy exercise." I would have accepted a lift from almost anyone else. The air stuck to me like a damp, sour washcloth, like a whole mildewed laundry basketful dumped on my head. We needed a cleansing storm, a King Lear kind of production number, to wash away this oppressive atmosphere.

But I, with my prejudice and prejudgment now extended to

his possessions, didn't want to encounter the inside of Lowell's car. I knew it would contain the automotive equivalent of unshaved patches.

"Mind if I walk with you a while, then?" he asked.

Could I say no? I didn't want to hurt him gratuitously. A parallel walk was just that and nothing more.

One of the problems I had with Lowell was that every time I saw him, I could imagine my mother saying "What's so bad about him? Give him a chance." So even though I didn't want to give him the time of day, let alone a bona fide chance, my guilt at not wanting to obliged me to give him the chance I wouldn't otherwise have given him—if that's what my mother, even long-distance, wanted. Is that intelligible? How about mature?

"You seem down," Lowell said. "Not your usual cheery self, Mandy Pepper. What's bothering you, if I may be so bold as to ask?" He spoke his silly lines with jolly ineptness. I thought of all the girls who must have turned him down, and I tried to be kind, even though what was bothering me at the moment was, in fact, him.

"The weather. Fatigue."

"No, no, no," he said with a finger waggle. "I know you too well to believe that. Can't fool Uncle Lowell."

That did it. He'd had more than a fair chance and had blown it. I opened my mouth to say something scathing, but he interrupted.

"Besides, you don't have to tell me. I already know."

"How would you?"

"Because you are a sensitive and caring person, so of course you would be affected by the evil you feel encircling us."

"The—" Us?

"The girl who was stolen, and Flora, what was done to her room. Well, to her, really."

"Are you saying the two events are related?"

"Many events are related," he said in a solemn, albeit high-pitched voice. "Don't you feel the rising tide of evil? I don't believe in coincidence."

"Like, um, what other things are in the tide?" I eyed him nervously. People don't talk about evil. Not people I want to hear. Even Lowell hadn't talked about it the other times he'd intercepted my walks and lunches. He'd talked about math, computers, and his aunt Melba. He'd even talked about the woman who'd unceremoniously shaken free of him three months ago. So what had provoked this? I checked out Lowell's small, gray eyes, made sure they weren't spinning.

He shrugged. "There's much more in the tide. Vandalism. The old graveyard that was spray-painted. That wasn't random violence. That was hitting a definite target."

Rebecca Gratz's grave. Weeks ago. Old news, nearly forgotten. Lowell was paranoid. Graffiti in a graveyard is, unfortunately, nothing exceptional. Graffiti anywhere is, unfortunately, unexceptional.

There were spray-painted stigmata all over the city. I couldn't believe some people wanted it classified as art. If so, then every time a dog lifted a leg and marked a fireplug as his turf, that, too, should be declared a work of art. There's no difference between that and the taggers' sprayings—except that the dog's product is biodegradable. In any case, graffiti isn't a sign of conspiracy or evil.

"It was a Jewish cemetery. Are you aware that Pennsylvania has more racist and anti-Semitic activity than any other state?"

"Oh, Lowell, surely not. That's the job of the South, isn't it? This is Pennsylvania. Quaker tolerance and all."

"You're an innocent. There's even an anti-Semitic group who believe that the computer bar codes on food packages are part of a Jewish plot to kill Christians."

The idea was ludicrous enough to be funny. Where did Lowell do his research? In an asylum for the incurably wacko?

"There's more evil on the loose than ever," he said firmly. "Often in disguise. Be careful who you befriend."

Meaning what? Whom? Himself? That was the trouble with being nice to people you didn't like. They turned out, too often, to be people you didn't like.

"I can trust you, Mandy Pepper," he said. "After all, we're friends."

There was no empirical basis for his feelings, but I couldn't think of a humane way to say so.

"Which is why I want to warn you about our Five, as he likes to be called."

Enough of the search for polite ways to handle this man. "What are you saying? Could you be more precise?"

"I understand. You women like him. You women are overly influenced by classic features and a smooth manner. In your biologically programmed imperative to find excellent specimens to father your children, you're too often attracted to superficial qualities. But Satan can wear a handsome face, you know."

"I'm really uncomfortable with this, Lowell." He was pathetic. Painfully obvious and pitiable. And still unlikable.

His face took on a fanatic's glow. "He's cunning. Nothing you could link directly to him. But *things*, Amanda. Trust me. He is not what he seems."

"People seldom are." I could, for example, have pointed out to Lowell that I had taken him for a poorly groomed bore, while he was actually a poorly groomed madman. I wasn't sure this man should teach anybody's children.

"Don't judge a book by its cover."

"Thanks for sharing that." I took a deep breath. "I'm sure that as a mathematician, you require proof. You want things to add up." I was proud of my analogy, and I savored it before continuing. "Well so do I, and I'm sorry, but you aren't offering anything tangible." Except jealousy. Understandable, but repugnant all the same.

"You're a bright woman, Mandy Pepper, but childish in many ways." His tone was darkly disappointed.

We had reached the corner where I should have turned right toward home, but I was sure Lowell would escort me, and I didn't want him overly familiar with my address. "I nearly forgot where I was going," I said. "I'm supposed to meet my friend Sasha. We're having dinner." I took a deep breath to stop the babbling that usually accompanies my lies. "This has been a real treat," I said when I was ready to speak like a normal person, "but I'm going down to Society Hill. Sixth Street, quite a way off. I'll see you tomorrow."

It should have worked. It would have, if he hadn't been Lowell. If I hadn't still been aiming for nice-girl politeness. "Get lost" would have been less ambiguous. As it was, he claimed that he was invigorated by the exercise and the scintillating—truly, he used that word—company, and he'd walk a bit longer, if I didn't mind. He even patted his spare tire and said the exercise would do him good. He was much too sedentary, he told me, spending all his free time keeping up with the literature of his field and working at his computer, surfing the Net.

I wondered what I'd do when we actually reached Society Hill. I wasn't sure whether Sasha was in town, let alone home. And in fact, Mackenzie was coming to my house for a dinner for which I was totally unprepared. How would I get out of this? Get rid of Lowell and turn back without antagonizing him, without putting pennies in his insane-o-meter?

So on we walked. It wasn't all that unpleasant. I didn't have to utter a syllable. Lowell waxed poetic about the Infobahn, as he loved to call it—many times.

I was relieved to see no one I knew. In particular, I cringed at the thought of a student seeing me with Lowell and making drastically wrong assumptions. It was very third-grade of me, I know, but it was also the truth.

However, I didn't recognize a soul, and Lowell wasn't overly interested in either architecture, history, or fashion, so he didn't dawdle or stop to admire or despair of anything along the way and our progress was speedy. I, on the other hand, studied the ever-increasing displays of personal flags hanging out of homes. Close to the Fourth, as we were, some were patriotic fantasias in red, white, and blue. One was a sunflower. Presumably, in autumn, the owner changed it to corn or chrysanthemums. Some reflected private passions—a fish biting a hook, a sailboat against the sun, a golf ball and club. I wondered what the one with a whale meant. Maybe Ahab lived there.

And although the custom flags were too expensive a decorative object for me to consider, I still wondered what I'd put on one if I could. The question used to be what your sign was. Given these outfront signs all over town, was the question: What's your symbol?

"Your friend lives in Society Hill?" Lowell asked.

That was indeed Sasha's address—but only when she was in town. We turned right on Sixth Street while I considered my options. I thought of the dire warnings I'd been given as a child about the snare we set when first we tell a lie.

I could go in her building and wave Lowell off. I could buzz somebody else. I could . . . I could perhaps stop acting as if this were an old *I Love Lucy* script? Maybe I should just come clean. Admit that I wasn't to meet Sasha, after all.

Except there she was. Big as life—which is quite big, indeed— and in Technicolor, a camera balanced near the tip of her nose. She was in front of Mother Bethel, the church that former slave Richard Allen began two centuries earlier, when he and other black members knelt in the *white* pews of their Methodist church and were told to leave in mid-prayer.

"Sasha!" I called. "I thought you'd be home, whipping up dinner. I'm starving. What are you doing out here?"

She lowered the camera and looked at me intently.

"This is Lowell," I said. "He graciously kept me company on my walk here to my dinner date with you." As blatantly put as I dared. She either got the message or was off my list of friends.

Lowell studied her warily. Dressed in a fuchsia scarf criss-crossed around her chest and what seemed a bedspread, emerald and ocher this time, draped into a sarong low on her hips, she towered above him, her six feet enhanced by clogs that looked like hand-me-downs from the Wicked Witch of the West.

"I told you dinner would be casual," she said. "I'm using the kitchen as a darkroom today. Which means takeout. Thought we'd hit Reading Market and make a choice. Hi, Lowell. Pleased to meet you."

"The pleasure is all mine," he said with mortifying earnestness, as if he'd just invented the phrase. "Besides, any friend of Mandy Pepper's . . ."

His approach was a little backward and a lot overconfident. I'd known Sasha since elementary school, and Lowell superficially for three weeks.

"Oh," he said, "well, not *exactly* any friend of Mandy Pepper's, because we were just talking about *one* of her friends who isn't as worthy as others."

"You were talking," I said. "I wasn't."

"No problem," he answered.

Sasha blinked. "Well, sure," she said. "Whatever you say. I'll be with you in a sec. I've been trying to catch a sense of it on film. I'm not sure it's possible, though."

Surely, the African Methodist Episcopal mother church was too massive in its High Victorian brick and stone for Sasha to capture at close range.

"So violent," she said. "And meaningless."

The street was deserted, the only oppressive element the heat. Violence seemed far away in spirit and geography.

She waved toward the recessed entry, dark in shadow. "Come look if you want to be depressed."

I came and looked and was depressed. The building had an arched doorway with a stained-glass window over it. Its doors, designed to be solid and welcoming, ready to swing open and admit the visitor, had been defaced. Rough red circles with a spray can's aureole of fuzzed spatters, and one long drip, like a bloodstain, down to the threshold.

"I tried to get into the pure aesthetics of it," Sasha said. "The brightness of the red, red blood, rebellion—but I couldn't. It feels like violation."

Lowell squinted in the direction of the doors. "You're wrong about one thing," he said. "This isn't meaningless." His face was flushed, not from the heat, I feared, but from unwholesome excitement.

I wanted to warn Sasha about Lowell's fixation on evil, and I raised my index finger and pointed it at my temple, meaning to spin it in that universal body-language indication of craziness. But Lowell straightened up and looked at me with a bright and expectant expression. I put my index finger to work scratching my eyebrow.

"Further evidence of the pervasive menace that sprayed those graves, Mandy Pepper. Perhaps related to the mud in Flora Jones's room today as well." He sighed and grew silent.

"Did you finish that thought? Are you going to?" Sasha felt no need to suffer fools gladly, or at all.

"Those aren't circles." Lowell pointed at the doors.

They surely weren't squares, or stars, or random shapes. There were four circles—ineptly drawn, but circles nonetheless.

"What do you think they are, Lowell?" Sasha asked with absolutely no inflection in her voice.

Lowell looked at her with a poorly shaven face full of contempt. "I don't *think* they are. I *know* they are. And what they are is eights."

That didn't sound nearly as crazy as I had feared. Eights weren't much. I'd never cared for them particularly, had trouble with their times tables, never got excited about Crazy Eights, either. But still and all, two eights seemed fairly innocuous.

"Eight-eight," Lowell said.

"Really," Sasha said. "I would have sworn it was just a swing or four of the spray canister."

I didn't get it. A lot of taggers used their neighborhood, their street number, for example, but there wasn't any Eighty-eighth Street that I knew of.

"It's part and parcel of the evil encircling us," Lowell said. He was obviously fond of that image.

I wondered if Aunt Melba knew what a sicky her nephew was. Worse—I wondered if my mother knew, and was so desperate about my single status that she didn't care.

"It's their mark." Lowell's voice trembled with emotion. "*H* is the eighth letter of the alphabet. Two eights represent two *H*'s."

My irritation with his pseudodrama, with his entire being, must have been visible at this point, because Lowell pointed at me and with still-greater dramatic flair. "I am not crazy!" he shouted, or as close to a shout as you can get in a tremulous, whiny voice.

"Of course you're not," Sasha said. "But you're not comprehensible, either, sweetie. Aren't you going to tell us what's the big deal about those two eights that might also be *H*'s?"

"Aitch, aitch," he yelped, like a yappy dog. "It's code! It stands for, 'Heil, Hitler.' "

I stopped laughing, even silently, at him.

The shadows of the recessed entryway of Mother Bethel, symbol of human dignity, reached out to the sidewalk, blotted away the sun and spread darkness over the street. And deep in its shadow, I thought I could see Flora, screaming.

I backed off from the building, from the bloodred loops on its doors, before they encircled me as well.

Eleven

"I STUDY the phenomenon," Lowell said.

Sasha was still trying to document the outrage on the church's front doors, twisting to the left and right, moving in for closer angles, back for the play of light and shadow.

"This is the fourth recent eighty-eight sighting," he went on. "Previously, there was a rash in Bucks County, but it's spreading, growing evermore powerful. And you, Mandy Pepper, could be in danger because of your open friendship with one of their targets."

"Flora?"

He nodded. "You appear a sympathizer. You put your arms around her today. You comforted her. Everyone saw."

"Please."

Lowell's zealot's eye and mouth were not to be stopped. I was being punished for hypocrisy. I vowed to never again try to be nice to anyone I instinctively disliked. Even if they were shaving-impaired.

"Or perhaps this is a new group," he said. Sasha clicked a few more times. I wondered how many shots of a door one person could take. "A more subtle, and therefore more dangerous cadre." I was no longer sure what Lowell was talking about, only that I didn't want to hear it. "After all, nothing is signed per se, and there are none of the indications that it's one of the groups with which I am familiar. Still, the defilement of graveyards, the harassment, the abduction—"

"April's abduction doesn't fit," I said, rather snappishly. "It doesn't make sense in your context."

"In what context does it make sense?"

"I didn't mean it that way. But it only makes sense in the way that nothing makes sense today. In the sense of urban crime, in the sense of bad things happening to good people, as random, senseless violence. That's where it fits. Nobody left a note, or made a phone call or gave it any symbolic, larger meaning, the way they did on the doors."

"That sort of naïveté lulls people like you into a sense of false complacency," Lowell said. "As your friend, I have your best interests at heart, and I'm warning you: be alert. Sometimes, their only goal is chaos, so of course, you can't figure out the sense of it."

He gave me the creeps, and I wondered if he wasn't like the pyromaniacs who started fires and even fought them, like the preachers who railed against the very sins of the flesh that occupied their free time. Lowell doth protest too much. What made him obsessively interested in hate groups? Was he really only a worried observer? "There isn't a single skinhead at school, if you're saying that the business with Flora's classroom is a—"

"They've gotten craftier. You can't identify a neo-Nazi by a look or an outfit anymore," he said. "It could be the clean-cut young man next to you, the ordinary-looking—"

Sasha snapped the cap back on her lens. It sounded like a sonic boom. "I hope you don't think I'm rude, Lowell," she said loudly, "or frivolous to think of food given the state of the world and the many plots against its people, but Mandy and I, we had this date and I've made us late already, so if you'll excuse us?"

"I could walk you to Reading Market," he said. "That's where you said you were going."

"Well, see, the date includes . . . there are others involved," Sasha said darkly.

He didn't get it. "This is a big, mean city. Sometimes, even in broad daylight, it's smart to have a male escort."

"You don't have to convince me of that," Sasha said. "I'm a male escort enthusiast. Wherever. But today we have to stop off at my apartment and do girl-things, you know?"

Lowell, master of evil, protector of womanhood, blushed so hard that even his unshaven facial hair took on a rosy hue. "Oh, yeah, sure." But he didn't move, except for his brow, which furrowed. Then he remembered what men said when taking their leave. "So I'll see you tomorrow, Mandy Pepper, right? And a pleasure to have met you, Sasha."

We watched his stooped shuffle for a moment, then we turned and headed north, toward the market.

"Is he by any chance your mother's handiwork?" Sasha asked.

"How did you guess? Her two latest suggestions have been Lowell and—get this—that I join AA to meet men."

"That idea finally reached Boca Raton?"

"You've heard it already?"

"Heard it, done it. It's *ancient*. First you meet them in a bar and then in AA. It's very Eighties, though. The bookstore's the place this decade. Better pickings and more to talk about than his recovery. My advice? Don't fix what ain't broke. Mackenzie ain't broke, except for his leg. Wait till he is."

"Speaking of which, want to come to dinner? The slightly broken Mackenzie is limping over."

A while back Sasha would have gagged before suggesting I stay with C.K., and I'd as soon have invited her to join us as I'd have brought home a strange cat to share Macavity's Tuna Delite Dinner. Which is to say, Sasha and Mackenzie spent a long time snarling, hissing, and swiping at each other, albeit metaphorically, before bonding. But now they'd forged a grudging peace and respect which made hostessing easier.

"Couldn't you pick him up in your car, given that he's crippled?" she asked. "Cut him some slack?"

"Oh, please. Nobody's crippled anymore. He's ambulatorily challenged. And bullheaded. Insists his sweaty walks are aerobic exercise."

"I think he's crazy," I said a minute later as we walked toward the market.

She knew I didn't mean Mackenzie. "Scary, too," she added.

"Not that it isn't creepy to see a reference to Hitler on a church door—if we can believe that's what those numbers meant."

"I still think they looked like swirls. Or four of the five rings of the Olympic symbol. Lowell seems the kind who'd find evidence of the devil in a bad hair day."

"But even if those were eights, and even if they meant what he said, I can't believe everything is linked. What would April's disappearance have to do with Hitler?"

We walked up Sixth Street and through the Historic Park, passing Independence Square and Hall, the glassed-in Liberty Bell, and the Free Quaker Meeting House. I loved this part of town in this season, with its grassy brightness against the weathered reds and oranges of the buildings. A brick city, built so as not to burn by colonists haunted by memories of the Great Fire of London. I watched an unashamedly hokey horse wearing a flower-bedecked hat pull a buggyload of tourists, clippety-clop along the cobblestones. There was a long line curling out of the Liberty Bell's home, and park rangers talking to groups at Independence Hall. The echo and sense of crucial events was so thick it became part of the atmosphere. Here, it isn't the heat or the humidity that gets you, it's the history. Splendidly. All that yearning and work and struggle to build something new, glorious, and free.

Which made the graffiti on the church doors even more revolting.

Then I thought about April, the wretched refuse paper. "What about Chinese food?" I asked.

"Really? Of all the options at Reading? I thought—"

"As in Chinatown. Let's get it there."

"Too far."

"A few extra blocks."

"I'm lugging this camera and the temperature is five hundred degrees and . . . why?"

"Because the missing girl worked there. And was abducted there."

She stopped walking. "That's disgusting! Ghoulish! I never imagined you for one of those people who buys the maps of dead stars' houses."

I trudged on. Eventually she dropped the pose and caught up with me. "What is it?" she asked in an almost normal voice.

"It doesn't make sense."

"You're going to snoop? Give me a break! What do you expect to find? A vital clue that escaped everybody else, Sherlock? A matchbook from a notorious nightclub with a scribbled message only you can decode?"

"That used to happen a lot more than nowadays. Everybody's given up smoking. Not many scribbled-on-matchbook clues."

"Then what?"

"I want to find out where she worked."

"Why?"

"I don't know. Because the place she said she worked at doesn't exist and they're making it sound like she worked in the massage parlor, and I'm sure she didn't."

"So this is to update her résumé?"

"People search more intently for a lost student than for a lost sex worker."

Sasha turned left on Filbert, in the direction of the terminal, but sighed histrionically and turned right two blocks before it, toward Race Street. En route she decided that much as she loved both me and Mackenzie, she wanted to eat at her apartment and she wanted only soft pretzels with mustard as her meal. Feeling as if I were dealing with a toddler, I promised we'd go to the market for fresh-baked on our way back.

"What now?" she asked as we crossed Arch and went through the gilded Friendship Gate that spanned the street.

I didn't know. The force and inertia of the walk ran out and I stopped. Two stories up, carved dragon heads looked down at me. Fool girl, they seemed to say.

Star's Café didn't exist. What were the odds of finding a non-existent place? We were on Race Street, near where Thomas used to drop off April. "Hey!" I said with a flare of anger. "How can they call the boundary of Chinatown *Race* Street? Talk about a lack of sensitivity—I don't want to be the morality police, but honestly, in this day and age you'd think—"

"What I think is that he really got to you," Sasha said. "That creep from your school. I happen to know why it's called Race. Remember Harry from maybe two years ago?"

I did not. It was nearly impossible keeping track of the male ships that passed Sasha in the night.

"One of the pompous ones?" she prompted.

"Which type?"

"Pompous despite having achieved nothing special."

It's sad when a woman has endured so many losers that she has given them taxonomic categories, phylum, class, family, genus, and species. In any case, I still didn't remember Harry. I shook my head and continued to scan the restaurants dotting the street, as if I could X-ray them and find out which one held the afterimage of April.

"No matter," Sasha said. "Harry lived on Race Street, but being Harry, his stationery and his card gave his address as: Race (formerly Sassafras) Street. Which it was, but the name had been changed in the 1850s, so it wasn't as if lots of hundred-and-sixty-year-old people who knew good old Sassafras Street needed that reminder. However, it was, as he said, a conversation starter. And since I therefore endured many a conversation about it, I know this street is called Race now because—are you ready?—races were held here. It was a track. Up Sassafras and around City Hall. Sorry. Nothing to do with sensitive issues. Just sensitive horses."

I guess Lowell had made me twitchy. Or Phyllis.

"And that still doesn't answer the question of which restaurant the kid didn't work at," Sasha said.

"All I know is . . . she worked for a man."

Sasha whistled and clapped her hands. "Great!" she said, hands on hips, camera dangling from a thick strap. "That narrows the field, since it's so unusual for a man to be the boss. Good gracious, we could probably just stand on the corner and ask the next passerby—'Excuse me, do you know of a place where the supervisor or the owner is a *man*? And a girl works for him?' "

"That's all she said."

It's amazing how little curiosity a lot of people have. An eighteen-year-old girl had disappeared in their neighborhood the night before last, and yet when Sasha and I entered a place and asked whether an April Truong had worked there, we were more often than not answered with a hostile stare, a head shake, and nothing more. Never a question as to why we wanted to know, or who April was. It was still early, not yet six P.M., and the restaurants were sparsely populated, yet there was always a great deal of plate-banging in the recesses of the dining rooms and a frenzied air to the proprietors, as if we were interrupting a particularly busy night with frivolous questions. We trudged from place to place, turning corners, exhausting a block's possibilities and turning a corner again. "I'm sure she said it had to do with food," I said. "She had cut herself one day. Slicing something the night before."

"Then she'd be a chef," Sasha said, "and that doesn't make sense. And why are we doing it this way, instead of asking her family?"

"Because the newspaper said her parents knew she had a job—a respectable job, they insisted—but they thought it was at Star's Café, and that doesn't exist."

"Her brother, then? You said he picked her up."

"And dropped her, he says, at the corner of Tenth and Race. Where we've been."

"No wonder it's assumed she worked at the massage parlor. To put it mildly, it sounds fishy."

"Are you saying we should try seafood restaurants?"

The man who seemed our last hope was high-strung and less than hospitable. "You want to eat?" he demanded. "Come in. You want to ask questions? Go next door!"

"He meant that metaphorically," Sasha said.

But he'd gotten me staring at his next-door neighbor's establishment. BUDDY'S, it said. I went in.

"Why?" Sasha asked as she followed me in. "It isn't even a restaurant."

"Why not?" We were near the end of the grid of streets that comprised the neighborhood, almost back to the start point, the place where April had disappeared, and we hadn't met with one friendly let alone helpful face.

Buddy's was a shabby convenience store, a hole in the wall, with a few cans, boxes, and shrink-wrapped basics. Aspirin, salt and milk, white bread, peanut butter, and cigarettes. A store for people who couldn't think far enough ahead to shop at a cheaper, better-stocked place, or who needed credit more often than not.

Anywhere but in Pennsylvania, where all liquor is sold in State Stores, Buddy's would have been well-stocked with cheap alcohol. Instead it featured bagel dogs, fried chicken, pizza, and enchiladas. Ethnic diversity meets the microwave. There was also a small copy machine, a check-cashing service, a case of canned soft drinks, and a row of periodicals, most of which featured cleavage or cars.

A flat-faced teenage girl stood behind the counter, next to a tiny TV emitting squeals of canned laughter. "And what did you think when you saw her for the first time?" a host-type deep voice asked.

"To tell you the truth, she wasn't anything like the way she described herself," another male voice said. "To say she exaggerates ..." The audience bellowed. "False advertising." The audience gasped with laughter.

"Yeah?" the girl behind the counter squinted and twirled a tendril of frizzed red hair, as if both bored and deeply suspicious of our motives for entering.

"Mandy," Sasha said, "this is most certainly not Star's Café."

The redhead sniggered, as if that were a very funny remark, but only she knew why. Sasha and I reacted by swiveling toward her and tilting our heads in unison.

Body language worked where direct questions might have failed. "It's only that ..." She shrugged and seemed to remember that she was supposed to be scowling. "Like my name's Star. My last name, and this isn't exactly a café if you haven't noticed, more like microwave takeout heaven, which made what you said sound pretty funny."

"Did—do you know a girl named April Truong?" I asked.

She squinted so fiercely she must have lost all vision. "You cops?"

"Teachers. Her teachers," Sasha said. I wondered what subject she was going to pretend to teach.

Ms. Star didn't ask. "She's missing," she said. "All over the news."

"But do you know her?"

"Why should I? Just because maybe I did a favor for a friend who was until then my boyfriend and got her a job and then she gets like really palsy with my friend? *My* friend."

I could hear April's voice reciting the exercise on what she had wanted. "Yesterday, I wanted to see my friend." She couldn't have meant this girl. But this girl's boyfriend? I didn't ask her to go on or explain more. This was a TV watcher, a person addicted to noise. Maybe she'd feel obliged to produce her own.

She did. "I have this friend Woody and he asked me to find a job for this poor girl in his school. April. So, like I did. As a favor. I didn't even know her."

"Here? She worked here?"

She nodded. She might have been pretty, or at least interesting-looking, if she'd added variety to her expressions, if she could reduce the storehouse of anger that blurred her features.

"Did you tell the police?" I asked.

"Why should I?"

"Because they think she worked—"

"At a massage parlor. Maybe she did that, too. She was a tramp. Besides, the cops didn't come here, and my father says don't push your nose where it isn't requested."

"Was April here the evening she disappeared?"

She shook her head. "Never showed. I had to come in. The whole point of getting her the job was I don't want to be here. Now I'm stuck covering for her."

"That isn't exactly her fault. She was abducted."

"Like I believe that. I'm sure she freelanced, moonlighted—know what I mean? Guys cruise by and you get in the car. She probably made a bad choice that night, is all. My father says girls like her who act like nuns are really sluts."

"He's a lousy kisser!" a woman's voice said on the TV. "If there's one thing I can't stand, it's a wet, drooly kiss." The audience squealed and shouted approval.

"What's going on here?" A man with the same rusty hair, flat features, and scowl as Ms. Star appeared in a doorway behind the counter. "What you blabbing about, Lacey?"

Lacey Star. Somebody had a romantic-poetic bent, but surely not this man.

"What you saying to these people about April?" he demanded.

"Hello. We're teachers, April's teachers this summer. I'm Amanda Pepper and this is Sasha Berg. We were wondering . . . you are the . . . manager of this store? Mister. . . ."

"Star. Yeah, right, why? Manager and owner."

Star's Café. April's little joke, although I still didn't understand why she simply hadn't told the truth. This place was pathetic but not shameful.

Mr. Star, I feared, was the man she worked for and intensely disliked, owner of the sweaty, roving hands. "April Truong worked for you?"

"I'm not saying yes or no."

113

"Maybe not officially?" I asked quietly. "I'm her teacher, Mr. Star, not an IRS investigator."

"Maybe we had an arrangement, okay? Maybe it wasn't on the books exactly, except I don't feel like talking about it. If that was the case, of course."

"Of course. I understand she wasn't here that evening at all."

He grimaced. "That's how help is these days. No work ethic. What can you do?"

"Do you have any idea who might have—"

He shrugged beefy shoulders. "The point of having employees, ladies, is that you don't have to do all the work. I come and go, you know? Didn't really know the girl. Chilly number, anyway. Not a friendly type. Truth is, I was ready to let her go. Not good for business to have an icicle behind the counter."

His daughter was not exactly Miss Congeniality. But then, we both knew that this was not a store that specialized in customer relations. This was a semi-embarrassing last stop before the lonely rented-room kind of store.

"April's cold unless you're somebody else's boyfriend." Lacey nearly spat the words out.

"My daughter," the man said. "Lover's spat, you know? Pay no mind. Even though that chink girl was a tease, know what I mean?" He directed the family scowl toward his daughter.

"Did April usually close up the store?"

"Assuming she worked here at all, you mean? Because you can check my books. Strictly a ma and pa—"

"And daughter," Lacey said.

"—operation. Period. Except my wife, she gets these spells and she can't work."

"Until her hangover clears up," lovely Lacey muttered.

I felt pity for drunken Mrs. Star, who must have envisioned something better than what she wound up with in the form of a life, a job, a husband, and an optimistically named child.

"Assuming, then," I said. "Would you have an employee close the place at night?"

He shook his head. " 'Specially not one of them, and not a girl one of them not yet out of school. It isn't so safe to be

114

carrying money in this neighborhood late at night. She's just a little thing. I come back," he answered. "Every night. Place is a boulder I carry on my back."

"So you were here when she left each night. Did you walk her outside? Did you see where she went, what she did, who she was with? How did she usually get home?"

"Whoa!" he said. "Who you think you are, lady? This isn't your schoolroom, and you don't get to quiz me. I didn't commit no crime, and I don't know the answers to that, anyway. She used to leave when we closed. I did the night deposit and things myself after. Nobody else, not even when my wife's here. I didn't want no outsider doing it or even watching. Not that I'm saying the kid wasn't honest, but it's hard to really, really tell with them shifty eyes they have, you know?"

The TV show was over, and a solemn newscaster promised the details of something horrific at eleven. It wouldn't be April's story anymore. That was old news.

I wondered if the Star family ever permitted absolute silence. They didn't glance at the TV, or seem to wonder what the catastrophe was that the newscaster dangled like bait for late-night. They played the voices like Muzak.

"So that's it, then," Mr. Star continued, "unless you're buying something. My employees—if I had any—would leave when I was ready to lock the door, around ten, give or take a minute."

Ten. She'd told me she worked until eleven, when her brother picked her up. Where had she spent that extra hour?

And what did I have? A letch with an off-the-books employee who worked until ten, not eleven, and his daughter, who was convinced April had stolen her boyfriend, Woody, a boy who, back at school, denied even knowing April. Was there anyone among them telling even half the truth?

Who was April Truong?

Why had she lied about her job?

Where had she gone after work each night?

Where had she gone the whole night she was abducted?

What was going on?

Twelve

I DON'T know what causes it, heredity or environment, testosterone or playground taunts, but men seem to equate okayness with any number of ridiculous activities, and there is no talking them out of it. Why else would Mackenzie, his right leg still encased in plaster, consider cross-city crutchwalking the mark of a real man? He didn't put it quite that way, but you could feel the unspoken laws that dictated this fixation. I found it a pretty stupid and exhausting gauntlet to run, or hobble, but then, I cannot comprehend most male rituals.

He was already there when I brought home the bacon or, more accurately, the sausage, chicken, shrimp, ham, peas, artichoke hearts, and peppers. Some domestic spasm had convulsed me at Reading Terminal, making me desperately need these things. Plus saffron, those tiny threads of gold that cost more than the original and that I hitherto considered one of the world's great hoaxes.

"Are you crazy?" Sasha had asked. "What is this?"

"I am suddenly dying, absolutely dying, for paella."

"That's why God invented Spanish restaurants."

But I had to do it myself. Maybe it was the female equivalent of staggering cross-city in a cast. So, a bulging grocery bag clutched in one arm, I opened the door onto my little family, as it were. A portrait suitable for framing, and a welcome relief after the Stars' idea of family.

One good-looking tall man with curly salt-and-pepper hair slouched on my sofa, face still flushed from a long, hot lurch to my house. He wore a black T-shirt and cutoff jeans that revealed one splendidly muscled and operational leg and one grubby plaster log with toes stretched onto the coffee table. An enormous, purring dust bunny teetered on top of it.

Mackenzie waved and smiled greetings. The cat was too preoccupied to notice me. His purr faded. It couldn't be snuggly to sit on a leg cast. In fact, it looked tenuous and treacherous—little by little his hind legs lost ground, slipping over and down the side of the cast. Obviously, even though Macavity's masculinity had been surgically reduced, this grim joy at the taking of new territory was a feline guy thing.

I balanced my shopping bag and leaned over to place a kiss on the man's lips, and then heigh ho, it was off to the kitchen. The air conditioner wheezed and made the first floor bearable.

Mackenzie slammed the book he'd been reading, startling the cat. It was a collection of painfully with-it short stories about people who understood the tragic futility of getting up in the morning and the need for highly styled shoes. And in spite of my contempt for them, they were so *now*, so *there*, so highly praised by critics who obviously also know the brand names of the right shoes, that they made me feel excluded and inferior. And bored.

117

"Donate this book to charity," Mackenzie said while I pulled edibles out of bags and onto the kitchen counter. "Yellow fever's more interesting. Besides, as a homicide detective, I find it offensive when people imply that being alive is about as much fun as being dead."

I put on water to parboil the sausage and dropped a mix of lettuce—pale green pronged leaves and purple ruffles—into the spinner. "There's no Star's Café," I said. "There's a hole-in-the-wall convenience store called Buddy's, which closes at ten, not eleven the way she said. I feel sick-dizzy, like when I was little and I'd spin until the playground whirled. Only this time, I'm not trying to spin anything except lettuce."

I fantasized a Moment of Understanding, an epiphany wherein sensitive hero embraces troubled woman and promises they'll make sense of everything together. And troubled woman believes him and is greatly comforted.

I squelched the image. Even in fantasy, it required too many clumps and grunts and crutches and contortions, and then downright lying. There was no ready consolation in any of this, and nobody was going to make sense of its contradictions.

Mackenzie contracted his brows. I was afraid he was going to tell me that I ought to grow up, stop being gullible. Wasn't it painfully obvious that I had misread her and April was a liar, that she had a secret and dangerous life, and that I was a fool?

He would probably be right, and I'd have to hate him for it.

"I trust your instincts," he said instead. "Some day I'll regret admittin' that to you, but the fact is, I do. Things that don' seem to be what they should be probably aren't what they seem—or don' seem to be."

It took me a moment to almost decipher that. What I did get clearly is that we were both on the same side.

"She must have had a good reason for creatin' this confusion," he added.

We had just experienced a customized but genuine Moment of Understanding, and even without the clinch, it had been exquisite.

118

Then I giggled, ruining the moment and displaying unbecoming behavior for Troubled Woman, even when relieved. But the laugh was on behalf of Macavity, whose rear had slid all the way down the side of the cast. He hung by two paws, legs and tail dangling while his front nails scritched tracks into the plaster in a desperate and futile attempt to regain his perch and dignity. He fell to the floor, turned his head and viewed me balefully.

Contrary to pop psychology, it is not always best to be completely open in every relationship. By carefully averting our eyes now and then, the cat and I have learned to coexist. I pretended I hadn't seen him slide and splat.

"Lowell says it's connected," I said. "He's paranoid, but—"

"Whoa! Who is this Lowell and what is connected? Thought we were talkin' about April."

I explained the whats first. "We wound up outside Mother Bethel," I said midway through this part of my tale. "And to my amazement, Sasha was there, photographing the doors because—"

"Did you know that when everybody else fled and panicked during the yellow fever, Richard Allen and Absalom Jones, the two men who started alternative congregations, stayed in the city and nursed people?"

Imagine, before this summer I'd not known that all roads lead to yellow fever.

"Okay," Mackenzie said after I'd glared awhile. "What about the doors and what about Lowell?"

I completed the explanations of the whats, and then tried to explain Lowell, a much more difficult topic. "And somehow, because his aunt knows my mother," I said, "he has acted from day one as if we have a long-standing and meaningful bond and a future."

"Awful," Mackenzie said.

"There've been times I've felt bad because I was rejected, but Lowell makes me feel rotten because I'm accepted. Welcomed with open arms. He's alternately silly and scary. Either making really inept flirtatious noises or uttering dark warnings about evil."

"Th' awfulness to which I alluded referred to your mother,

119

although Lowell doesn't sound like much. But she's relentless, isn't she?"

"Like a hurricane." I presented him with a glass of sangria and a plate of olives and sardines. "Tapas," I explained. "Kind of. We're having a theme dinner. Maybe I should find some classical guitar as background music." Maybe I should run out and buy some, as I knew I didn't have any.

What the devil was happening to me?

"You must really hate summer school. You've gone all of a sudden homey," Mackenzie said. "You'll be Philly's answer to Martha Stewart soon, gildin' pinecones and makin' quilts."

I was stopped in my tracks, although there isn't that much tracking that one can do in a minuscule living-dining-kitchen room. But I had suddenly understood what was going on. Mackenzie and I were engaged in an odd and surreptitious contest, two birds finding the best twigs and bits of fluff. We were doing parallel nesting, not living together, but preening, showing off to each other how exquisite a life we could design if we wanted to. He did margaritas and ratatouille and I did sangria and paella.

We scared me.

"An' here I thought I'd charmed your mama. I feel like a failure."

I didn't bother to console him. What would charm or at least placate my mama was nothing less than a wedding ring, a mortgage, and two point three grandchildren, or whatever the national norm called for. And I wasn't ready to suggest a single one of those factors.

Still, this cooking thing was a step in that direction, wasn't it? I chopped onions and sniffled, then browned and steamed and suddenly wondered why I hadn't ever thought about spending my time doing this, instead of teaching. Not always have papers to mark, lessons to plan.

I could shop for food, chop food, cook food, then clean up from the shopping, chopping, and cooking of the food.

And on those nights when nobody murdered anybody in Philadelphia on Mackenzie's watch, midway through that process we'd light candles and play appropriate background music and eat the food. And I wouldn't have papers to mark.

But on those nights when somebody did opt for murder, I'd do what? Go into a state of suspended animation? Learn to freeze and can and make TV dinners out of my day's work? Resent Mackenzie's day's work and create humongous problems? Wonder what portion of my existence was actually mine?

Now I remembered why I'd never considered it before. I was destined to be a once-in-a-while kind of homemaker. Not themes to meals, but themes to mark. "As soon as I get this into the oven, could you do me a favor and read something?" I asked. "A poem, I think."

"You think?"

"I'm sure it isn't the essay he was supposed to write, but I'm not sure what it is." I browned the rice in a second pan, added the tomatoes and wine and the precious saffron threads. My enthusiasm was already waning, and this effort feeling like an excessive amount of labor for something that would disappear in a matter of moments.

"What were you doin' in Chinatown this afternoon, anyway?" he asked, apropos of exactly nothing. "Not on your way home, is it?"

"Lowell wanted to walk me home, and I didn't want him near here, so I pretended to be on my way to Sasha's, and then, when he was finally gone, I thought I'd get Chinese takeout for us."

He raised an eyebrow. "Then what is it you're whipping up back there? Uncooked takeout?"

"I *thought* takeout. Then I was possessed by the Happy Homemaker Demon, and I couldn't help myself. I needed an exorcist."

He shook his head for a little too long. I like verbal despair. The silent variety drives me up the wall with its chattering white noise, full of accusations. I was halfway up the wall when he finally spoke. "So," he said, "somewhere between Chinese takeout and Spanish from scratch, you found a convenience store called Buddy's."

"The trouble with official investigations is that you don't know the players," I said. "You get cynical about what people tell you. I say she's a good girl—but even I know that's what everybody says about people who turn out to have chopped people in their basements. 'Oh, but he was such a good neighbor. Gave generously to every charity.' So, of course, you discount such banality, but what if it were true in this case? What if a certain action, like any connection with a massage parlor, was sufficiently inconsistent with her personality as to make it impossible? What if that inconsistency were important?"

He petted the cat, who had resigned himself to settling on lap, not cast, and he said nothing. His drink could have used a refill, but my domestic demons had gone off duty and I didn't feel like waiting on anybody, even though I knew it was reprehensible being mean-spirited with the serve-himself challenged.

"You don't accept that, do you?" I said. "You think that sooner or later truth will out, even in officialdom. But I think that by then it could be too late. Other ideas would have been built on top of that missed idea."

"And I'm sayin' your expertise is in the classroom, an' I don' make big suppositions about what tragic errors you could be perpetuatin' there. Look, you need to show me somethin' because you aren't even sure if it's poetry or not, but did I cast aspersions? Why do you always assume we all flunked Thinking 101?"

"I don't. But nobody questioned Buddy Star, and somebody should have."

"Why do I have the feeling you already did?"

"He won't cooperate. April didn't officially exist at his place. She wasn't on the books and he didn't pay any benefits."

"Maybe he made her lie—make up a place," Mackenzie suggested.

I liked that explanation, although it still left the extra hour unaccounted for. "Do you know Officer Deedee Klein?" I asked. "She came to school today, about the disappearance."

He shook his head. "Not Homicide."

"I knew that. She was in uniform. And nobody in my class had a thing to say, as far as she was concerned. They were quieter than they've ever been."

"Maybe nobody in your class knows anything relevant. Isn't that possible? But I'm glad you're aware of Officer Klein and I hope you understand that it's *her* job to find April Truong, not yours."

We were back to that. My turn to use my right to remain silent. A man who is used to questioning suspects is going to make his point—and too often yours, too—whether or not you like it. I combined my two skillets worth of sauté into one large flat casserole and put it in the oven. "I'll get that paper," I said, and I rummaged through my briefcase until I found Miles's exam. I read it to myself again.

> Who's supposed to say whether present guilt lies with
> A group? An idea? A tradition? A
> Person? Not Romeo, Juliet or that gang. They're dead.
> Assigning blame is useless, something he wouldn't dare.
> Would he?
> Ask him.
> Perhaps he is
> Afraid.
> Probably is, because
> Reality
> Is too much like fiction and
> Life sucks.

I still didn't get it. I could sense something whiz by, but it only grazed me and kept moving. I handed the page to the wounded cop. I even felt a flutter of mercy and poured him a sangria refill, then busied myself with setting the table and phoning Flora.

The message on her machine was cryptic, merely repeating the number that had been reached. "Call me if you need anything, please," I said. "I'm at home."

"I don't think this is likely to find its way into the anthologies of immortal verse," Mackenzie said. "It's more a coupla sentences with weird punctuation. Some people think poetry's a matter of not letting the lines reach the right margin. There's no logic to what's where, or how he breaks these lines. I mean, couldn't this be one sentence? 'Who's supposed to say whether present guilt lies with a group, an idea, a tradition, a person?' "

"Sure," I said, "but not a good sentence. Needs a conjunction."

"Or this one—these two. Why are they split? 'Not Romeo, Juliet or that gang, they're dead.' Or the next—I think this kid divvied up his few sentences to make you think he's written more than he has. Listen, 'Assigning blame is useless, something he wouldn't dare, would he?' What's with that rhetorical flourish? Why's it have its own line? It weights itself down. Don't need it."

But as soon as he'd said it, as soon as I'd heard it rather than read it silently, I understood why he'd needed it, why it had gotten its own line. I pointed the fork in my hand at Mackenzie. "Woody," I said. "It's about Woody Marshall."

"Why?"

"Listen to that line about assigning blame, about how he wouldn't dare. I kept wondering what *he* Miles could have meant—but the next line tells me who. 'Would he?' That's his name and that has to be what Miles means. Woody's guilty."

"He's only one option here. Prob'ly no more than a coincidence."

"Another knee-jerk reaction, because I said it?"

"First of all, it's real hard for me to jerk my knee these days," he said, "an' second, even when hale, I am not guilty of any kind of jerkiness, and third, there's somethin' else altogether goin' on here. Those broken-up ideas, split sentences—is this Miles illiterate?"

"No. Just unconventional."

"Yeah, but this is more than needing to be different." And then he scowled. "Except it doesn't work that way, either."

"What doesn't?"

"I thought maybe the point wasn't in the words but in their first letters, that they spelled something. An old poetic tradition. Except these first letters don't work. Wa Paw A Papr Il? Or maybe they're scrambled. A papr a paw wil? Law Papa Rail. Warp a lap pail. None of them seem real high on the sense scale." I heard his intake of breath. "Except for the last five lines."

April. They spelled April.

"That can't be coincidence," Mackenzie said.

"Romeo and Juliet and April and Woody," I said. "And blame—as in that disappearance."

"And fear," Mackenzie added. "Obviously, this kid was afraid to say whatever it is openly. Wrote it in code. You should show this to Officer Deedee."

"Sure. I'll give it to her."

"After you've copied it, I'll bet," he said without a smile. My toes were across his line again, on his turf—even while he was disabled and not using that turf—and he was ready to book me for trespassing. A cop in the manger.

Of course I'd duplicate the poem. So what? "I'll give her the poem in exchange for a list of what was inside April's backpack."

I'd taken him by surprise for once. His superior disdain was gone and he looked at me with open curiosity, waiting, but surely I didn't need to explain silly amateurish theories to a Real Pro. "It interests me," was all I said. "It's one of those assumptions, one of those things we could too easily take for granted and build on—all in the wrong direction. The leaning tower of presumption. *You* know."

But he didn't, and I was a sufficiently mean-spirited and un-saintly person to be glad. We had lots of contests going, Mackenzie and I. Only one was about cooking. More important others were about smarts and expertise and other subheadings to be filed under: power. Either this was a sign of an unhealthy relationship, or couplehood boiled down to one long balancing act.

"This ending worries me," I said. "About life being too much like fiction. The fiction in question ends with two dead kids."

"Let's stay with reality, then. At the moment, there is one missing, not dead, kid, so don't make any great and scary leaps."

"There's two kids. One dead. Vanny Tran."

"Don't count somebody you didn't know. There are lots and

lots of dead kids. But for right now, just take the next step. You are going to turn the poem over to the police, and confine your questions and curiosity to the classroom."

"No problem."

"That was too easy. What's the catch?"

"There is none. Luckily, all my questions—and people I need to question—are already in the classroom."

"For Pete's sake, Mandy—" He was interrupted by a formidable buzz.

"Saved by the oven timer," I said, glad again for my domesticity fit. What would have saved me if I'd gotten takeout?

Thirteen

HELGA can sour even feel-good mornings, and this most definitely wasn't one of those.

She seemed surlier than ever, so I grabbed the contents of my mailbox and left the school office as quickly as I could. Flora's door looked locked shut, and when I got to my room, the one student I needed to talk with was nowhere to be seen.

"Anybody know where Miles is?" Why had he chosen to break his perfect attendance record today?

"I heard he always misses a lot of school," a girl in the back said. "I guess he's got some kind of condition."

"Some kind of *aud*ition." Carmen Gabel actually interrupted her third lipstick application of the morning to say this.

"He has like an agent," Toy Drebbin added. Miles must really be something to have engaged the minds of two apathetic seat warmers. "He'll be famous someday. In fact, I think he had like a tryout this morning. Some movie that's shooting here."

The girl across the aisle glared at him. "No," she said firmly. "Today he's sick."

Toy's narrow face flushed and he sputtered a bit before getting words out. "He shoulda told me it was a secret," he finally said in a loud hiss. "Now I remember. Yesterday afternoon he was all splotchy and coughing and his stomach hurt."

I didn't know if Miles was exceptionally beloved, or whether I was especially disliked, but they were uniformly hell-bent on protecting him from me. I hated being the opposition, but that was my role. I was the law, the organization, officialdom. I was rules and regulations and prohibitions.

And to think I'd imagined teaching as a helping profession.

I squelched further discussion of Miles's whereabouts and pushed the group toward the syllabus. Today's activities included working on dangling participles, discussing "Sonny's Blues" by James Baldwin, which they were supposed to have read last night, and SAT vocabulary building.

While they worked on analogies I flipped through the memos and notices that had been in my mailbox, tossing most directly into the circular file, then picking out one that looked slightly interesting, mainly because it was printed on bright yellow paper, folded in thirds, and stapled shut. It suggested somebody had cared about protecting whatever was inside.

Reading it was like being punched in the stomach.

STOP LOVING MUD PEOPLE OR ARE YOU ONE TOO, A JEW? YOUR KIND HAS TO GO. NO MORE NIGGERS AND GOOKS. NO MORE WARNINGS.

"Miss Pepper?" Carmen said. "Are you okay? You look sick." I must have looked like death itself to have roused her out of her makeup fixation. But, in fact, why, for the first time this summer, was she paying attention to me? Was she concerned about me or was she checking to see if her flyer had worked?

What about the rest of them? Several sets of eyes watched me. Why? I could feel the near-hysteria I'd witnessed on Flora the day before take hold of me.

Maybe she'd been right. Maybe my class was my enemy in a new and chilling way. The note was made of cut and pasted letters in a sickening familiar typeface. The school newspaper again.

Who was it? Why?

I heard echoes of Lowell warning me that being friends with Flora could bring me grief from *them*. Was Lowell *them*? And what sort of grief came next? And it wasn't only about Flora, it was about April, too. It was against *their* rules to care about anybody whose skin wasn't exactly like mine.

"Miss Pepper?"

I looked at her almost blankly, and then I remembered what she had asked. "I'm fine, Carmen," I said slowly. But I wasn't. I was hot inside, and chilled as well. And I was furious. "No," I said. "No, I'm not. I'm sick. Sick of the hate and poison in a note I was sent. Sick of the kind of ugliness that hit at Miss Jones. That should never be in this school. That should never exist anywhere at all." I was shaking under my skin, each nerve echoing the pounds of my heart. But I kept my voice from quavering. I was willing to show my anger, outrage. I wasn't willing to show my terror. Just in case there was one among them who would gloat over it, delight in it.

"I'm going to trust in nursery rhymes. Names can never hurt me," I said. "Because I don't care what anybody calls me. I will *never* let anyone intimidate me out of what I know is right. I will never shut up and stand by, go along with something loathsome. I will never be a 'good German'!"

I hoped that what I was saying was true. I had had to hear it out loud, but it wasn't easy getting it out. It had to make its way bumpily up through my vocal cords, over the bangings of my panicking heart. But the more I said, the more words demanded airtime. "These days there's too much tolerance for hate and no tolerance for anything else," I heard myself say. "My car radio's broken, and I don't mind. I don't want to hear it. It's all about hate—all sorts of hate, who wants to make cruel fun of whom. Why doesn't anybody call in to say it's *wrong* to be so ugly, so undemocratic, so *un-American*? When did it get fashionable to hate and to be right out front about it, to *sell* it, even? The rappers, the INS, the Limbaughs, the skinheads, the woman haters, the anti-Semites, the gay bashers? This isn't how it's supposed to be. This is too cheap, too easy, too ugly, too ignorant and stupid. I refuse to be any part of it!"

I was close to shouting. Going to flunk deportment, if we still had such niceties. I took a series of deep breaths. Slowly, my blood level simmered down until I could see my class clearly again. Not a one of them spoke, or moved. They were gape-mouthed, incredulous.

I didn't know if they'd heard or cared about a single word I'd said, or if they'd merely been dazzled by the sight of a teacher going stark-raving mad.

I sighed. "This city started as an experiment in tolerance. Now, we've been voted the Most Hostile City in the United States," I said. "Please don't think the new title is something we have to keep justifying. That's all I was trying to say."

And that was that. Despite my rhetoric, I spent the rest of the interminable morning fighting and defeating—then fighting again—the urge to give up. I wanted to be out of the mix, out of the messes people made. Uninvolved and absent. Unafraid.

But capitulating out of fear meant I was letting the anonymous *them* call the shots, and I'd be damned first. I took more deep breaths.

"Woody?" I said at the end of class. "Could you stay a moment? I have a question about your exam."

His eyes widened, then he flicked a glance from his buddy across the aisle back at me. Woody did not look well. His skin had a jaundiced undertone and dark shadows under his eyes. Earlier in the summer he'd looked frighteningly angry. Now, he looked just plain frightened. "Yeah," he said. "Okay."

His buddies, accepting the idea that he was in academic trouble, didn't question me when I closed my classroom door to have privacy.

Woody slouched in a front row chair, legs straight out. His T-shirt was black, against which a single large red rose glowed. But what initially appeared to be a pearl of dew on one petal was actually a drop of blood. The image reminded me of the dark side of fairy tales—the pricked finger, the deep sleep.

Woody was trying hard to look bored, tapping his fingers on his black jeans and keeping his eyes focused on the ceiling.

"Tell me what's going on," I said. "Be straight with me."

He stared as if I'd spoken in tongues. Then he took a deep breath and leaned forward. I felt a flutter of optimism. "I don't have stuff to say. *You* said you wanted to talk about my paper."

My optimism collapsed in a dusty heap. "Cut it out. You didn't hand in an exam and we both know it." He had gone on automatic pilot, looking outraged by the suggestion of a no-exam scam, but his eyes dulled and he shrugged and closed his mouth as if protest weren't worth it. "And that's not the issue now," I continued. "You were distraught. I'll let you make it up."

He still said nothing, but he looked willing to listen, so I kept going. "Yesterday you said you felt responsible for what had happened to April, that she was dead and it was your fault. Why? What happened?"

He shook his head and redirected his eyes to the tips of his clunky shoes.

"Okay, then I'll suggest something. You and April spent time together every night."

He settled back in his chair and looked like his formerly smug self. "How could we? She worked, you know."

"Yes, and I know you got her the job. Is that why she made up a name for the place? Or because it was a sleazy operation?"

His smirk faded and he swallowed before he finally spoke. "Both. And because Buddy was white and her brother didn't want her to work for whites. And because Buddy didn't put her on the books and he said she shouldn't say she worked there. Okay, now?"

"And—look, I can't resist—did you really date Lacey Star?"

He rolled his eyes. "Not exactly *date*," he said.

I didn't ask for further clarification. "But about April—you must have known she didn't work the hours she told her family. All I can figure is that you saw each other, secretly, from ten to eleven, until her brother picked her up."

He sighed. "You aren't making sense."

"Then help me out. The day I saw the two of you on the bench, she was upset. It didn't look like a casual encounter. In fact, it looked deadly serious. She disappeared that night."

"Are you saying *I*—"

"Not necessarily, but I have to believe you had more than a casual relationship, and that you know a whole lot that's important. What I can't imagine is why, if you didn't hurt her yourself, you aren't telling the police."

He shrugged. He was a virtuoso with the gesture and used it much too often, as if it summed up his entire existence.

"So are you saying the rumors are true?" I asked. "Did she have a second job at a massage parlor?"

"April? No way in hell she'd—you knew her. She was going to go to college, be something. That's all she'd talk about, almost. How could you believe that kind of . . . of stuff?"

I waited.

"Okay, listen." Woody leaned forward in his seat. He looked drawn, much older than his years. He sounded that way, too. World-weary, ancient. "Yes. I have a part-time job at a gas station. I get off at ten, too. I used to meet her and spend an hour with her before she was picked up."

"Her brother picked her up every night?"

"Him or somebody else he knew. Her family wouldn't let her ride the bus at that hour. I'd have driven her home, but it would have made too much trouble. But we didn't do anything wrong, her and me. We had a lot to talk about. She knew things. She was wise in a way that . . . Anyway, we kept a low profile because there wasn't any time, really, and because—"

"Your father. I remember."

He looked surprised. "But the night she disappeared? I didn't see her. I went where we met, except she wasn't there. I waited fifteen minutes, then I went to Buddy's, but it was locked up. I figured maybe she hadn't worked that night—she was upset after school. Maybe Thomas had come early, that she'd gone home, so that's what I did, too. Go home. Don't blame me for not wanting to tell the cops. You really think they'll buy that story? Even if it is the truth? How about my father? Or Thomas, who was doing everything on earth to keep us from each other?"

"Where did you meet every night? Maybe she went there, got there early—she never went to work that night—and maybe there's a witness who saw her there and knows what happened."

"We met at the corner where she *was* seen. By the witness. The one who saw her get into a van."

"At eleven."

"Lookit," he said. "I know you mean well. No offense, but you don't understand a thing that's going on and you'd be best off if you didn't push, you know? It's not something you can make better. And I'm not talking about April and me. All I can say is no matter what you might hear or think, I never would have hurt her. I never put a hand on her or took her anyplace in that van or in anything else that night—I didn't even see her—and that's the truth. We were close, but I would appreciate it if you didn't spread that around, okay? To my pals, the Vietnamese aren't . . . And April didn't like my being with them, either."

"But I still don't . . . you said you were responsible . . ."

"For her being killed." He swallowed hard, then nodded. "I'm going to feel rotten about it until I'm dead, too. But not because I did it."

"Then what? How?"

"Why aren't you asking the creep she worked for? Telling the police about him?"

"I did."

"Good. He was always coming on to her, touching her, making bad jokes. Big mistake, my listening to Lacey and getting April that job. I told her to quit, but she needed the money. She was going to go to college, no matter what."

133

His words hung in the air. *No matter what* couldn't include the *what* of being abducted. That *what* mattered.

"This is making me crazy, Woody. All other issues aside, I have to say it again, I know what I saw on the bench that afternoon, and—"

He stood up, and I realized with a start how large and menacing he could be. *"No!"* he said. "You *don't* know what you saw, you only think you do." His skin grew paler and the premature lines on it seemed to deepen before my eyes. "Look, Ms. P., there's this story my last English teacher told us about a bunch of blind people trying to see an elephant. One touches a leg and says oh, yeah, an elephant is a tree trunk. And one maybe touches the tail and says you're wrong, it's a snake. And one touches a side and says it's a wall, and—"

"I'm familiar with that story."

"Then you should understand. No offense, but you're like one of those blind people. You saw a little piece of something and from that you made up a whole thing—only the thing you made up is wrong. Not the real thing at all."

"Then tell me what I saw."

"I can't. I swear it. It's a matter of life and . . . I sound like bad TV. But we're talking about something serious. What you should understand is that those blind guys who thought they saw the elephant could feel real good about their tree trunks and their snakes. But if they didn't get out of the way, the thing they didn't see—the elephant—could kill them." He paused and folded his arms across his chest and waited for some kind of response.

I stood up, too. I resented having him lecture me from above, which provided a sudden moment of insight where I saw myself looming over students day after day. "Meaning what?" I asked Woody quietly. We were still not nearly at eye level, and I had to tilt my head back a bit.

"Meaning you have to stop thinking you know what you're seeing. You could get trampled. You're not a bad person, and neither am I. I'm trying to help you. You could get in trouble. Real bad. Please don't." And without waiting for my response, without even a flicker of interest in how I would respond, he walked to the door.

"Is that what happened to April?"

He turned back, one hand gripping the doorknob. "What do you mean?"

"Did she see too much? Did she ask the wrong questions? Does what happened to her have to do with those other things I don't understand?"

"Please," he said. "Please. I'm taking care of it myself. Trust me. I'm doing what she wanted, doing my best already. Don't push me."

But I had one more push left. I picked up the yellow paper from my desk. I hated to even touch it, to reacknowledge its existence. "Is this the elephant?" I asked quietly.

He blanched. "Jesus, Miss P., don't—what *is* that? The thing you were talking about? Why're you showing it to me? I feel like I'm going crazy! How'd you get that? Where? Why does everything have to do with me?"

He looked enormous—and fragile. A brittle tree about to topple. Either I was seeing him for the first time or something had changed about him, drastically. He seemed a victim, not a thug. "Woody," I said in a near whisper, "are you in trouble, too? Do you need help?"

He rolled his eyes, raised his brows, almost grinned, then grimaced as if in pain. Expressions spilled one into the other, combining shock, near-laughter, the suggestion of tears, and, I thought, fear—all at once, as if I'd said something so beyond belief—and perhaps also so true—that there was no possible response except incredulity.

"Thanks for asking," he said in a strained, low voice. And then he was gone.

So much for my *Would he? Ask him.* It hadn't worked the way I'd hoped, to put it mildly. I sat back down at my desk, semiconvinced that if I waited long enough, some all-encompassing idea would come along, something that clarified the situation. I wanted to feel more certain than I did that Woody truly had nothing to do with April's disappearance—but he had such an air of desperation clinging to him and was so adamantly close-mouthed that I wondered. Had he done it? If not, did he know who had? Did he know why?

And what was the greater, further danger he repeatedly warned me about? What was the elephant I couldn't see?

My thoughts circled, swallowing themselves like cerebral serpents. Give it up, I counseled myself. Maybe April had truly gone for a kinky joyride. There'd been a recent news story like that. An entire town searching for a girl thought abducted by a stranger. She came back—at the stranger's insistence. She refused to press charges, because she'd willingly, enthusiastically, gone.

Maybe April had, too. Maybe the rigid pressures of her life, the careful monitoring by her family, and the dark side of all her self-discipline had been too much. Maybe she well and truly needed a break for freedom so that she didn't break instead.

Except that she'd been seen struggling. Was it an act? A cover-up?

I should let go of futile and directionless speculation about April Truong, and direct all future futile and directionless speculation to my own life. And be safe.

And give up Flora, too? And anything else I wanted that didn't meet with my anonymous censor's approval?

Finally, I stood up. I was getting nowhere here, except closer to the fear again. Back off, a part of me insisted. The adult part, I feared.

But the two-year-old in me dug in and refused. I was going to do what I thought was right. There was nothing else I could do.

I walked down the hall. Bartholomew Dennison the Fifth, approaching from the other direction, waved. A sign, I decided, that I had made the correct decision and I was on the right track.

"I'm still thinking about April," he said when I caught up to him. A perfect opening.

"Me, too, and feeling really sorry for her family," I said. "Whatever hullabaloo or concern there was that first night is over. No yellow ribbons on trees for her. The Truongs must feel abandoned. I'm going to make a—not a sympathy call, but a sympathetic call, even though I'm a little nervous about going."

I'd thought I'd have to sell him the idea, but he nodded immediately. "Great idea!" he said. "Want company?"

I was enormously relieved. I didn't know whether April's parents would welcome our concern or consider it an intrusion. I didn't know if they spoke English, or whether April's sullen brother would willingly serve as interpreter.

"When?" Five asked.

"Tonight, around eight? The Truongs work all day, so after school wouldn't be any good. I'll call them around six, see if it's okay. If it's not, I'll call you. Otherwise, does it sound all right?"

"Fine," he said. "I'll meet you here, at school."

I walked taller, felt just a tad John Wayne-ish. No yellow-bellied sheet of paper was going to tell me what I could or could not care about.

My momentary elation ebbed when I reached the back stairs and realized that sour Aldis Fellows had been watching me. She had a gift for creeping up on a person. "For a minute I thought you were part of the man's midday mob," she said.

"Five's?"

Aldis nodded. "Current events, my foot! The man's blind and has no sense of discipline whatsoever. Did you hear the noise from the room while he was out there with you?"

"I'm sorry. I'm not following you."

"He thinks they're reading magazines and having small group discussions, but just ask around. They're using him. He doesn't understand what kind of boys they are."

"Using him for what?"

She looked at me as if I were pathetic. Then she looked around. "Drugs," she whispered. "That room at noon is ground zero for dealing and making plans, talking over strategy, distributing."

I must have looked dubious.

"He's a dupe. A nice enough man, but a fool. People must have fawned over his good looks his whole life, and he's gotten too used to it. He would never wonder what those boys actually want from him, just take it for granted that they like him."

Was it possible? He had joked about how little actual attention he paid the group. He thought of it as insulation against Phyllis and Edie, so maybe . . . I felt sorry for him if it was true, but worried, too.

"I'm sorry to drag a nice man like that into this, but I am going to have to report it, and anyway, if he's that stupid and lax, he deserves it."

"What made you think that drugs—"

"I thought it would be different here, this summer. I was looking forward to it, but it's all the same, everywhere." She gestured in the direction of Flora's closed room. "She still in hiding? Still in a righteous sulk?"

"I wouldn't call it . . . it must have been—" I was having trouble shifting gears, still worrying over the possibility that Five was an unwitting front for student crime.

"Those people," Aldis said with a weary shake of her head. "Anything that happens to them becomes a major issue."

"But having your room trashed—"

"Look, it happens. We're way past the sweet little schoolhouse of yore." She clomped down the stairs behind me, lecturing. "You've lived in an ivory tower here with your privileged students."

"I thought you just said things were the same everywhere."

She ignored my point. "Now," she went on, "what with the people who were let in this summer, you can see how the world really is. And it's her people who are responsible for a lot of the change, too. And not for the better, either."

"I don't feel comfortable with this talk about Flora's people, as if she's an interchangeable—"

Aldis simply didn't care what I had to say. "Some people should wise up and smell the coffee," she continued. "Maybe other people who are tired of what's been going on in this country for the last twenty years are trying to get their message through."

"What do you—"

"Don't you just get sick of how everything gets twisted into a big civil rights case?" she demanded from behind. "I mean if a white teacher is hassled, who would care? You'd look to see if they had *caused* their problems in some way, antagonized somebody. But with *them*—it's all a great meaningful outrage, a hue and cry. Poor me, poor me, I'm so oppressed. Meanwhile, who made the problem in the first place? I tell you, this minority business has gone too far. Time to put on the brakes."

She was so sure of the universal acceptance of her words that when we reached the bottom of the staircase and we were again side by side, she almost saluted me in a burst of camaraderie. "Good talking with you," she said as she strode off and out the door.

I stared at her retreating back, her sensible shoes, wondering just how intensely she believed those brakes had to be applied— and where—and whether mudslinging and mail, phone, and in-box terrorism were a part of the braking apparatus.

Aldis, her dark suspicions about student drug-dealing and her ugly assumptions about Flora, became part of the note, of the mud in Flora's room, of the desecrated church.

Too much, I thought, my breath short. My short-lived self-confidence had gone through meltdown and there was no oxygen left in the building.

I needed air. Desperately.

Fourteen

I MEANDERED through a specimen noon for half an hour, wishing I were in a better mood, because the weather deserved it, could in fact be bottled and marketed as Essence of Summer. Its blue and gold perfection balanced out mosquitoes, flies, broiling, muggy, steamy days, thunder and lightning, and summer colds. I was sorry I had driven to school. This was a day to walk straight over the horizon.

Nonetheless, I was *not* in a better, or even a good, mood, not even when I forced myself to stop thinking about Aldis. The yellow warning note haunted me, and I couldn't stop the low-grade shaking deep inside me.

140

How *dare* some anonymous coward tell me who and how I should be or live! Except—one had, and as enraged and combative as I felt, I also struggled against the urge to run for the hills and hide.

I needed help. There was no time for a shrink, and the best the weatherman had to offer wasn't doing it for me. Time to try retail therapy. It supposedly works for many of my sisters.

I tried, but stores, in their ineffable wisdom, live a season ahead, and the displays were filled with falling leaves, itchy-looking sweaters, tam o'shanters, and thick knit stockings. Even with plate glass separating us, the ensembles gave me prickly heat.

Their *tempus fugit* message layered misery on top of my anxiety. Each wooly-warm window along my route sang the same rondelet. Summer's no longer a'comin' in, hey, nonny nonny. It's here, and it's a-going out, and you've missed it!

As the Chinese have long warned, I should have been more careful about what I asked for, because I'd gotten it: Mackenzie without the commitments of his often-draining job. What I hadn't gotten were the delights of his companionship or of the season: the swims we could be taking, the walks on the beach or in the park, the picnics, and even, let us be frank, some uncomplicated, logistically simple shows of affection.

Happy student sounds came from the square as I made my way back toward it. That didn't seem at all fair. I looked yearningly across the street and did a double take as I saw Miles Nye, gesturing with great animation for one so ill this morning. That seemed even less fair.

"Sorry I missed class," he said when the warning bell had rung and I intercepted him on his way in. "An abscess." He waved authentic-looking letterhead. "Dentist wrote me an excuse."

"Did you get the part?"

"I got a toothache. Honestly."

"You're a good actor. I'm sure you'll make it. But I need to talk. Can you spare a minute?"

"I have class."

"Your dental appointment took four hours, Miles. Must

have been pure hell. Maybe it took four hours and five minutes?"

He lowered his head in an eloquent show of submission, and, gesturing him to follow, I moved to the side of the hallway. "I want to know about your exam. About the 'Would he?' and the spelled-out name." I was trying to be discreet, not mentioning April directly, as students made their way past us. Every one of them checked us out and then moved on, the way a herd might glance at one of its members that had been seized by a lion. They felt sorry for their captured kin, but they had their own skins to protect. "What about it, Miles?"

The normally voluble boy said nothing.

"You sent a signal. I caught it. What sense is there in being coy now?"

"I wanted you to get it, and you did. What else is there to say?" He was bleating for rescue, but the laws of nature are relentless, and self-preservation is its bottom line. The uncaught moved on past us.

"I talked to Woody," I said. "He didn't see her at all that evening. Isn't that what you were saying with the 'Ask him'?"

"No. That was about assigning blame. That was about Romeo and Juliet."

"But Woody said they weren't . . . um . . ." In love? Girlfriend and boyfriend? I mentally stammered, unsure of what terminology played with these kids now. Lovers? Significant others?

"*Romeo and Juliet*, the play," Miles said. "It was an exam, remember? I was talking about the play."

"What about it?"

"Oh, Ms. P., if anybody here knows about that, you surely do. What could I, a mere student, possibly say that would add to your vast storehouse of knowledge?"

"Anything, Miles. You're being smarmy. Devious. Of no help. Why? Don't you care about April? Care what's happened to her?"

"Sure," he said. "She's my friend."

"Are you sure she still can be anybody's friend? Some people

142

think she's dead. If you know something and don't do anything about it, maybe it's past tense now for her. Maybe she *was* your friend, but you let something bad happen to her."

His nostrils flared as he flashed a look of pure resentment. And then, with a breath, he was again bland and noncommittal. "If I were you," he said, "I wouldn't get into an uproar. What's done is done. Go with the flow."

The crowd around us had thinned to three stragglers, shuffling toward their classrooms. I couldn't believe how heartless Miles had become. The class jester, overflowing with emotions and quick, mostly joyous reactions to life, had turned into permafrost. "How can you say that? Maybe she's being held somewhere. Maybe it isn't too late."

"Please, Ms. P., I can't say anything else. If I could, I would have already. And I'm in big trouble with Miss Fellows. She has this rule that she drops you a half grade for every tardy. No exceptions."

I envy the self-confidence of despots. Rules with no exceptions, no room for human error or happenstance. A part of me wants to be like that, wielding my pathetic power for all its worth. But the other parts of me are too lazy or rebellious or democratic.

"I need a good grade in Modern History," Miles said. "I don't want to take it during the winter. I want to be in the school play and it takes up a whole lot of time. That's why I'm here, mostly."

Grilling him was getting me nowhere, even though I was still sure he knew something important. "I'll take you to Miss Fellows and explain," I said. I thought of Aldis's accusations again. "Miles, did she ... did you ever hear anything funny about Mr. Five's noontime sessions?"

"Funny ha-ha?"

"No ... odd."

Miles stared at me with laser intensity, then shook his head. "Don't know a thing about them."

I returned to the subject at hand, the one I was sure wasn't pure speculation. "One more try—when I saw April's name, and those allusions to guilt, I was sure you were trying to tell me what had happened, or who was responsible."

"And you were right. Correct." He tilted his head, waiting for more, but that's what I had. April. Woody. Present guilt. Romeo and Juliet. A mess.

Speaking of messes, I had a class upstairs, undoubtedly raising hell in my undespotic absence. "Okay, let's go face Miss Fellows," I said. "By the way, are you enjoying her class?" It was a mean-spirited question asked only because I wanted to hear what a rigid bitch she was.

"Oh, yeah," he said. "We're doing the Third Reich. You know, the rise of the Nazis. Every old movie you ever saw."

"History is interesting stuff," I murmured. Had I expected Miles to click his heels and give me the secret Nazi handshake? Maybe not that, but I'd have liked a hint that Aldis Fellows was so into her subject matter that she incited her students to reenact fascist history, to sign their papers with eighty-eights. Something subtle like that.

"Of course, some people say the stuff about the Jews and concentration camps didn't happen." Miles sounded considerably more at ease now that he was on his way to where he was supposed to be.

"Oh, God, Miles, who's telling you that? Of *course* it happened. You're too smart to pay attention to lunatics who deny the Holocaust, aren't you? It's history—documented. We're supposed to learn from it, not say it never happened. Does Miss Fellows say it never happened?"

He glanced at me sideways and walked up the stairs. "I'm not talking about me. I know the truth. That's what's interesting, that some people can actually doubt it happened." He spoke in a small, rational voice. "I was making conversation." Trying to placate me. I must have sounded on the verge of hysteria, which was a realistic estimate of which verge I actually was on. All the same, he hadn't answered my question.

I tapped twice, then opened Aldis Fellows's door. Miles

turned to me. "Read the poem again," he whispered. "Not the April part, the other part."

"What other part? The Woody part? What do you—"

"Miles Nye!" Aldis said. "Seriously late." She raised her wrist with a great flourish and considered an oversized watch. "Seven minutes," she announced. Then she spotted me and came over, and once I'd explained that I'd detained him and he was quite worried about it, she was forced to flex her rule. Not at all happy about it, either. Her class slouched lower in their seats. Miles had gotten away with something they hadn't been able to swing. Yet.

I got to my own classroom nanoseconds before my students had destroyed life on earth as we knew it.

From then on the afternoon oozed forward, each minute sweating into the next. Luckily, we had an *American Playhouse* video—the dramatization of a Steinbeck story—to occupy the first hour. Even more luckily, videos do not need the TLC that films used to require. Nothing snapped, blurred, or popped off its sprockets. I zoned all the way out, back to festering about the note this morning, until I realized that the next business of the day was not in the room with us.

"I'll be back in two minutes," I told the class. "I left your job applications in my car." They were well into couch-potatohood and amenable to anything, as long as it didn't require effort.

Outside the room I felt like I had as a kid when the teacher had allowed me the big wooden hall pass and I alone owned deserted corridors, thrilling at not being where I should be.

The three flights of narrow stairs were, as always, furtively underlit, and it was a relief to get down and out, to step into open space, fresh air, and pure light.

Except that, in the midst of the afternoon's dazzle, there were human silhouettes where only my car's should have been. Hulking, half-bent figures surrounding the vintage Mustang, one bent over the driver's side door.

"My *car*!" I screamed. On automatic, I ran toward them, going to save my baby. Those who would pirate her had their backs

145

to me. Four of them. Too large a contingent for a '65 Mustang convertible. How the devil did the stupid thieves plan to fit in and ride off? "Help! Police!" Stealing my car in broad daylight! "Hel—"

I never finished the thought, or even the breath, or got to them. In a fragment of a second the figures spun, arms out, weapons gleaming in the sunshine. Wrenches? Bombs? Guns? It—They—Whatever—took aim, and even as I reflexively screamed, a burst of something alien hit my face. I spat, but it was in my mouth, a poisonous chemical taste, but I couldn't keep myself silent. I raised my hand to my mouth and screamed again and again, and felt the hot-cold blast hit my arm, then my forehead, my eyes.

I stopped screaming. I dared not blink and barely breathed. I was blinded, skin pulling and mouth burning, caged in by my own skin, trapped.

I heard footsteps, but my eyes were sealed shut and I dared not open them—something was running down my forehead. I had no way to know if the men were gone—all of them—or if they were regrouping or circling me.

I didn't risk opening my mouth, either. I was afraid to swallow, to let in more of the poison. Couldn't shape words, call for help or demand the police. I merely let out the noise I could produce, a thin, tight-lipped wail. My skin was stiffening, getting hard. I was blind, burning, choking, terrified. The alleyway was appallingly silent. I put one arm out and felt the rough surface of the brick back wall, then edged along it until the temperature dropped and the facing turned a corner and I knew I was in the shade of the recessed entry.

Five steps, I told myself. Somebody will hear you once you get inside. Four steps. I told myself not to think of my assailants smiling among themselves, waiting to pounce again. Three. Don't panic. Two more steps. Okay, panic, but *move*. One. I groped until I found the handle, then pushed.

Help me, help me, I'm blind and poisoned and sprayed with I don't know what—I said, my lips still held tight. "Mrrree!" I heard myself mewl. "Gleeek!" Wasn't anybody there? The janitor? Anybody? I cried out. "Deeeiiii?" I heard.

I sounded like a stray animal. Nobody was going to come.

Do not panic. Your brain was not sprayed. Use it. Think.

I was getting good at groping walls, rough cool plaster this time, and I moved to the right. It should be there. Near the framing of the first door. A small box, glass-fronted. Poorly placed, Havermeyer had often lamented. Too accessible. He wanted it where nobody could ever misuse it. Unfortunately, that meant nobody could use it, either.

I opened the little glass door and pulled, mentally apologizing to the fire company for breaking the law and wasting their time.

The alarm sounded throughout the building. We'd had a drill the third day of summer school, had shown that we could get ourselves outside within five minutes. Havermeyer had been quite proud. That meant I didn't have long to wait for the sound of hundreds of feet making their exit.

Then it hit me. The feet would pound out through the *front* door. Down the wide, safe, marble *front* steps. Down and out the *first* floor onto the street. I was another story down, and at the other end of the building. The back stairs were narrow and wooden. A fire hazard. Not to be used by students.

I had just arranged my own demise, gotten rid of any possible rescuers. I was too stupid to live.

But sometimes life is kind to the seriously stupid, because it turned out I was not all alone there in the basement.

"What's going on? I heard a— Oh, my *God*!" A pure, ear-piercing scream that would have shattered crystal, had there been any. "Oh, my—Jesus, Mandy, what—you're covered in—oh, my *God*! You're—oh, God—she's—you're—"

Flora? Flora? "Bluhah?" I said.

Another scream. I wouldn't have thought she'd handle shock this way, the way I would, the way mere mortals would. "You're *alive*," she shouted. "Thank God! I thought you were—wait right there—" as if I were likely to race off. "I'll call for help. Don't worry, baby, it's okay now. Things'll be okay."

I doubted that, but I didn't correct her. It didn't seem the time to quibble. Besides, I still couldn't speak.

* * *

IN A WAY, it was lucky I hadn't known what I looked like, because I would have scared myself right out of my few remaining wits. No wonder the unflappable Flora had flapped. She told me I looked like a corpse, a vampire's sundae, as if I were dripping gore, as if I'd been exsanguinated.

Crimson paint, the E.R. doctor said, rather quizzically. I'd been spray-painted, like any other piece of urban architecture.

Unfortunately, it seemed no easier to remove oil-based graffiti from flesh than it was from the walls of buildings. My skin felt abused, though valuable, like the Sistine Chapel ceiling being slowly cleaned and restored.

"Thank you," I said when my mouth and nostrils were refinished.

"Welcome," the doctor said in a rough voice.

"And thank you, Flora. You were my guardian angel, appearing then. What were you doing there?"

"I needed things for my room. To replace the ruined stuff. Havermeyer said to check out the storeroom."

"Then you didn't quit, after all. I'm really glad. I would have missed you terribly."

"Three computers were goners, and a couple of posters and books, but most of it was saved. And Havermeyer said they'd replace the machines. He spent half last night begging for my return. Face it, I'm a twofer, black and female. I provide staff diversity almost single-handedly. Plus, half you idiots don't know the first thing about computers anyway, so you need me. And the truth is, I need the job. Whatever we say about Havermeyer, he arranges my hours so I can take my courses."

The doctor pitty-patted around the tender flesh on the sides of my eyes. Must be hard getting paint out of crow's-feet.

"Besides," Flora said, "I hated myself for backing down. For being hassled into retreat. I'm not giving them that."

"How did such a thing happen?" the doctor asked. He sounded seriously perturbed, perhaps feeling he hadn't gone to school for twenty years in order to remove paint. "We get Krazy Glue on the eyes. People mistake it for eyedrops. People with bad eyesight. But a face full of red paint?"

"People were stealing my car."

"Painters stealing your car?"

"I don't think they were stealing it," Flora said.

"Then I don't understand," I said.

"Working on the eyes now," the doctor said.

"Good. Crimson mascara is not overly flattering," Flora said.

The doctor was still not amused. I didn't blame him. I wasn't, either. I was terrified that my eyes would never open again, or that they would—and have been burned blind.

"Nobody was stealing your car," Flora said. "They were painting it. I saw it when the ambulance came."

"*Painting* it?"

"Stay still!" the doctor said.

"Painting *on* it," Flora said.

"On my car?"

"Please! These are your eyes I'm working on. Either your friend leaves or you get quiet or you need sedation."

"Sorry." I kept my head rigid and spoke in a flat voice, as if that would help. "They used red on a burgundy car."

"You don't like it aesthetically?" Flora asked. "They used red and black."

I imagined the Mustang looking like a checkerboard.

"I don't think they got to finish what they intended," Flora said. "You interrupted. It's nonsense—squiggles, zeros, and a set of stairs."

I felt a hot rush of fearful rage. "It was them."

"Who?"

The doctor stopped doing whatever. I almost suspected he was interested.

"I don't know names. The haters. Those circles are eighty-eights, like on the church. For Heil, Hitler."

"You sound a little crazy, girl."

"I'm going to try and manipulate the lids open now," the doctor said. "I don't think there's any paint in the eye. Good blink reflex. But these lashes are pretty much . . ."

"And the stairs?" Flora asked. "A step, maybe."

"Half a swastika," I whispered.

The doctor tsked, then cleared his throat. Then I heard snips, very, very nearby. "What—What are you doing?" I asked softly.

"Clearing the affected lashes so your eyes will open." Snip. Snip.

He was cutting off my lashes. I was going to look like Yoda, or an earthworm. I almost told him to leave me alone. Let's see if I could popularize the bright red shut-eye look.

"Don't let them win," Flora said. "I'm not going to. I'm going to find him. Or them. Or her. Or it. I'm taking countermeasures. Nobody's going to push me around. No more retreats or yelps—this is war."

Snip. Snip. Shame on me and my vanity. I was under attack by neo-Nazis, but all the same, I winced each time I heard the tiny click of his microshears.

"Now you've got your own battle scars," Flora said.

More than she knew. I'd tell her about the note later.

I couldn't see her face, read her expression, but her silence coated me as thickly as the paint had. Finally, she cleared her throat and spoke. "So push comes to shove, doesn't it? You going to run away, or stay the distance? You have the choice, you know. It isn't about you, isn't your battle the way it's mine."

The clipping paused for a second so he could work at prying my remaining lashes apart. "That's where you're wrong," I answered Flora. "It's about me, too. About who I am. About who I'd be if I didn't speak up. Besides, if you think I'm going to let some left-brain computer-nerd bean counter like you show me up, you're dead wrong." My lashes parted a bit and I saw a glimmer of light. It was artificial, fluorescent cold, and illuminating a blank ceiling—and the most beautiful sight of my life.

"I'm not running anywhere," I told Flora, "even if," my voice nearly broke with joy, "even if, as it appears, I wouldn't be running blind."

Fifteen

"THIS expedition is stupid," Mackenzie said. We parked his car in my spot in the alley behind the school. The Mustang, not sufficiently damaged to be covered by my insurance, had been towed to a semischlocky body shop that promised overnight magic, and Mackenzie didn't think graffiti would strike twice in the same parking spot. "I'm only going along because I don't think you should be going anywhere at all tonight. And surely not alone."

"I'm fine," I muttered.

"Yeah, right. You still have a patch of bright red in your hair, as if your scalp were bleeding. And red dots around your eyes."

"They said they'd wear off."

"An' you don't have much in the way of eyelashes."

"That's not a real handicap, is it? Besides, the sunglasses help." I looked like a termite, but I was trying to be gallant about it. My eyes were working—working well enough to make out a fine spray of pinky-red paint on the ground near where I'd stood this afternoon.

"The point is—somebody's after you," Mackenzie said in a low and lethal voice. "You're a target. You could at least lay low."

"Back down, be intimidated? Play by their rules? I can't. It would make the future much scarier than anything happening now."

Five was picking us up around front. I would have gladly chauffeured, but Mackenzie's VW does not seat a trio gracefully, particularly when one of the group has a log leg. "What is my cover story for going there? Who am I supposed to be?" he asked petulantly. This was accompanied by grimaces and grunts as he insisted on extricating himself from the car without assistance.

"Look, C.K., I'm glad to have you along, but it was your idea, remember? You're going as my friend, if you go—but you don't have to. I asked to borrow your car, if you recall. And even with that, Five could have picked me up. This isn't going to take long. I want to see what I can find out, and nothing would be made better if I sat in my home instead of the Truongs'. And Five's along. I can manage."

"Five," he muttered. "What kind of name is *Five*?"

I glanced at him. Some macho competition was in progress even before the players met. "A man without a name is not in a position to challenge somebody else's nickname." I wondered how I'd manage the introductions. "C, this is Five" sounded like inept spy-talk. I nonetheless explained the Bartholomew Dennison business. "Maybe you'd like to decipher your lack of a name while we're at it?"

"I don't like the sound of this guy. Too hail fellow well met." Mackenzie was finally out of the car. "Oh, forgot to give you

this in the confusion," he said. "I got what you wanted, the contents of April's book bag."

The slip of paper he passed me listed, in his handwriting, a ce-
rise canvas wallet with two dollars and thirty-seven cents and ID,
a dark pink lipstick, a student assignment calendar, a paperback dictionary, a rolled up rain hat, a three-subject notebook,
house keys, seven student discount bus tickets, an apple, a copy
of *People* magazine, a flyer advertising a series of Taiwanese
films to be shown on Penn's campus, an environmentally correct spray bottle of something called Hair Scruncher, and
Huckleberry Finn, property of the Philly Prep library, not due
for another week.

"Where's her work?" I asked. "*Romeo and Juliet* and something about immigration—the paper she was writing? See? The
newspaper said her backpack had schoolbooks in it, but *her*
books aren't actually here. This doesn't make sense."

"Uh-huh," Mackenzie said with little interest. He was looking
behind me. "You know her?" he asked.

I did, to my regret. I watched her squatty figure determinedly
bear down on us. "Evening!" Aldis Fellows said.

I made introductions, and took a step away, toward the front
of the building where Five would be waiting.

"Would you look at that!" Aldis gestured at the unimpressive
back of the school. "That's what eats the budget and doesn't let
us have books or films we need. A disgrace!"

"You mean the paint spray?" I asked.

"The what? I mean those lights!"

Three barely visible bulbs illuminated the recessed back door.

"This citadel of learning does not seem to know that the days
are longer in summertime. The sun has not yet set, and yet lights
blaze away, burning energy and limited funds. No one has the
intellect to reset the timer! It's all wasted resources around here—
false alarms ringing midday, lights on before dark—"

"I'm sorry," I murmured. The woman had the ability to make
me feel responsible for the decline of western civilization, as
demonstrated in the three wrongly burning lights. I was relieved

she didn't seem to know who'd set off the afternoon's false alarm.

"Excuse us, ma'am," Mackenzie said softly but firmly.

Aldis nodded, and we made our limpy, slow way around to the front of the building. "She may be the single angriest woman I've ever met," I said.

Five's dark green sedan waited at the curb. "A narc car," Mackenzie said. "What's the guy afraid of?"

Two teachers on a mission to console parents, and Mackenzie behaving as if Five and I were having a tryst. "It's hard to buy a Maserati on a teacher's salary," I said. "He has an ordinary car, what's it to you?"

"Five, this is my friend, Mackenzie," I said as I tried to hold the backseat door open for the invalid. However, he looked affronted, his manhood questioned, so I left him on his own.

"Mackenzie?" Five asked. "Sorry, I didn't catch the first—"

I climbed in the front. "Crispin," I said. "It means curly-haired, and isn't that appropriate? Did you have lots of hair when you were born, Crispin?"

The detective arranged his right leg in a diagonal across the back of the car. "Hitting *What to Name Your Baby* again?" he murmured.

I had, indeed. At least the C's. "St. Crispin was the patron saint of shoemakers."

"Then are you a cobbler?" Five asked. I couldn't tell if he was joking. "Scion of a shoemaking dynasty, perhaps?"

"No," Mackenzie said.

Rude, rude, which prompted a need on my part to make social noises. "Or like Crispus Attucks, the first man killed in the American Revolution. That'd be a name you'd know, Five, wouldn't you? Five teaches American history," I babbled. "Knows all kinds of things about Philadelphia, too, even a poem about Peppers!"

"Interesting," Mackenzie said. "Well, I'm not of the Attucks branch. Not the scion of a slave dynasty, either, far as I know."

Five's laugh was forced.

"Mackenzie's been reading a lot of history this summer, while he recuperates." I sounded like a nervous hostess at the start of a bad cocktail party. Come on, somebody, pair up and mingle!

"I noticed. Ski accident or what?" Five asked with minimal interest. It doesn't take a whole lot for men to feel slighted, and somehow, both men already did.

"Or what," Mackenzie said. "Bullet misplacement. Into my leg. I'm the scion of a bullet-ridden branch of the service."

"Sorry," Five said. "I'm not following."

"Special division of the Philadelphia Police. C.O.C.—Cops on Crutches," Mackenzie said. "You know these new laws—can't discriminate against us crips. Our motto is: We're hobbled but hot."

We were silent most of the rest of the ride into the Southwest section of the city. Five gallantly, I thought, did not comment on my splotched skin, mottled hair, or missing eyelashes. Nor did he comment on the outside scenery, which was no more aesthetic than my recently painted face was.

We drove up Woodland Avenue, past boarded and steel-sheathed stores. Past paving dense with broken glass and wire-fenced playgrounds that looked like Bosnia on a bad day. No one needed statistics to know this was one of the most economically depressed neighborhoods in the city. And no one needed to point out that this was not the Southwest with which decorators had fallen in love.

There was a pervasive grayness despite the orange sunset sky, the leafy attempts of curbside trees and the occasional hydrangea on a tiny front lawn or pot of petunias hanging from a porch support. And the tension was almost palpable. We were a nondescript car with three riders, but a great deal of curbside energy went into checking us out as we passed.

"A lot of ethnic strife around here in the past," Mackenzie said.

I remembered ten years ago, when I was in college, a black family had bought a house on an all-white block around here and they were burned out. Thugs set the house on fire. After we'd thought the Civil Rights Movement had to do with the South.

"Right," Five said. "Ever since the influx of Asians and blacks. Used to be Irish, Italians, Russians, Germans, and Brits, then, mid-century—"

"I meant in the *past*."

I felt yellow fever approaching again.

"Swedes took it from the Lenni Lenapes, then the Dutch threw the Swedes out, then the Brits threw the Dutch out."

"When?" Five asked.

"Sixteen hundreds." My history's older than your history, so there. That ended that conversational tack, and all was silence until we reached the Truong home.

April's parents were small people who looked as if they'd been sandpapered close to the bone by time and circumstance. They lived in a narrow brick row house that had seen better days inside and out, and they sat close together, hands clasped, on a love seat that had probably been nondescript when it was in its prime.

We were seated across from them, on unmatched straight-back chairs. Cups of tea and a plate of delicate cookies were on the table in front of us. A photograph of April in a bouffant white dress—first communion, perhaps?—was on top of the TV.

I apologized for my dark glasses and said I had an eye problem. They looked confused. I moved on and said how fond I was of their daughter, and how I wanted to do anything I could to help her family and the search for her. I said what a bright student she was, how much I expected a good future for her, how impressed I'd been by her work and her attitude.

Her parents smiled weakly and nodded. Now and then her mother wiped at her eyes and swallowed hard.

April's brother Thomas, pencil-thin, wore a T-shirt that had a painted tombstone with VO VAN TRAN written on it. Custom-made mourning shirts were a local growth industry. Thomas sat on the worn arm of an overstuffed chair and helped his parents with their conversational English. I had the distinct impression that he'd been coerced into being part of the gathering, but I had the equally distinct impression that Thomas Truong wouldn't be an easy person to coerce.

April's parents spoke in a mix of English and what I assumed was Vietnamese.

"My parents explained that the police have not been back," Thomas said when they were finished. "Not since that first time."

"Did they question other people who knew—know—April?" I asked. "For example, the boy who was killed outside the school—the one on your shirt—Vo Van—could there be any connection between that terrible event and April's disappearance?"

The older Truongs inhaled in unison at the mention of Vo Van, and watched their son nervously.

Thomas's posture became defiantly rigid, his chin tilted upward. "My sister's disappearance is not the fault of a Vietnamese, of our neighbors," he said. "There is an unfairness toward us, toward my people. The truth is that while my sister has very little sense about the people she favors, Vo Van was not one of the people she favored. There can be no connection."

"Of course, we know April only through school," Five said quickly. "And only for a few weeks. She was—is—a promising student, but I—we naturally feel deep concern about her disappearance, and wondered if perhaps there was anything she had said—about school—that might help the police find her."

Thomas sat up even straighter and spoke. "I do not understand."

"Do you feel the police were thorough enough about April's life outside your home?"

Thomas translated for his parents, who looked at each other, then shook their heads. How would they know if the police had failed to ask something significant about a portion of April's life they didn't share?

"Perhaps something about school," Five said. "Did she mention anything that worried her?"

"Many things worry all of us, including April. But my parents are tired when they come home," Thomas said. "And then there are the little children. April did not return from her work until nearly midnight, when they would be asleep. I do not think there were many long conversations about school."

157

"Then with you? You picked her up from work."

"Many times," he said. "Not always. We did not talk a great deal."

"Why did you pick her up?" I asked.

"My sister had no car. It is a dangerous city. She might have made an unwise choice of transportation otherwise. She did not always have sense about the people she favored. She needed to be protected. From herself."

From Woody. Thomas had thought he was making sure they didn't see one another.

"Do you think she might have meant to go away?" Five asked his question slowly, with deliberation and consideration of each word, and he watched intently as the Truongs responded.

He was being the detective. Mackenzie was being nothing, his entire self as inert as his leg.

"April is a good girl," her mother said.

"Why would she want to leave us?" Thomas sounded as if he were issuing a challenge. "Why do you ask such questions? What do you think about this, Mister . . ."

"Dennison," Five said. "And I don't know what to think. That's what I was hoping you'd help with."

"The police have already asked all the questions. Over and over. About worries, fears, problems."

"And they've come up with nothing," Five said. "That's why I thought together we might have extra insight."

I could see the hint of a lip curl on Mackenzie, and I could read his thoughts as if his skull were transparent. Another wannabe sleuth, he was thinking, and not with admiration.

"But if we of April's family are content that the police are doing their best, if the police are content with what they know, why should not you be?" Thomas asked. "Is it not wrong for citizens to try to be the law keepers? My parents do not blame the school. This did not happen on school time."

"I didn't mean—" Five began.

"We are confident that all will be well," Thomas said. "And that all effort is being made in the meantime."

The older Truongs did not seem to share their son's serenity.

They looked wracked, devastated, had winced with pain each time April was mentioned, and they had been wringing their hands throughout the visit. But they didn't contradict their son. I hoped their silence was due only to a problem with the language, or to a point of Vietnamese etiquette.

"It is kind of you to have come all this way and made this visit," Thomas said, rising. "To have put yourself to this inconvenience." His parents also stood and nodded, nearly bowing. "It is good to know her teachers care about April."

"But—"

"We thank you." And then Thomas quite literally showed us the door, and used it, too.

We stood on the street, the night close around us. "Was that peculiar or what?" I said. I expected no more response than grunts of assent, so Five startled me. He had been so intent inside the house, so much more aware of possible holes in the search than Mackenzie or I had been, so tuned into each answer given.

But what he said as he unlocked the car was, "Maybe I've caught their Asian sense of fatality or something." He sounded relaxed, relieved, almost happy. "I think we should let go of it, too. Leave it to the pros."

I could almost feel him slough the residue of all those questions without a backward glance. Case closed. Leave *it* to the pros. It?

But April wasn't an *it*, and what about her? Suddenly, I heard echoes of Aldis's judgment of the man, and I, too, wondered just how bright or observant Five really was, and how much he'd let slip by without his notice or comprehension.

Sixteen

"**U**P for a nightcap?" Five asked as we drove around the edge of Penn's campus and started for center city.

I was. Not particularly for the drink, but for the talk. I wanted to gnaw this over, pick apart strands, get to its center. But as I opened my mouth to accept, I turned around and saw Mackenzie's eyes, even in the dark car, shouting absolutely not.

"Thanks," I told Five, "but I'm exhausted. Those hooligans today . . ." The official story was that my car and I had been the victims of random violence. Same old, same old. Nobody questioned it.

"You sure? Maybe it'd be good to unwind. Plus, it'd be a chance to toss the topic around."

"You said we should let it go," Mackenzie said.

"Maybe not till we know what we're letting go of." Five's voice filled the car interior. "I'd especially like to hear what a pro thinks. Unless you were pulling my leg about your leg, so to speak. The cops on crutches division? I know the division is a joke, but you are a cop, right?"

You tend to forget that even a handsome, all-American specimen such as Five could be lonely. The man needed friends, needed to feel comfortable in his new environment. He was trying. You could hear it in every word. The least I could do was not be a card-carrying example of why we were the Most Hostile City in the U.S.

"Of course I want to know what you think, too, Mandy," he added, rather lamely.

"Well, then, sure. A quick one."

At that exact second, Mackenzie's slurry voice came from the backseat. "Some other time."

"Not you, Crispin? No problem. We'll drop you off first. Whereabouts do you live?"

I watched the words drop in front of Mackenzie like flags in front of a bull. "Changed my mind," he said. "A quick drink'd be good." And then he suggested a place about two blocks from the school. It was charming—dark, sleek, and cool, but not overly chilled. In the far corner a woman in a plumed extravaganza of a hat played piano just loudly enough, and more than well enough.

I'd never been there. I wondered when Mackenzie had. I knew that if I asked, he'd say he read a review or mention of it in the paper months ago, and that might be true—he had an amazing ability to store abstract knowledge. But still I wondered.

"Quite an interrogation you gave back there," Mackenzie said when we were settled in and our orders taken. "Very smooth. Professional."

Mackenzie had a keen appreciation for language. *Interrogation* wasn't the right word, unless he meant to insult Five. Maybe an extension of the evening hadn't been the best idea, after all. It was unwholesome fun, having two men circling each other because of me, and not particularly pleasant, not even in a guilty, secret way, since I wasn't part of the game. At least not consciously.

The woman at the piano played "As Time Goes By," but we were not the stuff of legends, not up to the standards of the *Casablanca* threesome.

"Interrogation? Did I seem to be drilling them?" Five sounded truly concerned.

"Didn't mean it that way," Mackenzie said. "Jus' interested in your questions. Very systematic approach."

"I should have let you do the asking," Five said. "I'm not good at it, and it's definitely more your line."

Mackenzie shook his head. "Wouldn't have known what to ask. Didn't know the girl or the circumstances."

Five's eyes flicked from Mackenzie to me, then back. He was translating knowledge of April into mating data, deciding whether Mackenzie's know-nothing stance meant we didn't see each other much or that we saw each other a whole lot but didn't confide in each other much.

But we *had* talked about the missing girl. We'd talked it through a dozen times. So why, after practically putting yellow tape around me that said POLICE LINE: KEEP BACK, would Mackenzie lie in a way that was almost a quitclaim?

"What was your take on what they said?" Mackenzie asked Five.

"Not much. The parents didn't know squat about their daughter, and the brother didn't care. How about you?"

"You think they were tellin' the truth? That nothin' bothered her, she didn't fear anybody or like anybody in particular?"

"Why would they lie?" Five asked. I wondered if he realized who was now the interrogator, whether he minded.

Mackenzie's shrug was barely perceptible. I'd known him long enough to translate it as All Kinds of Reasons, but he didn't choose to share any of them.

"I can understand now how she might well go off on a joyride," Five said. "Anything would be better than going back to a house where nobody talks to you. Nobody's even awake when you're there."

"She didn't see it that way," I said. "There are younger children she cares for, and that didn't seem a chore. They were a team, the family, and that was her job."

"Surely Thomas isn't playing on that family team of theirs. He's in a gang that runs massage parlors. Not a wholesome lot, that group. Not exactly family values."

"Where'd you hear that?" Mackenzie asked, but with curiosity, not hostility.

"Somebody told me." Five looked at me. "Was it you?"

I shook my head. Even though I'd heard about Thomas from Woody or Miles or somebody, I'd never passed it on. Except to Mackenzie, who was choosing to play dumb.

"But I'm interested how you relate that to April," Mackenzie said. "You think a gang member snatched her? Revenge against brother Thomas, maybe?"

"It sounds possible, doesn't it? And then, it gets really murky when you get into the possibility of her being a . . . a harlot."

Five obviously wasn't into PC talk, but even so, I was surprised by his choice of words. "But you knew her," I said. "Didn't she seem the least likely girl in the school to be a sex industry worker?"

"Sex industry worker," Mackenzie grumbled. "Hard hats and pasties. As for the sex industry itself, the smokestacks and Environmental Impact studies show—"

"I didn't know her well," Five answered me. "Only through her classwork. We never talked about her personal life. We didn't have that kind of time you must have had with her. She didn't do special sessions with me."

"Never at lunch?" I asked, hoping to relocate the conversation to the issue of what went on at noon. "She wasn't ever part of your fan club?"

"My what?" His eyebrows rose.

"No false modesty. The lunch bunch. The summer scholars."

"But I told you what really—"

"I'm teasing." I decided on another tack. "Remember how you were asking me about April and drugs?" I said.

He nodded.

"Do you think much goes on at Philly Prep that way?"

"Drugs? There? I didn't mean that—I meant in her neighborhood, with her friends," Five said. "Not at your school!"

"Why not?" Mackenzie asked, semibelligerently. "You think Philly Prep has some special dispensation, that rich kids are exempt? Who'd you think can afford the stuff?"

"I didn't mean, I only . . . No." He relaxed, looked at me and answered my question. "I don't think so. If there is, I'm unaware of it. Jesus, if I thought for one minute—I have zero tolerance for that business."

But perhaps he was just naïve. I pressed on. "I'm still so jealous of whatever it is that makes your extra time with the kids work. Would it be possible—be honest, if this would be an imposition—could I visit some noon? Observe for a while?"

"Observe? Well . . . sure." He seemed ill at ease, and I wondered what really was going on. "Except it isn't like a lesson. I told you. So don't expect too much," he added. "And more important, I can't let it establish precedent."

"Meaning?" He'd lost me.

"Phyllis," he hissed. "What if she decides to observe, too?"

Phyllis. That was all it was about. Not drugs but predatory females. Nonetheless, I'd pop in someday to set my mind at rest.

"Hate to backtrack," Mackenzie said, lumbering into the talk. "But I'm still not clear on the gang connection. Did you think the brother seemed put off by your questions? You know, how he was about the cops having already asked about what they needed to know?"

"I'm sure he's nervous about anybody asking anything that might involve him," Five said. "He definitely wanted the interview closed. And who knows what the parents really thought?"

"I keep wondering if Thomas is at all connected with her disappearance," Mackenzie said. "What's your take?"

"I don't know as I have one. I don't think I knew what I was doing in there or where I was hoping to get. Looking back, I'm really embarrassed to have hogged the floor. I hoped that maybe asking around would get me somewhere, and then I'd know where to head from there, but it didn't happen."

"Why?" Mackenzie asked abruptly. "Why do you care so much?"

We were back to rude, and I didn't see why.

"Be-Because, she's—I—"

I really disliked my detective at that moment. "For heaven's sake!" I said. "You can tell you're not a teacher. And thank goodness for that. We *care*. Forgive me for speaking for both of us, Five, and feel free to disagree, but the question doesn't make sense, Mackenzie. I don't want to sound simplistic, but a young girl is gone. Swallowed up by the earth and somebody she struggled with. That's scary. She's our student. If there's something to be done, then we'd want to do it. There's a damn fine possibility that the police did not sufficiently question the people who were with her every day. Deedee Klein was nice enough, but nobody wanted to talk to her and she let it go at that. So there's a good chance that they—the police—are missing something important that a lowly teacher might know. It's as simple as that."

"Didn't mean the question to sound like a challenge," Mackenzie said mildly. But I thought he had. He is a man who generally sounds precisely the way he intends to. "It's real impressive that you care about your kids. But depressin' as this is going to sound, she's a girl who is not underage, who got into a van."

"Was forced into it. She struggled," I said.

"The witness thinks. For all we know, she was giggling hard, play-fightin', or just shrugging off her backpack."

"And leaving it there?"

"And leavin' it all behind," Mackenzie said. "The sad truth is that people take off and disappear all the time. Like that, and for keeps. Because they want to or because they don't want to. But there is a spectacular lack of evidence here, of meaningful clues. Of anything. And this is an enormous country, and she could be anywhere in it by now. Legally. In places where nobody's given a thought to looking for her. I'm going to be real surprised if she is found. Ever. Or at least, in time."

We both stared at him.

"Get on with your lives, you two," he said with supreme calm. "If anything solves this one, it'll be time. Your first reaction was the right one," he said directly to Five. "Adopt that Asian fatality. Leave April to destiny and the police. Let go of it."

I opened and closed my mouth like an oxygen-starved fish, but my protests remained empty bubbles of silence.

"Thanks," Five said. "You're right. Thanks a lot." He picked up the check. "On me," he added. And Mackenzie, obviously no longer proving anything, let him pay while he and I waited outside. The balmy day had melted into a mild and delicious night. Not the right setting for talk of abductions or runaways or gangs.

"Should I drop you off at your place, or, um, your places?" Five asked with little subtlety once we were all outside.

"We can walk from here," Mackenzie told him. "I'll see her home." I could almost feel his glee at avoiding the issue of where, or in what combination, we lived. "But thanks," he said with a minor reprise of his customary charm. "For the lift and the drinks and the company."

"You'll walk home on crutches?" Five said doubtfully.

"Good exercise," Mackenzie insisted.

Five waved as he walked off toward his car. "See you, then."

I stopped gritting my jaw. The imagined contest was now on hold, if not over. "I'm glad you eased up at the end," I said as we walked back toward the school. "I think he's a lot more shy than he seems, and maybe not too bright. He was just trying to make friends. Basically, he's a decent guy."

"Likable," Mackenzie said. "But decent? I don't know . . ."

"Come on," I said. "This imagined rivalry—"

"What are you talking about?"

"Mackenzie, you can be so perceptive about other people's motives, but you are in such denial about your own that I can barely believe you function on this planet."

"Rivalry? With whom?"

I waved him away, crutches and all.

"What's happened here?" he asked. "Blindsided by a square jaw?" Crutch-clump, crutch-clump.

"Jealousy is a worse handicap than a shattered bone," I snapped. "And a whole hell of a lot uglier." And so we might have continued, escalating to new heights of bickering, had not Flora Jones come marching around the corner. Flora and a high-spirited brown puppy who looked as if someday, when he grew into his feet, he planned to be a formidable Doberman.

"Well, hey!" she said. "It must be somebody famous wearing those shades at night."

"We're playing charades," I said. "We're the blind leading the halt. Get it?" The evening was becoming a mobile PTA meeting. Philly Prep faculty were everywhere, taking over the city. Once again I made introductions, and watched as Flora evoked a differ-ent Mackenzie than Five had. This one was cordial, indeed gal-lant, radiating charm and beguilement. He made it clear, in a soft, Southern way, that never before had such a charming woman and puppy crossed his path.

Now I was the one to flash with jealousy, to fight the temp-tation to give his good leg a solid kick.

"Meet my bodyguard, Lamont," Flora said. "As in Cranston. He knows what evil lurks in the hearts of men."

At the moment, Lamont looked as if all he knew was the pure joy of being alive and out on a summer night. "Pleasure to meet you, pup," I said.

Lamont wagged his tail, his hips, and his hind legs. In fact, he wagged his head, too. This puppy was going to have a hard time learning what evil lurked anywhere.

Was this what she'd meant by taking countermeasures? I didn't see how a dog, even the future fierce one, could prevent vandals from spray-painting a door, or leaving ugly phone mes-sages, or mailing threats, or defacing a classroom. But it seemed cruel to say so. Besides, Flora had intimated that she had a whole arsenal, a multifaceted plan.

"Mr. Cranston and I have just completed our evening constitutional," Flora said, "and we were heading home and probably should continue doing just that. Pleasure to meet you," she told Mackenzie. And, "See you in the morning," she told me. "Both of us. I'm bringing Lamont to school."

"Wow," I said, "does Havermeyer—"

"Let him try and stop me. Let anybody try and stop me from now on. I am nobody's willing target anymore." And with a smile and a quasimilitary salute, she and Lamont continued on, Flora walking, Lamont experimenting with a canine version of skipping.

"Nice woman," Mackenzie said.

"Amazing woman. And gutsy. I'm not as sure about Lamont."

"But your Bartholomew Dennison the Fifth is a different story. Charming, sure. Good company. But I think the man was lying." He spoke in a flat voice as he moved, little-crutch-clump, little-crutch-clump, down the sidewalk.

I walked beside him, trying hard to think of what, if anything, Five had to lie about, or when he might have done so this evening. He hadn't made any statements I could remember, simply asked questions. Except, maybe, about drugs at Philly Prep? But even so—and I didn't want to think it might be—why would that bother Mackenzie so much?

"Something about what he was doin' was a sham."

"What?" I really didn't get it. "Questions simply *are*. They can't be a sham." The word *sham* began to sound silly.

"Motives for askin' questions can be fake. Bet my entire sick pay that nothing Mr. Five said tonight is one hundred percent the way he made it sound. That he didn't want to know what he said he wanted to know, and he didn't care about what he—or you—said he cared about."

"You forget. The outing was my idea. That's for starters. It isn't as if he had some big secret scenario in which he involved us. And if he wasn't doing exactly what he seemed to be doing, then what was he doing? Getting kicks in a particularly boring way? There's nothing nefarious about running out to Southwest for a strained session with a sad family. Your professional skills have atrophied." Instead of having insights, he was indulging in spite.

The sight of the school across the street sent a blip of panic snaking through me. I was glad I wasn't alone, even if I was with an impaired member of the C.O.C. He could swing a crutch if anything once again lurked in the alley behind the building.

Mackenzie sighed and clumped along. "The man has a definite agenda," he finally said. "Not necessarily one that's about April."

"Look, I admit he's good-looking. Exceptionally so. And maybe a little bit interested in me, too. And there were questions that annoyed you—probes for whether we lived together, what our relationship was. But that's no reason to smear him. I'm a grown-up. You can trust me, and you'd better. Honestly, if we're to have any kind of—"

"He wanted to know something—wanted to know it a whole lot. Only not what we were supposed to think he wanted to know. He found it out, too. Tha's why he was almost giddy with relief. An' I'm sure it had nothing to do with April's welfare."

But I remembered the conversation in the bar, and Five's concern, and I told Mackenzie so.

He shook his head. "*I* was the one kept going back to the issue at hand."

"No, he did—remember? He said we could have a drink and talk about it and you asked him why he'd changed his mind."

"Fact is, Five didn't give a damn about the Truongs by then. Nope, there's some other story there. He's slick, too. Good at hidin' it, all smooth surfaces, no edges to grab hold of."

Which is to say, there was nothing Mackenzie could name or identify. There was, in fact, nothing. Mackenzie was paranoid. Jealous.

It's a shame how quickly a perfectly good man could spoil in the heat.

Seventeen

WE crossed at the corner, like good citizens. Whenever I approached the school in less than my usual double time, with no students or classes looming, I was able to appreciate what a handsome building housed it. Its turn-of-the-century brownstone walls and carved facades spoke of a very different city and social class than my small brick *trinity* house did with its three rooms, named for faith, hope, and charity. By the time the Philly Prep building went up, history and philosophy had marched way past the deliberately understated Colonial ethic, and new millionaires flaunted their success with expensive materials, carved stonework, gilding, sweeping staircases, and imposing entryways.

I've tried to envision the successful brewer who built himself this palace, and wondered what life was like when only one family lived inside its walls. I imagined them enormous in number and girth—and the paterfamilias a strutting, proud fellow as he left his oversized front door each morning.

And as if bringing my idle thoughts to life, a figure exited the building. Down the front stairs, onto the sidewalk. The ghost of brewers past? Except that instead of a swagger there was a hunched-over slump.

"Lowell!" I called out before I could censor myself. No matter. He continued walking away from the school and us.

"Lowell? Of Aunt Whatsis and Mom?"

"What's he doing here at this hour?"

"Well, hey, I'll prove my skills haven't rusted. Let me demonstrate an advanced police technique of findin' stuff out. Lowell!" he shouted, "Hey, there!" He turned his head toward me. "Should you happen to want to study up on it, the technique is called *askin'*." He looked back down the street.

Lowell continued to shuffle along, shaking his head from side to side. So much for advanced police techniques.

"Lowell!" Mackenzie called one more time without any response.

"Doesn't matter." We turned left, beside the building, toward the back alley and Mackenzie's car.

"Look at that," I wailed as we turned again. "Somebody broke the lights." The recessed back entry was dark. "The vandals are back. Who *are* they? What do they *want*?"

"Probably they've been out for a while," Mackenzie said, consolingly. "It was still light when we parked, so who'd have noticed?"

"Aldis. Remember her ranting about how stupid the school was?"

"I pretty much tuned her out."

"The lights made her irate because—"

171

"Because pretty much anythin' could, was my impression."

"Correct, but it was those lights this time, because it wasn't dark yet and they were on, wasting money."

"She busted them to make a point? It couldn't have been easy." The bulbs were set in mesh protectors. Somebody would have to poke and prod and stab at them. Two of them looked as if somebody had. With the third, the one directly over the back door, it appeared the vandal had lost patience—the entire mesh cage was crushed along with the bulb. "Cost more to replace them than to keep them off two more hours would have."

But of course, Aldis wouldn't really have smashed the offending lights. She had her own kind of craziness—rigidity, bigotry, and narrow-mindedness, discipline and efficiency to excess. But that was the sort of outrageousness that wrote petitions and harassed city hall, not the sort that smashed lights.

I took deep, even breaths to control a mild attack of nerves. I reminded myself that broken lightbulbs were not cause for alarm, or preface to anything worse, but a basic city fact of life.

Mackenzie, meanwhile, stood back on his crutches, leaning against his car and regarding the broken lights, the door, and then me. He smiled invitingly. I moved away from the school, closer to him. Very close. He smiled again.

"What?" I said.

He kissed me. Balanced against the car, he was almost as able-bodied as he used to be, and he had full use of his arms and hands.

"You are a world-class kisser," I whispered.

He kissed me again, both his hands cradling my face, and it finally did seem summer with its soft, dark nights and sultry charm. Then he pulled back and looked at me, almost quizzically. "Listen," he said, still holding me, punctuating his words with kisses on my temple, my nose, my mouth. "I have this idea . . . Don't laugh, okay? You think anybody's in there?"

"In school? I didn't see anything posted for tonight. No plays, no paper, no games." I waited for the *don't laugh* part.

"Never told anyone before, but I have this fantasy. Had it since junior high, which is a difficult time for a growin' boy.

172

Made more difficult in my case by the existence of Mrs. Taubman. She was quite a voluptuous woman, teachin' basic biology, and I spent all class weaving ornate reproductive fantasies about her and me. Alone in the lab." He pulled back a bit and looked at me. "I still have the fantasy."

"I hope you've noticed that I'm not Mrs. Taubman."

"I hope you've noticed I'm not in junior high anymore."

"I don't have a lab, and you do have a broken leg and a cast up to yay."

"I also have a fantasy about makin' it with my teacher in her classroom, test tubes and periodic chart of the elements or not."

I loved the idea. My classroom! Shakespeare and Hawthorne and Virginia herself on the walls! Havermeyer got upset by uneven window shades in a schoolroom, so think how he'd be if . . . And Helga, the office witch with her rules and regulations.

I knew it was more than a little sick to stoke sexual fires with the image of my principal and his secretary. I hoped that someday we grew up enough so that we were beyond being thrilled like adolescents by daring the forbidden, by breaking out of assigned roles.

But not quite yet.

I opened my bag, extracted the school key, and handed it over. "Consider yourself Taubmanned," I said.

Mackenzie retrieved his crutches, hobbled to the back door with me, turned the key in the lock, then pressed the latch.

Nothing happened.

He frowned, then turned it back, to where it had been. And the door opened. We looked at each other with some dismay, then in unarticulated unison decided to think about Mrs. Taubman, not the issue of the unlocked door. "Good thing we happened by," Mackenzie murmured.

Inside, we stood at the base of the steep back staircase. Mackenzie took a deep breath and put his crutch on the first riser.

"There's an elevator," I whispered. "How important is climbing three flights of stairs to your fantasy?"

"Why are you whispering?" he whispered back. "Where is it?"

I pointed toward the other end of the hallway. The brewer had designed this floor for out-of-sight, out-of-mind activities. Some were still housed here—the janitorial staff had its office, and most out of season equipment was stored down here. But my journalists also had a basement room during the school year, the summer kitchen now housed home ec and child-care classes, pantries and storage rooms had become science labs, and a great warren of rooms for washing and polishing and ironing and preserving had been pulled apart and reshaped into a large basketball-court–sized gymnasium and locker rooms. And at the very end of the hall, a small, slow elevator had been installed a few years earlier, to meet the rules for handicapped access. The brewer would have had a fit had he seen what became of his palace.

We tiptoed toward the elevator, or rather, I did. Mackenzie click-shuffled on the hardwood flooring. I turned to see if he was following me and to check how he was doing with his lopsided shuffle.

Something registered as not right, but too quickly to be translated into words. Simply ... something. I stopped all motion and tilted my head, my breath immediately catching and growing rapid. But the hall was empty, its only occupants the two of us.

"What?" he asked as he approached.

I slowly swiveled back, so that I was facing the way I'd been before. Facing the elevator. And in the swing I saw what was wrong and laughed out loud with relief. "It's nothing," I said. "The light's on in the gym, that's all."

It was difficult to tell, because the glass squares in the doors were heavily covered with mesh on the inside, making them useless as windows. But they were able to let a thin wash of light through.

"Aldis would be infuriated," Mackenzie said with a grin. "Better turn it off before she sues the school." He reached up with a crutch so as to push one of the double doors open. I moved to hold the door so that he could walk through.

So I was in position to hear his immediate reaction. It was nothing so mild as a gasp. It was a combination groan, swallow, and choke. "Jesus," he said. "Oh, my God!"

By then I was into the gym, too, and I understood.

Woody was at the far end. Up high. Suspended. Woody, in ripped jeans and no shoes or shirt, arms up and tied with solid-looking ropes to the two sides of the basketball backboard, both bloody palms nailed into the backboard, body hanging limply, head lolling, eyes closed.

Woody, crucified.

Woody, who had told me he was going to make everything all right himself. That he was handling things. Today he'd told me that. And tonight, tonight . . . "His chest," I said. "The blood."

"Superficial cuts, I think," Mackenzie said. "But the hands, the arms . . ."

We gaped and gasped. Time ground to an absolute halt. Epochs passed before either Mackenzie or I moved. Millennia before my brain began to process what it was seeing, let alone recover from the incomprehensibility of it and think of what to do.

But finally we both inhaled long, jagged breaths and spoke at the same time, neither one of us completing a thought. "Nine-one-one—gotta get him—do you think he's still—is he breathing?—need a ladder, something—cut those ropes—but can't let him fall—a phone is where . . . ?"

And all of that interrupted by frequent, stupefied reality checks back to the dangling figure on the backboard. And yes, each time it was still, incredibly, horribly there.

"There must be a phone in the coach's office. I'll—"

"Wait a minute—what if whoever did this is still here? I'll go," Mackenzie said. "Just in case—"

"What kind of deluded—you're on *crutches*—"

"Do you think I don't know that?" He glared at me, then clomped across the gym.

I looked wildly around. How to get up to Woody—and then what? If I could find something to cut the ropes, he'd crash to the ground—what about after only one rope was cut?—and hurt whatever might still be intact. If he was alive. Should I check that first? But how?

I needed a basketball player—a pro—one of those slam-dunkers who could levitate to Woody's shoulders and cut away the bindings. And I needed a linebacker to catch the falling body. And I was neither. I hoped that Mackenzie was telling the dispatcher what, precisely, we needed.

But meantime I couldn't let Woody hang there, life dripping out of his palms. He could die in the few minutes' difference.

There was nothing in the gym except ropes and basketballs and risers along one wall. I had no time to find tools to pull the banks of risers apart, so with great screeches and groans of the wood, I pushed and pulled and dragged a long section that felt like a freight train. I was barely able to breathe as I did it, crying in short dry sobs until my cargo reached the end zone—was it called that?—and provided a makeshift series of steps up to where I could be almost eye-level with Woody.

When that was done, I dragged mats beneath him, stacking them until they nearly reached him and would cushion his eventual fall.

And then what? I looked around frantically, but a gym is not a place one is likely to find sharp objects. And what was Mackenzie doing? Wasn't calling 911 a quick business? Wasn't that the point of it? Or, dear God, had the maniac who'd done this to Woody—the maniacs, it must have taken more than one person—been in the office and hurt Mackenzie, too? Had I heard him call?

No, because I'd been too busy and too noisy with the risers. "C.K.!" I shouted, and nearly wept with relief when I heard his "Can't find a thing that'd cut—"

"I'll be back." I raced down the hall, into the model kitchen—the nutrition center—amidst the sinks and ovens and scrubbed pots. I pulled open one bank of drawers then realized with fury that knives must be in a locked cabinet. Because of midnight raids such as mine, or suicidal teens. Whatever—I couldn't get to the knives.

Upstairs to the office? Surely there would be scissors—but Helga was impossible about locking things away. Everything. Even nonlethal items like pencils and hall passes.

My thoughts ran in hysterical circles. I could not think clearly, wanted only to protest—to have a screaming, fist-banging tantrum. Don't let this be happening!

But I had to find something that cut. Up in my room? I had scissors. No—damn it! Mine had been *borrowed* and not returned, a memory of recent frustration prompted. Then what?

I could feel Woody's time tick out with each beat of my own heart—if, indeed, he was still alive. He'd looked waxy and unreal. What did having your arms up in that violent position do for your heart, even without the spikes? I gagged at the memory of his hands and side and had to shake my head to clear it of the crippling image.

In desperation I grabbed a food processor, twisted off the top and pulled out the blade. It was not handy, nor meant to be held, and it'd do a better job of chopping onions than slicing rope. It had a center post with two curved blades, smooth on one edge, serrated and dangerous on the other. But it would have to do, because it was in my hand, and it would cut, and Woody was hanging from the basketball backboard.

Of course, Mackenzie and I squabbled about who should saw and who should catch, even though my arrangement was the only logical one. I would cut and Mackenzie, able to sit on the high bleachers so that his leg wasn't a major impediment, would brace Woody's fall, gentle him onto the mat. And while I worked he propped the body so that there was less tension in Woody's shoulders. This made slicing more difficult, but that was the trade-off.

"Can't you go faster?" Mackenzie called up to me. I was standing on tiptoe on the top riser, trying not to sever my own hands as I sawed back and forth. "This is supposed to process food," I shouted. "Not ropes. Why don't you carry a Swiss Army knife like men are supposed to?"

"Don' cut the knot, okay? It might be relevant."

As if I would aim my untrusty nonknife at the thickest part. "Where are the police? The ambulance?" I asked. "Did you tell them he was tied up here? That he had those—"

"Mandy," he said quietly.

It was the tenth or eleventh time I'd asked the same question. I couldn't stop myself. It was like having chattering teeth in the cold. It just happened. My mouth muscles took over and those words came out. "Okay, look," I said, "both sides are nearly through." We'd been panicked about having Woody dangle by one arm. "I'm going to do the right side now. You'll brace him, and then real quickly, I'll—"

"Yes," Mackenzie said wearily. We'd also gone over the logistics of this rather primitive drill a dozen times, but repeating it like a mantra almost reduced my fear.

I cut through the last filaments of rope holding up Woody's right arm, and his hand flopped lifelessly, a dead weight, down onto my head. I screamed as the palm and its spike cut the side of my face. Mackenzie half stood and nearly let go of Woody.

"No!" I shouted, "I'm okay—hold him!" I braced myself and moved sideways to cut away the last of the rope on his left arm.

This time I ducked, then grabbed his waist to help Mackenzie with the weight of him. And as we settled him as best as we could onto the mats, he moaned and his eyes opened.

"He's alive," I whispered. "Thank God." He blurred as my eyes filmed over with tears of relief. "Woody?" I asked softly. "Say something. Tell me you'll be all right. Oh, poor Woody, what happened? Who did this to you?"

The eyes stared blankly. His breath was shallow, the skin pasty. His whole body suddenly and uncontrollably trembled.

"He's in shock," Mackenzie said.

We heard the siren, and then the back door opened. "Here!" we shouted. "In here! Hurry!"

Paramedics and police entered almost simultaneously.

"Mother of God," the first paramedic said. His skin was the color of rich coffee, but it nonetheless seemed to blanch. He looked up at the backboard, then at Woody, quickly crossed himself, and then became all efficiency. He took out a blanket.

"Oh, hell," he said. "Hell, hell." All the while, with speed-of-light efficiency, he was attaching monitors and tubes to Woody.

"You found him when?" a uniformed cop whose name tag said RAMIREZ asked Mackenzie after they'd shaken hands and established professional kinship. His voice had none of the suspicious hostility I was willing to bet he'd have shown a citizen.

"Ten minutes ago, max," Mackenzie said. I could barely believe that what had seemed endless had really been so brief.

"And why did you enter the building?" Ramirez asked.

It was hard to tell in the gym—the lighting wasn't all that brilliant, my eyes were bald and tired and shielded by dark glass, and Mackenzie was suntanned and always had ruddy cheeks. All the same, I thought he blushed.

"I teach here," I said quickly. "We'd been out, and I realized I'd forgotten something I needed upstairs. The key I have is for the back door, and Mackenzie needed an elevator, so we didn't use the stairs, and—" What was I going to say I needed? I had to think of something—anything—but I couldn't even think of what courses I taught, what subject, let alone what equipment or texts they might require.

Saved by the paramedic, who motioned to Ramirez. "Better look. There's carving on this boy."

Carving. As if Woody were . . . what? A block of wood, an artifact, not a human being? The cuts—the *carvings*—had shapes, zigs and zags and a rounded segment. Blood, now dry, dripped from them like the runoff of spray paint. I had a sick sense of familiarity, but since they weren't eights or swastikas, even half swastikas, I kept quiet.

"Superficial, but they look like letters, not wild cuts," the paramedic said. "Thought they might mean something."

"W-A-P-A," the officer read.

"That's what I read, too."

The zigzag—a W, not lightning. Those initials—hadn't they been on Flora's door? The front of her building? Or on those graves, the photo in the paper? Small hammers beat against my temples, and with each drum, a letter. W.A.P.A.

"Damn it all to hell!" Ramirez said. "I was hoping you wouldn't agree, that it was my own—so it's those damn fascist—"

"Who?" The paramedic's motions never stopped. He and his partner had Woody hooked up and insulated in a blanket and they were about to wheel him out. His spiked hands were hidden inside the blanket. He looked almost normal, if a clay adolescent could be considered normal.

"WAPA. White Alliance to Preserve America." Ramirez spat out the words. "Vicious lunatic white supremacists. But what in God's name they want with him? This boy looks to be or to have been, at least, precisely what they so horribly want to preserve."

And from Woody's silent, waxy mouth, I heard echoes of him telling me I didn't understand, that I was seeing only part of the elephant. I could see his eyes begging me to leave him alone, his fear that others would find out about his involvement with April.

Would he? Woody. I hadn't left him alone.

NO MORE WARNINGS my hate mail had said.

Would he? Woody. I had asked Miles, asked Woody himself. The only thing I hadn't done was leave Woody alone.

This had to do with April, with Flora's mud message.

I hadn't seen the elephant, I still didn't. But I hadn't left Woody alone.

Had I put him in jeopardy? Pushed him toward this?

I felt faint as I watched Woody wheeled out.

Eighteen

I COULDN'T stop crying. Woody, the paramedics, and the police were gone. The school was locked up, and Mackenzie and I were in the VW, ready to go back to my house.

Except that he couldn't drive with his leg, and I couldn't stop crying.

One reason for remaining optimistic about our personal future was that he didn't try to make me stop crying and didn't act as if there weren't good solid reasons for the tears, useless though they might be.

I felt overwhelming sorrow, and not only about my own unwitting role. There'd been so many minor and major indignities in the past few weeks, all of them motivated by somebody's inability to see somebody else as fully human. I felt as if I couldn't bear it.

The haters polluted the world more effectively than toxic spills because they spread their filth with no sirens and no warnings and precious little outcry. Ordinary poisonous by-products don't think. The people who splashed paint and trashed Flora's room and defaced cemeteries and churches and snatched April and sent me threatening notes and sprayed my eyes and crucified Woody and carved their initials in his side were supposed to be able to think and make moral choices. That's what made us human.

I cried still more because Woody's life had been saved—if indeed it had been, if indeed he'd ever completely recuperate—by chance. A whim based on an urge based on a junior high fantasy.

Mackenzie said he understood—not only about happenstance and sexual fantasies, but about the uncommon accumulation of perversity, here and everywhere, which made me even more sorrowful because I knew he really did understand. Consider his work, look at what portion of mankind and mankind's passions he saw every day.

Then I cried because despite what Mackenzie knew, he was *good*, so different from the haters. Such a decent person that he didn't even mention that I was something less than coherent as I snuffled and bawled and blew my swollen nose and wiped my termite eyes and blubbered about things he'd known for too long.

The crying ran its course. "I'm okay now, I think," I said.

"You always were okay." His voice was calm and semidetached. "Just less painfully aware of reality, maybe."

"I liked it better that way."

"Who wouldn't? An' if we'd been born eggplants instead of people, we could have it that way forever. But we weren't and can't, so now the big question is—What do you do with the knowing? Wallow in self-pity or terminal bitterness? Go catatonic? Become a survivalist and hide in the hills? Arm yourself?

182

Preach fire and brimstone? Pick a crazy theory to explain every-thing? Climb up to a bell tower and take out half the city?"

"None of the above. I give up. What's the answer?"

"Beats me. All I know is mine, which is pathetically simplis-tic. Balance the scales best as you can, but not with more of the same. Bring the one who unbalanced them to justice, then go home, play good music, drink good wine, be kind to the kitty and try to readjust the imbalance by adding to the world supply of love, instead of hate."

"Somehow, I think I'm being led back to that unfulfilled fan-tasy of yours."

"Now that you mention it, wasn't there somethin' about Johns Hopkins makin' a university out of two people sittin' on a log and talkin'? A great schoolteacher can make a classroom out of anyplace she finds herself willing to teach," he said solemnly.

"Right now, she finds herself in a quandary."

"A great schoolteacher could make a classroom of a quandary, too. Or a foundry or a laundry or—"

"A quarry? A . . . ?"

"Tannery?"

"That doesn't work, poet-man. Breaks the meter. A great schoolteacher wouldn't dare do that." I felt as sexy as lint. But Mackenzie deserved points for getting me to think, at least for a moment, about something besides the world's rottenness. Along the way, I even remembered how to drive.

I HAD GIVEN the police Woody's last name. I had his phone number home in my roll book, so I'd told them how to reach Maurice Havermeyer, who could actually extract information from Helga. At least, he was authorized to do so, and I thought she might let him.

"We should be at the hospital," I said once we were in my house.

"It'd be intrusive on his parents," Mackenzie said. "They need privacy at a time like this."

"His father," I said. "I don't think his mother's alive, or at least not around." His father existed, I knew, because it was he who would have killed him for being with April. I had no idea how close or estranged father and son had been, but I hoped Woody had communicated something of what he feared to someone. "Maybe we should call the hospital."

"How 'bout we give them a few minutes to reach a decision about his condition before we ask them for it?" he said mildly.

Macavity rubbed my ankle. He considered our return a bonus day, necessitating another feeding. I let him purr and seduce me for a while—made the kitty foreplay last, as it were, then I gave in. "Only a snack," I told the cat.

"Machine's blinkin'," Mackenzie said while I pulled back the tab on a can of food. "Want to play your messages back?"

"I have no secrets. Go ahead."

I was immediately sorry. I should have secrets, and one of them should be my mother. There was her voice, still heavy on the Philadelphia accent despite years in Florida. Her "A-*man*-da" has a metallic edge like no other's. Luckily.

"A*man*da," she said, "I was hoping to catch you, but maybe you're out at one of your meetings?" Overlong pause while she must have wondered whether she was happy or upset about my not being there if it meant I was following her advice.

I wished I had listened. An AA meeting surely beat finding a student nailed up in the gym.

"Well," she said, "when you have a chance, let me know how the meetings—how *you* are. I certainly hope you're more comfortable than we've been. The air-conditioning conked out yesterday, and I could just about breathe. But it's back on again, thank heavens."

Macavity purred like a buzz saw and wrapped himself around my ankle. I reluctantly put a portion of the can in his dish, and with one grateful look for getting what he wanted—wham, bam, he was through with me, just another conquest, like Mom had warned.

"I spoke with your sister," she went on. I'd have to change my machine so that it cut people off sooner. "Baby Alexander has two new teeth. Oh, and how could I forget? Daddy hit a hole in one yesterday. It's made him impossible to live with. The phone didn't stop ringing last night. I thought maybe we hadn't heard from you because you were trying to call during all those congratulatory calls."

I wondered why my mother pushed marriage so resolutely when she made it sound excruciatingly dull. "She makes me want to drink. Maybe that's part of her plan to get me to AA," I said when her message finally ended. Mackenzie nodded, and I poured us both wine. I would have poured something stronger if I'd had it in the house. I was functioning on the surface, but when I lifted my wineglass, my hand shook.

"Any theories?" Mackenzie asked.

I shook my head. I was beyond exhaustion, and I still had to go through the day's papers so that I could coherently continue the lessons tomorrow. I unsnapped my briefcase and dumped its contents onto the kitchen counter, then stared at it blankly. I couldn't. Simply could not do another thing that involved thought.

"What about that Lowell person—the one that left the building just before we got there?" Mackenzie said.

I was ready to object—he was such a nerd, such a noodle—but on second thought, Lowell with his conspiracy theories, with evil under every stone . . . Lowell, who protested too much . . .

"He didn't turn around when I called. Odd time to be leaving school, don't you think?"

"Maybe he'd had an assignation with his very own Mrs. Taubman up in his classroom."

"An' there was that woman complained about the lights."

"That was hours earlier."

"Door wasn't locked when we arrived, how do you know where anybody was in between? Includin' your friend Flora and her doggie."

I shook my head. "It's physically impossible. No one person could have held somebody as big as Woody down, or up, and done that to him at the same time. Certainly not Aldis, Flora, or Lowell."

"Any of 'em could give directions," he said softly. "Be part of a group."

185

"I don't think Flora—" But I did think. I thought about Flora's grim determination to not take anything from anybody anymore. I thought about her having been in the basement this afternoon when the vandals hit my car and me. Had I been a diversionary tactic? Was it possible that she'd determined that Woody had been the one to trash her room or terrorize her at home, and she'd arranged revenge?

And I thought about Aldis, who reminded me of central casting's concentration camp guard, female variety. Aldis, with her rigid assurance that whatever she believed was a truism. Had she felt the need to teach Woody a lesson? Punish him?

But why? Why him? For what?

Why any of it? The past weeks had been like an experiment in disorientation. One thing happens, and just as you adjust to it and prepare against its recurrence, another, completely different but not unrelated event takes its place, until the subject loses her handle on reality.

"These things have to be connected," I said. "Vandalism, nasty phone calls, cryptic notes, the mud, the paint, Woody. All ugly. And April, somehow, because she connects to Woody. And maybe even Vo Van, because he connects to April. And out of school—the cemetery and the church. And things I don't even know about that have the same mean spirit behind them." I felt as if I'd seen the ends of a creature, the tips of its tentacles only, but the creature itself was hidden, unknowable.

Despite everything, I had to teach again the next day, and had to get myself at least somewhat organized. I sorted through papers, separating must-do's from should-do's from who-cares-if-I-ever-do's. I had been derailed by the yellow warning note this morning and had never finished going through my mail. I passed the threatening note to Mackenzie. "Maybe it's students who did that to Woody. Who are doing everything. I hate to think about Miles, but all the same, he seems to know more than he's saying. . . . This came in my mail this morning. I forgot, after the spray paint. Meant to show you then. The letters were cut out of old school newspapers."

He sighed. "I don' like this."

"I'm not overfond of it, either."

"You'll give it to the police?"

"I just did."

"I wish . . ."

"I know." He wished I'd confine my interests to academics and pedagogy and him. He wished I'd make my life—and by extension, his—easier.

He knew that I knew. No need to spell things out. No need to explain that I had no more desire to box in my curiosity, ethics, or intelligence than he did.

I thumbed through the day's flyers, nervous, but sure that one piece of hate mail per daily delivery sufficed. And it seemed to have. I found one of Helga's incessant memos, this one entitled "Official Grade Entry Methodology and Spitting Regulations." There was notice of a fire drill scheduled for the next afternoon. I wondered if it would be canceled as redundant, thanks to me. Notice also of a woman's sports watch that had been found in the girls' room. A glossy ad from an encyclopedia that was now available on CD-ROM. "Hey," I asked. "Have any relatives named Rom?"

"Got a Ron and a Rhonda. Wait—there's a Romulus somewhere."

"This is a last name."

He shook his head.

"Well, there's a C.D. Rom here, I thought might be related. Named after the same C, perhaps."

"I will not honor that with even a groan."

I tossed an announcement of a glorious, new, fully illustrated nonsexist collection of scientific essays I assumed had been put into my mailbox by mistake. A gobbledygook notice from Havermeyer about "maximal" security efforts being implemented in response to the lamentable "defacing" and—I nearly choked—"desanitization" of the computer room and the consequent "nonoperational condition" of valuable school equipment. He also earnestly requested "immediate notification" by staff at the first sign of further "vandalistic impulses." His notices made me want to chain him to a heating pipe until he swore to foresake all words of more than one syllable.

And what were those *maximal* security efforts, anyway? On the day the gibberish went out, my car and I were spray-painted, and a few hours later the school's back lights were systematically smashed and the door left unlocked. And there was surely no evidence or sense of security in that gym. Havermeyer couldn't distinguish between larded-with-jargon promises and reality.

And that was it, except for another paper folded in thirds. I swallowed hard. It wasn't yellow or stapled, but it still produced an extra pulse beat or two. I forced myself to open it.

It was laughably unthreatening. A quote from Shakespeare, printed in Gothic letters. Somebody had a splendid graphics program.

> "O Woe! O woeful, woeful, woeful day!
> Most lamentable day! most woeful day,
> That ever, ever, I did yet behold!
> O day! O day! O day! O hateful day!
> Never was seen so black a day as this:
> O woeful day, O woeful day!"

I passed this page, too, to Mackenzie.

"This about what happened to Woody?" he asked.

"What else could it be?"

"Should be 'O woeful evening.' Or woeful night."

"Guess Will Shakespeare didn't plan ahead for all possible woe schedulings." I shook my head and got my brains closer in place. "But it was in my cubby this morning."

"How come you didn't mention it?"

"I didn't read it till now." I felt chilled. "Oh, God, was this a warning of what was going to happen?" A competent teacher—an Aldis sort of woman—would have read all her notices immediately, no matter what threat was tossed in with them.

Mackenzie shrugged. "If it was meant as a warning, then it was a singularly stupid one, like somebody wagging a finger and saying 'something bad'll happen at some point.' Like the daily horoscope. 'Don' do anything stupid today.' Big deal. It's too vague to mean anythin'."

I excused myself for a quick run up to the third floor, site of my home office, attic storage, guest room, and library. All of which were contained in one small sloped-ceilinged room. The air conditioner wasn't on up here, and the cubicle throbbed with heat. I grabbed the paperback edition of *Romeo and Juliet* from the corner of my desk and descended to the living room's relative comfort.

"Are there opposing groups at your school? Members of rival gangs?"

"I don't think so. I mean, I've noticed that the black and white kids don't hang out together this summer, but that doesn't mean all that much." Maybe they just plain didn't like each other.

"How about Woody?" Mackenzie asked. "Does he have black friends?"

I shrugged. "I never saw him with X or Lawrence or Warwick, all of whom are in his class. But I never noticed any particular tension between them, either. And all of that means less than nothing. There are obviously lots of things I never saw or suspected."

"I can't figure who would have done that to the kid. In the school, too, like a taunt, but for what purpose?" Mackenzie said.

I thumbed through the play looking for the event that had triggered those "woe is me's." A tragedy, it was chockablock full of woe producers. Mercutio's death? Tybalt's death? Romeo's banishment? Ah . . . Juliet's supposed death.

The cat, having eaten excessively, now resolutely ignored me and switched to his cop-groupie self, sidling up to and draping himself over Mackenzie's neck like a feline boa. I am not such a petty soul that I could be jealous of where a cat placed his no-good wandering sluttish affections, even though *I* am the one who feeds him and performs his unaesthetic custodial services.

The only thing I can figure is that the Macavitys and the Mackenzies go way back, maybe even share a tartan in the Old Country.

Besides, I had found the quote. "The nurse," I said. "She's the one with all the woes are me."

"So what? What's it mean? That we should wring our hands and gnash our teeth?"

"The nurse is carrying on because she found Juliet dead."

Mackenzie raised a single eyebrow. "That's less than astoundin'. Most folk would express similar sentiments when findin' a dead girl, particularly one in her charge."

"That word is supposed to have five syllables. There's no such word as *partic-ly*."

"All the same, what is *particularly* remarkable about that quote?"

"I don't know. I'm not the one who printed this out. Only there's all this lamentation—and Juliet isn't really dead at this point." The more I thought about it, the more I was convinced that had to be the message. "Juliet isn't dead. The young girl isn't dead. The charge isn't dead, she just seems that way." I stood up and paced my small first floor, sure with each step that a solid idea was only one more step away, which meant I circled my downstairs a dozen times before I said, "It's about April."

"It's about Juliet. How are you making the leap?"

"Of all the quotes in the play, it's one of the least memorable, so why put it in my mailbox? It has to be a message, and in context, it must be saying that our girl isn't in the trouble she appears to be."

"Be careful. *It* says, 'Oh, woe is me,' and *you're* sayin' all the rest."

"No, no, I'm sure. Somebody who's afraid to speak up directly is trying to tell me something."

"Woody?"

"I don't think so. Not this message. He's sure she's dead and he's somehow to blame for it."

"Then what are you sayin'? That April's alive and she nailed Woody up?"

I sat back down. The cat blinked at me warily from around Mackenzie's neck. "April didn't hurt Woody. Of course not. But she talked an awful lot about whether Juliet had done the right thing by deceiving her parents. She seemed intensely, personally, involved in Juliet's story because it obviously paralleled her life. Woody told me his father would kill him for consorting with a Vietnamese, and that her parents—her brother, actually, and Vanny, like Tybalt in the play, her kin in this sense, were just as rabid about her being with a white boy. In the play, Tybalt is so enraged by Romeo's being with Juliet that he fights with Romeo's friend and kills him, and then Romeo kills Tybalt, Juliet's cousin, in return and sets off the whole chain of events."

He put a hand up, like a traffic cop at an intersection. "Are you saying that Romeo Woody shot Tybalt Vanny? You're gettin' carried away with the analogy. Who are you in all this? The nurse?"

"I'm not saying there's a direct correlation with each plot turn, but ..." I was still working through the possible meaning of the note, but no matter how I twisted or detoured, I kept falling into potholes.

"But what?" Mackenzie finally said.

"What if April Truong wasn't kidnapped, just the way Juliet wasn't really poisoned? What if the bad thing that supposedly happened to her just plain didn't? What if she planned it as a deliberate attempt to get herself away, and if she's Juliet, then it had to do with Romeo—Woody—and saving the two of them."

"Whoa! We've leaped from Shakespeare to Woody. Why ascribe so much to that quote? For that matter, why do people keep sendin' you cryptic poems?"

"What do you mean?"

"That test? The thing with April's name at the end?"

I stopped all pacing and stared. "You're right. It *ended* with her name."

"You're maybe missin' the point of what I'm sayin'."

"He said to look at the part that wasn't about April." I excused myself again. Up to the desk where my copy of Miles's paper still awaited a decision as to grade. I read it again, and

191

realized I'd been right. Slow, but right. I ran downstairs and slapped it down in front of Mackenzie. The cat deigned to leave his love's shoulder in order to sit on the poem, but we gentled him off.

"Okay," Mackenzie said. "What?"

"Look at the initials at the beginning. All the initials."

Who's supposed to say whether present guilt lies with
A group? An idea? A tradition? A
Person? Not Romeo, Juliet or that gang. They're dead.
Assigning blame is useless, something he wouldn't dare.
Would he?
Ask him.
Perhaps he is
Afraid.
Probably is, because
Reality
Is too much like fiction and
Life sucks.

"See that?" I said.

"I see it." W.A.P.A. Running down the side of the poem. Running, a second time, right into April. The same letters that had been carved in Woody's side, sprayed elsewhere. "Things are connected," I said in a low voice. "I was right." That didn't make me feel any better. I took a deep, deep breath.

Romeo and April Truong. All her questions about whether Juliet had done the wrong thing. I remembered asking her what other options she thought Juliet had. I'd wanted her to realize that acting without reflection—killing herself as Juliet had, as Romeo had, was juvenile. April's response instead had been that Juliet could have left sooner.

But Juliet had never left at all. April did, and saw it as a parallel. "She left to save them, to save Woody." My tongue felt thick, words hard to say.

"Then it sure was one sorry plan." Mackenzie looked at me. I could tell we were both remembering that boy, hanging from the backboard, arms up, hands nailed in a parody of an all-too-familiar pose that usually was accompanied by the idea of salvation. "But maybe," he said slowly, "the people who wanted to hurt that boy chose that particular method to make it clear that nobody was saved. Not at all."

Nineteen

WOODY was the only subject on the curriculum the next morning. It isn't often—thank God—that students are found crucified in a school gym. The late news and the early morning news had headlined the story and repeated it every five minutes. All three networks had called my house last night, but I'd refused to comment, let alone be photographed. This morning, CNN had phoned. Mackenzie fielded the calls.

Even though I felt as if I'd emotionally and intellectually exhausted the topic, it was obvious that I couldn't avoid it.

Five approached the school at the same time I did. I'd walked, because my car was still at the shop, the weather was fine, and I hoped exercise would keep me alert, maybe even reinvigorate me after a night of no real sleep.

I wasn't invigorated, but Five looked even worse. Ashen. "Mandy!" he said. "My God! I watch the news while I shave, and when I heard—" He shook his head, speechless. "I nearly cut my throat!" He had a Band-Aid on his jawline, but I permitted the hyperbole. That was nearly his throat. "Speaking of cuts—what's that on your face?"

"I'm auditioning for Bride of Frankenstein." I could not bring myself to describe the spike in Woody's hand cutting my cheek.

"They said you found him. Is that true?"

Why had they used my name on the air? Wouldn't a generic "found by a member of the faculty" have sufficed?

"What—Why were you there? When I left you, I thought you and Crispin were going home. What made you go into the school? Go looking for Woody?"

My mental screen flashed Mackenzie's grin, sexy Mrs. Taubman and our plans for the evening, and I felt my neck, then my chin, then my entire face blush. "I was, I—I didn't mean to—I wasn't looking for—I—" I forced myself to shut up until I was breathing normally. "I'd forgotten something, and since I was there, I thought I'd get it from my room."

"What?"

The police hadn't ever inquired what I needed to retrieve, but Five was a fellow teacher, and less likely to be satisfied with vagueness, and much more aware of the normal parameters of teacherly devotion. What was worth going back to school for at night? "My roll book," I said, "and I was in a real sweat—didn't want a student to get ahold of it and change grades or anything."

He nodded.

Stupid! The police had to call Havermeyer to get Woody's number—but if my roll book had really been in my classroom, I could have provided it. I need a lot more practice at lying.

But why would Five question how or where the police got their information? I relaxed. The trouble with lying is that you—I—become paranoid and excessively suspicious, jumpy and worried about loopholes in my story. Five had asked a casual teacherly question. A make-conversation question.

"They said—the TV—that he's going to live and probably will have full use of his hands," Five said. "But they aren't sure about damage to the shoulders and hips." He shook his head again. "Did he say who did it? The news didn't say a word about that, maybe for legal reasons."

"He couldn't speak. He was in shock."

Five's lips were clenched. There was lots to say—and no point saying it.

"They carved letters in his side," I said. "They stand for some racist group. Did the news say that?"

He shook his head, his mouth slightly open. His silent shock reminded me of Woody's last night. I thought about Mackenzie's unfounded suspicions of him and wished he could see him now.

"Something rotten's going on," I said. "And I hate to say this, but I think it's based here. In this school."

"Why here? Just because that's where Woody—"

"I personally think even April's disappearance is connected."

He looked at me with great concern, then shook his head. "Her parents didn't seem to."

I shrugged.

"I can only hope you're wrong," he said softly. He moved in the direction of the office, slowly, so I could accompany him. "You still didn't say why you think this thing, whatever it is, is based here."

"Have you gotten peculiar notes?" I asked. "Poems? Threats? Things that feel in code?"

"No," he said. "But obviously, you or somebody must have or you wouldn't ask. What kind? What did they say?"

I shrugged. "Nothing specific. Vague threats. A quote from *Romeo and Juliet*. The nurse saying 'woe is me.' "

"Maybe it has nothing to do with these . . . events. Maybe," he leaned close, "they're typically garbled messages from Havermeyer."

I smiled weakly.

196

"Might as well try for levity," he said.

"Isn't it *awful*? I'm just so *nervous* now. So *appalled*." It was Phyllis, swooping down on us in the office, all aflutter and batting rescue-me eyes in the direction of Five. I found her doubly annoying on a morning when I had almost no lashes to bat. "How could something like that *happen*?" She seemed about to swoon into his arms.

I took that as my exit cue, silently waving goodbye and backing off. Phyllis didn't care about me, or about Woody for that matter. She cared about appearing pathetic and in need of a great big history teacher to take care of her. She cared about Five. Dennison was sufficiently sibilant to add to her string of names.

"Dr. Havermeyer called me in the middle of the night," Helga announced as I passed the dark walnut barrier that shielded her from us. "Woke me up and nearly frightened me to death. What were you doing in the school at that hour?"

"I was . . . this is pretty embarrassing, but I was going to practice gymnastics."

"You? Here? Gymnastics?"

I nodded. "It's kind of a secret, though. I'm not very good."

"But those girls are tiny. Barely past puberty. You're a great big, tall—"

I nodded again. "That's why I only practice at night, when nobody's around."

She blinked a few times, and I turned to leave. "I'll have to check whether you're *allowed*," she called out. "You didn't ask permission. We could be liable if you got hurt."

I tried to slam the door behind me, but it had one of those whooshy tubes attached that made it impossible. Foiled again.

"Amanda!" This time it was Aldis, who already had her mail, and who looked honestly in distress. "I heard. Are you all right? Your cheek—what happened? Did he hurt you?"

I nodded, then shook my head. "Fine, thanks," I said. "Just a bit shaken. The cheek? I played with a cat that needed a manicure." I glanced at my mail. Nothing looked personal today.

Aldis fell into step beside me. "How did you happen to find him?"

This time I refused to think about Mackenzie's grin or his buxom science teacher and I didn't blush. I changed my story to a packet of tests I'd left behind. "I don't know when it happened," I said. "Did you hear or see anything when you were there?"

"That was too early. Nothing was going on then."

"How come you came back to school?" I asked in a noncommittal tone.

"I forgot my roll book."

Come on! I thought. That's cheap and easy—even I thought of that one right away, like a reflex. Surely, you could do better than that, or don't expect me to believe you.

"It is not like me to be slovenly and forgetful," she said. "I don't think I ever did that before."

I had a nasty if irrational moment when I was sure that Mackenzie had also told her the story of Mrs. Taubman, and that they, too . . .

"You know how these people are," she said. "Those grades would be switched in a second. I couldn't risk leaving it overnight. But I never went near the gym. Up the back stairs and down again." She didn't ask why I had gone to the elevator, which was lucky, because it might have sounded odd that I was taking along a handicapped friend to get my test papers.

We were quiet for about half the flight up, then Aldis *tsked.* "We shouldn't be surprised that something like this happened," she said. "All this overemphasis on equality—on mediocrity, if you ask me. And look where it's gotten us. Look what happens when you let that sort into where they don't belong."

"What sort is that?" I kept my voice low and sounded convincingly interested, if I say so myself.

"Do you really have to ask? The coloreds—pardon me, the blacks. Or are they Afro-Americans these days? And those Orientals who barely speak decent English and who even knows if they're legal? Or if they're communists? And the Filipinos and that Russian girl and those Spanish from what, Salvador? Where are the Americans? Except for that one poor boy, and look where he wound up! You see my point? I came here for this program because I expected anything but this! And look where it leads. I could have told you."

"I still don't get what sort of people—which of our summer school students—you think did that to Woody," I said. "He was crucified. Wasn't it the *Romans* who were into that? Their soldiers? Are you saying we let too many centurions enroll this summer?"

She looked at me as if I were not only insane, but criminally so. She looked at me, in fact, as if I were . . . that sort.

And then she huffed off.

I nearly made it into my room, but not quite, and nearly doesn't count. "Mandy Pepper!" a high-pitched male voice said. "Mandy Pepper, are you all right?"

Students stopped milling and turned to watch, no doubt formulating rumors about Lowell Diggs and me. The idea was pornographic. "I've been worried sick!" he shouted.

"Calm down," I said from between gritted teeth. The kids moved in for the kill. "I appreciate your concern, but I'm all right. I found him. He was the one hurt, not me."

"Your cheek! What about that?"

"I auditioned for a play. An all-female *Count of Monte Cristo*. This was a dueling accident. It looks worse than it is." I've never understood that expression, to tell the truth. By definition, aren't things precisely as bad as they look since that's how we're defining bad?

"I was so upset, I called your house," he said with arm-waving agitation, "but some *man* told me to get lost."

Great. Supergreat. I really wanted the student body to know the details of my personal life, like my having a male roomie now and then. "That's my security person," I said. "After all you told me about what's going on in the world . . ."

He squinted, considered, and nodded. "Talk to him about his attitude. How was I to know he was a good guy? I thought maybe he was a *thug*. I thought maybe you were being held against your will."

What was Lowell's problem? Me? Or something more? His shaving today had been even more impaired than usual, with several patches of stubble and one piece of toilet paper. "Why would you think that?" I asked. "Honestly, Lowell!"

"I was so worried, I called your *mother!*"

The air went out of my lungs. I had to remind myself to breathe. I shaped my lips to respond, to find out why on earth, what, why . . . but no sound except that of collapsing lungs emerged. I gasped and tried again. "My . . . my . . . you . . . my . . ."

"Thank goodness, my aunt knew what complex your parents—"

My strength and speech returned. "My mother lives in *Florida.* That state all the way at the bottom of the map. Far from here."

"Don't I, of all people, know that? That's why it took so long. I don't have a Florida directory." He looked even worse when agitated. His eyes bugged and he dribbled spittle. "I couldn't remember where, but my aunt remembered, but first she had to call—"

"*Why?*" A blonde girl stepped back a pace at my shriek. Her lids lifted until I could see white above her blue-blue eyes. What could be better than seeing a teacher have a nervous breakdown? I tried to scream softly, privately. It hurt my throat. "What on earth did you think my mother could do in Florida if I were being held? Which was a bizarre thing to imagine, anyway! And *who* are *you* to call her?"

He looked stunned—profoundly hurt. Uncle Lowell, he called himself with me. And must have believed we had some kind of kinship. Nonetheless, an unsolicited fix-up by my mom and her pal did not constitute the ties that bind, and it was now down to Lowell's emotional health versus mine. "You—You—" I had lost coherency again. And then I remembered who else had been at the scene of the crime last night. "*You!*" I said. "What about you?"

"Me? What?"

I lowered my voice still more. Students strained forward to hear. "Why were you here last night?"

"Are you accusing me of something?" His voice squeaked and broke.

"Asking. I saw you leave the building around ten. I called you by name."

"No, you didn't."

Was I supposed to say *did so* to his *did not*? He was lying, but why? "I *saw* you," I hissed. His face glistened with perspiration. Humidity, or nerves?

"I told you to be careful, didn't I?" he said. "When we saw the eighty-eight? I told you bad things were going on."

"Was that some kind of a warning? Besides, that's a non sequitur. How about last night?"

"What *about* last night?" he said, back to his loudest, most stupidly belligerent voice.

Students sniggered. Lowell knew precisely what he was doing—he had a reservoir of stupid cunning I hadn't suspected, and his object was to humiliate me, for whatever evil purpose. Lowell had no redeeming qualities. He wasn't even much of a teacher, from what I heard. At least, not of math. Maybe he was better at teaching hate. In any case, I was finished worrying about his ego. "I have to get to my class," I said softly.

Before I was inside my room, from across the wide landing, Lowell shouted at the top of his lungs. "Don't forget to call your mother, Mandy. She's worried sick."

I entered my room to a chorus of adolescents chanting, in singsongy unison, "Call your mother, Mandy. Oooh, Mandy—call your mother!"

Evil has many faces. Some of them are poorly shaven.

Twenty

THE day felt old by the time it truly got under way, and it wasn't helped by my morning session's two empty seats—April's and Woody's. We were being slowly decimated. Was it something I'd done? Planned to do? Somebody stalking my students?

In any case, not a soul in my room, including me, wanted to systematically build our vocabularies through synonyms, antonyms, prefixes, and suffixes. I could kiss the first forty-five minutes of my lesson plan goodbye.

To make matters worse, I'd forgotten my notes on *Lord of the Flies*, which we were to start reading and discussing today. And how applicable my talk on the dark potential of human nature would have been. My words shimmered much more brilliantly when out of reach than if I'd been holding them. As it was, while my clever insights took the day off at home, I stood in front of my class, dull with exhaustion and mind-numbing memories.

I had no choice but to wing it. We'd talk about the substance of the book, get into how the group defined *civilized* behavior, what bound us together as a society, what happened when the rules collapsed or people misused or overenforced them.

We didn't need a novel about boys stranded on an island to examine chaos. We could pull up the shades and look outside. Or keep them down and look inside, at ourselves. Boys and girls stranded—for their own good—in a seemingly benign private school, a little island of safety away from the world's insanity for a few weeks in summer. We could write our own story. We already had our own horrific sacrifice.

My attitude was not wholesome, teacherly, or optimistic this morning, but there wasn't a hope in hell of changing it. We staggered onward, minute by minute. We discussed *Lord of the Flies*, then wrote letters to Woody, swapped them, edited them, and rewrote them. That was a subversive way to have a writing lesson. Plus, the class discussion of what could or should go into such letters, what would or would not be beneficial for Woody to hear and know, unbeknownst to the oh-so-tough teens, was an actual, face-saving exploration of emotions. In the guise of discussing what they could or should say to their fallen classmate, they seemed willing to show themselves for once, to mention fears, anxieties, and guilts.

Nobody, seemingly, knew what to make of the attempt on Woody's life. Not even his best friends, Tony Ford and Guy, who remained tight-lipped and withdrawn and whose letters were stiff and formal. "I'm sorry this had to happen to you." That sort of awkward guy thing. They'd have been more at ease patting each other on the backside or delivering a mock punch to the biceps than saying how wretched this made them feel.

While they wrote I watched them as if I could X-ray their

minds. I'd even discarded the sunglasses, gone public with my crew-cut lashes, the better to observe with.

When the packet of letters was complete, I chose Miles to deliver it to the office. I walked outside the classroom with him. "Hold on, I'd like to ask you something," I said as he bolted for the stairs. We were nearing the end of the morning. If there were a few unattended minutes inside the room, then so be it. I didn't think the class was in a mood to riot today, anyway.

"I'm in a hurry," Miles said.

"Too bad. You sent me the nurse's quote, didn't you?"

"Me? Why me?"

"Bad answer, Miles. You didn't ask what I meant. Besides, you're the class's only actor, as far as I know, and the only person who probably memorized great chunks of that play—or at least read them so closely that you'd be able to find something relevant. Except maybe for April, and she isn't sending me notes lately."

"I don't know what you're talking about."

"You do, and you have to stop playing games because I don't know what to do with the messages you're sending, and I'm afraid somebody is going to die as a result. Last night, Woody was saved by"—once again I blocked the image of Mackenzie and Mrs. Taubman—"dumb luck. Pure chance. A few minutes later, I'm convinced, he would have been dead. As far as I know, April already is."

"You don't understand."

"I *need* to understand, and you already do. And you owe it to me—or to her—to explain yourself."

"I don't. I thought I did, but I don't anymore. Besides, they'll kill me."

"*Who?*"

"The ones who did that to Woody. The gang. The Vietnamese guys. Had to be them as revenge for Vanny."

"Against whom?"

He lowered his voice. "WAPA. I don't know their names. I just know they *are*. All over the city. You don't mess with them

204

if you're smart. And it doesn't do any good to know about them because you can't stop them."

"Did April know about them?" He said nothing. "I'm going crazy with this, Miles, and I think it's time I brought the police in to talk with you. I know that you know a whole lot. The difference is, the police know how to get it out of you."

His eyes, which were an interesting gray-green, grew large. "I thought you'd get it. I thought you'd understand."

"I think I do. I think April wasn't abducted. There's the quote—and the fact that her backpack didn't have any of the things she should have been carrying. The things that mattered to her. I think they're with her."

"You *did* get it. So why all this?"

"Because why should I believe it? How could you know?"

All his gangly youth, all his vulnerable, still-growing cells seemed to come forward, along with pure, undistilled fear. I felt sadistic, drilling him, but I didn't know what else to do.

He shook his head. "Please. I swear, until that happened to Woody, it seemed something that would all work out. Now . . ."

"Has it ever occurred to you that if I think you know things, that *they*, whoever they are, will, too? You may be in danger now."

"I know that," he whispered. He looked around furtively. Doors would open, students—*they?*—would see him with me any second now. "She's with relatives," Miles said. "Out of state. She didn't get into that van that night. I took her to the train station three hours before her brother, Thomas, pretended to be her, throwing them off the trail."

The lookalike. That was possible. "Who needed to be thrown off?" That was why her brother seemed apathetic about her disappearance, why Miles had seemed so indifferent. They knew she was safe. But why had she run that way?

"Her brother's gang. She dumped Vanny for a white, shamed him, and then he was killed. You see?"

I shook my head. "That was gang-related. A drive-by."

"That was because of April. So there has to be retaliation. The gang has to hurt Thomas for letting her do that, and Woody, for . . . being Woody."

"For being her boyfriend. Are you saying Woody killed Vanny? Shot him?"

He shook his head. "He didn't even know it was going to happen. But all the same, it was done to protect him from Vanny. April told me that. And she disappeared for the same reason—to protect him. And Thomas needed protection, too, because the other guys in his gang were angry about Vanny, about Thomas letting his sister cause that. So April got an idea from you. From Shakespeare. If people thought she was dead—they'd consider the score settled."

"Did Woody know that she wasn't really kidnapped?"

Miles shook his head and looked miserable. "It seemed safer this way, but we were wrong. Maybe it made him do something dumb."

"Against Vo Van's gang?"

He shook his head. "No more," he said. "I can't say more."

"Then what?" I was lost again.

But Miles had dissolved from the spot. He was at the top of the stairs when the noon bell rang and the first classroom door opened, and he blended into the crowd descending for lunch seconds later.

Once my class was gone, I went and sat in the square, needing a dose of nature—particularly the citified, cleaned-up, and domesticated variety. I put my sunglasses back on, and felt close to socially acceptable.

"Hoped I'd find you here."

The voice was honey-dipped, familiar and welcome, accompanied by the aroma of superbly dangerous food. Plus, the body that accompanied the sound and the scent had been newly renovated. "No cast!" I said.

"Look! Two whole legs—a pair!" Mackenzie leaned on a cane, but he had two feet, two shoes, long pants on both legs. "It's sickeningly pale," he said, "but it's there, every bit of it, and it works, too. I can wiggle my toes and tap my foot and bend my knee. And, I have a most impressive scar to put fear into people on the beach. What more could a man want?"

"Congratulations. I'd show my delight more obviously if we were anywhere else."

"I know." He sat down next to me on the bench, but didn't even take my hand. "The kids behave like bunnies, but we remain pristine, thereby confirmin' their opinion that grown-ups have absolutely no fun. Anyway, wanted to say hello before I return to the world of the workin' stiff."

Had I managed to shove that bit of information out of my brain? I did dimly recall his telling me, ages ago, that as soon as his cast was off, he'd go on light duty. "I hadn't realized 'as soon as' was to be taken literally."

"Well, hey, it wasn't. I've had two workin' legs for three hours now, and I'm still goofin' off." He looked at his watch. "Goin' soon, though."

Despite his no-hurry Southern-boy tempo, I could almost see the waves of excitement he was emitting, hear his soul tap dancing "Hi ho, hi ho, it's off to work I go!"

He winked at me.

I finally *really* got it. He loved his work. Was crazy about it. Required it.

And I had to accept that, cope with it and all the messy unpredictability it brought into my life—or back off and make my exit.

The sensation was not unlike, I suppose, having the bench suddenly collapse over the Grand Canyon. I tumbled through open space with no prospects ahead except a sad splatter.

Mackenzie squinted at me. I was afraid he was reading my mind, but it was the cut on my cheek he was examining. "Looks like it's healin'," he said.

"I told my class I cut myself shaving. The worst thing is, they believed me." And we were past my dreadful moment. But it was something that needed serious thought as soon as I had time.

We shared about four and a half minutes of chitchat and part of the hoagie Mackenzie produced from the greasy paper sack. I was just up to what Miles had and hadn't said when I heard the high-pitched, "Mandy Pepper!" I wondered if he could sing falsetto as easily as he spoke it.

"Mandy Pepper!" he repeated. He always sounded shocked that I existed, that I was to be found.

"Lowell." I, in turn, responded as if a low-pitched voice would cure him of his vocal affectations. It never did. "I'd like you to meet Calvin K. Mackenzie."

"Not," C.K. said softly.

"My bodyguard. He's with the police. Mackenzie, Lowell Diggs. He's teaching math at Philly Prep this summer."

"Glad to meet you!" Lowell grabbed Mackenzie's hand and shook it with excessive vigor. "I was relieved to learn that Mandy has a bodyguard. We have to take care of our little girl, don't we?" He smiled on me benignly. "Although a guard who is, listen, forgive me—but, ah, I can't help noticing that's a cane, which I assume is not decorative, and isn't that a little . . ."

Mackenzie stood up and leaned on the cane. "Speakin' of Miss Peppah heah, mind if I clear somethin' up? Last night, Miss Peppah and I, we were walkin' to the school . . ."

His accent was a *Gone With the Wind* high mutation. Surely the sight of Lowell, even the meaningless possessiveness of Lowell, wasn't stressing Mackenzie out, although tension was the usual accent trigger. I decided he wanted to prey on Yankee delusions. He wanted to sound Southern and, let's face it, stupid. To us fast-talkers.

". . . an' I do believe we saw you across the street from us? Comin' out the front of the school?"

"Oh, no!" Lowell shook his head so vigorously and overlong I was afraid his sharp nose was going to loosen and fall off. "She said that, too, but you're both wrong. It was somebody else."

"You sure now? It was Miss Peppah heah who recognized you and called out, you know."

Lowell's eyes flitted down to mine. "Mandy," he said in a softly accusatory tone. "I *told* you I wasn't there. Why would you?" Then he looked back at Mackenzie. "Is this official?" he asked. "What part of the police are you with? I mean when you're not off duty?"

"Homicide," Mackenzie said gravely. "Need Ah remin' you that there was an attempted murder in this school at about the time you were seen?"

"Why are you her bodyguard?" Lowell demanded. "Why do you need a homicide cop bodyguard, Mandy? What's going on?"

"I do believe our subject was not Miss Peppah, but you, Mr. Diggs."

From my vantage point on the bench, I could see color rise up Lowell's neck and onto what there was of an underjaw, as if some force were pumping red dye up through his gullet.

"Could we talk privately?" he asked Mackenzie. His voice squeaked on the last word. "Nothing personal, Mandy. Just . . . man-to-man things."

I nodded, unable to imagine what men-only act could have brought Lowell to the school last night. Or did he think teaching Woody a *lesson* was manly? I watched them shamble off, Mackenzie limping, leaning on his cane, Lowell more hunched and pitiable than ever, a condemned man off to the death chamber.

"Would it be demeaning to offer you a penny for your thoughts?"

I looked up at Five's craggy face. "No problem. I'm used to that kind of pay scale." I smiled back.

"May I join you?" He gestured at the bench.

I don't know what the absolutely correct etiquette would be. Saying that I was already semijoined and I was saving this seat for my semijoinee? That didn't sound sane or right, although I was sure Mackenzie would think it was. But Mackenzie was toodling around with Lowell, and I had no idea to what purpose or for how long, plus this whole issue was nonsense. What was it about Five that produced such exaggerated and ridiculous dilemmas in me? I gestured back and he sat down.

"You all right?" he asked. "I mean, of course, none of us are all right after . . . but are you going to be all right?"

"Good to be outside. Just being in that building where it . . . It gave me . . ."

"I agree. I'm not even keeping my room open today. Nobody had much to say, and all of us had the same impulse to get out. However, I note that you didn't say out in the fresh air."

"Well, it's fresh exhaust fumes. You must miss those wide-open spaces."

"Where I lived, Idaho wasn't that wide—lots of mountains. Spectacular, but not big flat spaces."

We both regarded the landscape in front of us. The only wild-life consisted of a few plants, some packed dirt, students, an enormous squirrel stalked by a cat wearing a warning bell, and an obviously amateur juggler who kept dropping the third orange.

"I called the hospital," Five said. "He's stable, whatever that means. Wish I could see him, but it's still only immediate family."

I nodded agreement. I eyed the remaining hoagie wistfully, but I wasn't going to be caught with cheese strings or shredded lettuce hanging out of my teeth.

"Too many of these kids are starved for family. We get so close that I start believing I am their blood relative, and it's a shock being reminded I'm not. Now Woody . . ." He shook his head and sighed. "That father of his . . . immediate family, sure, but not much of a parent. Drinks, ignores his son. The mother's dead. O.D.'d six years back. There are so many like him, needy, lonely children."

"Maybe by tonight he'll be able to have visitors. I'll call after school."

"If so, want to go together?"

"A deal," I said. We even shook. And as we did, I looked up to see my semijoined man and his prisoner returning.

Mackenzie looked peeved.

Tough.

"Well," Five said, with a glance at his watch. "I have to get going. Mandy, you'll let me know?"

I nodded.

"Good seeing you again, Crispin," he said to Mackenzie before he left.

"Crispin?" Lowell squeaked. "The guy doesn't even know your . . ." He stood awkwardly, eyes flicking over the two of us, then across the square, face oozing perspiration. "Well," he said in an overly enthusiastic voice, "if we've taken care of our business, Calvin, officer—Mister—if you don't need me, I have work to do before the afternoon session."

Apparently, Mackenzie was not going to slap him into leg irons, so Lowell, with one last frantic glance, waved goodbye.

"What did Mr. Slick want?" my semisignificant one asked.

"Funny, I never thought of Lowell as particularly—"

"Oh, Mandy." He sounded tired.

"Not a damned thing. He'd spoken to the hospital and he gave me an update. I'm sorry I let him borrow your piece of the bench. I'm sorry he makes you insecure. Bet you can't stand it that he can't be a suspect for last night's events because you and I are his alibi."

Mackenzie emitted a Southernized version of *hmmmph*!

"Hey, there," I said. "How about forgiving me for not treating your bench with proper reverence and tell me what's up with Lowell? Did he admit being here?"

Mackenzie nodded.

"Well? Why?"

"He forgot his Walkman."

"I don't get it."

"He came to retrieve his Walkman, then couldn't hear you call him because he was wearing it. Kind of dancing to it, too, as I recall."

"He came here at night for it? Why? He doesn't look like a jogger, and why would he deny he was here if that was it?"

Mackenzie sighed. "I can't tell you. He desperately doesn't want you to know this, prob'ly because you might call off the engagement—he practically told me you two are betrothed."

"Then surely I deserve to know."

"Surely, you do. To set your mind at ease, understand, I will divulge his dark secret for your ears only."

"I promise."

"Lowell's afraid of the dark, and night noises. Can't sleep. Truth is, the man is afraid of ever'thin' 'cept you, so he puts on the security system, slips a sleep mask over his eyes, then plugs himself in with his special music, and only then can he doze off."

"For real?"

"TV doesn't do it for him, nor do tapes of white noise, nor does a radio. Needs those earplugs to be safe. *Connected* is his word. And as of this summer, the tape has to be Barry Manilow."

"Not singing . . ."

He nodded. "Right. 'Mandy.' "

I felt personally ashamed to be, even if in name only, part of the ritual.

"Truly. An' even though he has a spare Walkman and an old pair of headphones, the Barry Manilow tape was erroneously taken to school yesterday along with papers he'd marked, an' in the confusion of the fire drill, he forgot to check for it before he went home. He was so agitated that he put on the headphones as soon as he retrieved the tape and therefore heard absolutely nothing—'cept Barry, of course—after that point."

"So now you know," Mackenzie said. "Jus' promise that if and when you break your engagement to the man, you make sure he doesn't think it's 'cause of anythin' I said. Be kind, you hear?"

Twenty-One

Iᴛ's either miraculous or horrifying to realize how quickly human beings regain their equilibrium. The worst happens, and if people don't throw in the towel and become catatonic, they carry on. Reorganize, regroup, and start again.

Which is why, I have to assume, my afternoon session was so much calmer and more *normal* than the morning had been. Of course, they were less directly affected, which always makes coping easier. Woody had been in the morning class, and most of these students probably didn't know him. Still, a major disaster had occurred in their school, to one of their own. But by afternoon the catastrophe in the gym was old news, a part of local history. There were no dramatic late-breaking developments. Woody was going to live. No further complications or horrors. Life and time and clichés march on. Even English class marches on.

We got through our four hours with as little awkwardness as possible, even during the necessary, but never-popular punctuation segment. I wrote the advice the oracle at Delphi had given an ancient Greek who was wondering whether he should fight in a battle:

Thou shalt go thou shalt return
never by war shalt thou perish.

"So he went," I said. "But he didn't come back. That Oracle was no good with commas. This should have read:

Thou shalt go, thou shalt return
never, by war shalt thou perish.

"Lack of comma sense killed him." I've scored a pedagogic touchdown when I see kids copying an example or exercise on which they'll never be tested.

The working portion of my day ended at about the same time that Mackenzie's reentry into employment began. We were back out of synch, and I already missed having him at the ready, there when I needed him, devoting his daily routine and all his energy to making my time at home pleasant and relaxing. Anxious for news of the outside world, a little depressed, but eager to please.

I'd had a gender-free retro housewife, and it was hard to give it up. No wonder so many men had been royally pissed since the Seventies.

I passed Aldis on the way down the back stairs. She looked at me with a cold, suspicious eye. I psychically frisked myself for guilt. She had that effect.

I had tried to be charitable for a long while now, but the woman gave me the creeps. The only attraction to teaching I could imagine for a chilly, single-minded woman like her would be the allure of control.

It has been my observation that it's next to impossible and downright heroic for a teacher to significantly improve a child's life, abilities, or mental health. But it's easy to use the bit of power you've got to injure that child, to do serious damage to growing egos. Our capacity to wound far exceeds our ability to do good, and "first do no harm" should be our motto as much as it is a physician's.

Aldis seemed likely to be a power monger sucking the joy from learning and leaving permanent scars in her wake.

I gave her a perfunctory nod. Once outside, we both slowed to look up at the slice of sky that showed between the buildings. Its earlier blue had turned sour, looked almost bruised and bloated. Rain skulked somewhere. Never trust the promise of a summer's day.

Aldis unlocked her car and removed an iron bar device from the steering wheel of her dinged, rusty red sedan. A city conveyance, kept in bad shape, below the standards of thieves.

My vehicle was due to be picked up in two hours, so I walked. What had Aldis been doing at school last night? I wanted to grill her under harsh police lights. Forget the bogus roll-book story, babe, and confess, I'd say. The third degree, whatever that was. I'd have to ask Mackenzie what the first and second degrees were.

On the other hand, I feared that this entire string of events was going to turn out to have been hideously ordinary. Nothing to confess, nothing provoking headlines. One gang killed a member of the other. The other struck back. The same story that ran last week and the week before. Use the boilerplate print. Just change the names of the victims and suspects. And what could be more depressing?

I should have suspected that Woody was in a gang, even if nobody mentioned it. It was too dangerous traveling solo in his world, and the only safety—albeit a shaky one—was in numbers. There were markers and monuments to dead children all over the city, and even as these dark images surged through my mind, I saw an example on a passing car. Its trunk had a white cross painted on it and the back window shelf had become a shrine with plastic flowers and a small crucifix. A driver grieving for someone close to him who was murdered, unnaturally dead.

The car, my thoughts, even the sighting of Aldis, left a bitter aftertaste. Going home to an empty house, a space absent of the immediate possibility of Mackenzie, felt purposeless and dismal.

The voice of my guardian nag piped up to ask whether I might deduce something from this reaction to Mackenzielessness. But what did she know? She sounded too much like my mother.

Mandy, call your mother! I had submerged Lowell's directive, forgotten that I was supposed to check in with Boca, to prove that I wasn't being held hostage. It still felt absurd to reassure her that something that had never even been suggested had, in truth, not happened. I hadn't been promoted or knighted or banished, either. Was I supposed to constantly call to catalogue things that had not happened to me? Hey, Mom—I haven't mutated or marinated or hallucinated today. Damn Lowell. It was too tempting to think of retaliation, of a public accusation of Barry Manilow dependency.

I trudged on. The humidity was like an overly affectionate, sweaty lover, refusing to let me out of its embrace. By the time I got home, I was slick and cranky.

My house wasn't precisely empty. Macavity, despite his fur coat, looked unfazed by either the heat or the humidity. "Hey buddy," I said. "I'm alone. Your hero is not here. What you got is she who provides your link in the food chain. Humor me." He yawned and stretched. I picked him up and planted one on his round forehead. He looked startled, then squirmed out of my hands and started furiously grooming himself.

"Right," I said. "I forgot. I didn't ask if you wanted to be kissed. I did not respect your boundaries, your otherness. You will probably take me to court for harassment, and I don't blame you." But I was just as bad as all the other rotters, because I winked at him, positive that he'd secretly enjoyed the nuzzle and guiltily aware that the next time I had an irresistible urge to kiss the cat, I would, no matter how he felt about it.

I was bucked up by the twinkle of my answering machine. Four messages. I felt loved, wanted. I pressed the rewind button and waited for life to expand and include grand surprises.

The first message was a desperately worried where-are-you-how-are-you post-Lowell cry from my mother's heart.

The second was a more puzzled, almost annoyed report that my mother had called the police, who, amazingly, had no record of anything like a hostage-taking happening, so where, then, was I?

By her third message she had regained enough equilibrium to remember where I most logically was, and she'd called the school. "The secretary wouldn't let me interrupt your class," she said, "so I asked her, 'Does that mean she's there, teaching?' and she was snippy. 'One must assume that, Mrs. Pepper,' she said. 'She went upstairs as did her students and none have come back down, so they are either there, or they've jumped out the window.' What kind of woman is that, Mandy? Anyway, I'm glad you're okay. I'm sorry I was so worried. Ignore my other messages."

The fourth message was also from Bea Pepper. It told me not to ignore the part of the previous messages that said to call my aging progenitors, because it was high time I did so, even if I wasn't being held by a masked gunman.

Good daughter that I am, I dialed my parents, although that is not completely accurate. I dialed my parent, since I can't remember when my father last lifted a receiver. He doesn't like phones and pretty much doesn't acknowledge that they exist. On the other hand, my mother more than compensates.

Multiply her four calls to me today by the aunts, cousins, and neighbors who had to be kept on ready-alert about all stages of my alleged disappearance, and you may understand why I nominate Mom as the long-distance vendors' poster girl. "Be like Bea. Live on the line." It makes a nice slogan.

The gods for once rewarded my good girl behavior. Nobody was home. I left my message. "Everything's fine, Mom. Except for Lowell, who has a few itsy-bitsy flaws. Like he's an hysteric.

217

And delusional. And obnoxious. And a pest. And afraid of the dark. And an alarmist. And he has bad taste in music, too."

Since I already had the phone in hand, I dialed the hospital again, and asked after Woody's condition. He had had microsurgery on both hands, I was told, and they were guardedly optimistic about the operation's success. Right now he was resting, and all his vital signs were stable. He was out of intensive care and could, indeed, have a limited number of visitors this evening.

I whooped and applauded. Woody hadn't paid with his life or his hands for April's misguided "escape."

Maybe we should stop teaching *Romeo and Juliet* to anyone under fifty. It was too adolescent and set a bad example, presented wretched ideas. April had cried at the ending, yet still adopted the tragic heroine's suicidal plan. It would work for *her*. Very like a teenager.

I could tell Woody she was fine and ease his mind. I was sure he wouldn't tell whoever it was that was menacing him or her, and I was positive his recovery would be quicker with the knowledge that he was guilty of nothing concerning her disappearance because she hadn't disappeared.

There was enough time to have something to eat before visiting Woody.

I lifted the phone again. "He's okay," I told Five. "Resting but alert. I'm so relieved! I'll aim for seven."

Woody was at University Hospital, which was not far from Five's apartment in Powelton Village, a semifunky collection of rambling Victorians near Penn's campus and hospital. I'd have my cleaned-up car back by then, so it made better geographical sense for me to pick Five up than the reverse, and with that decided, I hung up and, feeling cocky, walked over and again picked up Macavity and kissed that irresistible spot between his ears. And once again he gave me his yellow-eyed glare and squirmed out of my grasp.

"So sue me," I said.

THE CHEAP-AND-QUICK body shop had not done a great job. The car looked patched and makeshift. But you'd have to work

really hard to decipher the eights or the half swastika. I was glad
the light was so dim outside. It made my car look almost normal, even though it made finding Five's house difficult. His
neighborhood was poorly lit, the buildings not clearly num-
bered. Very Philadelphia.

The sky had lowered till its entirety sat on my car roof, con-
gested with incipient storm. Dusk felt like midnight. I cruised
his street until finally I thought I had it, a four-story shingled
and turreted building. He was apartment A, ground floor, which
was the only set of windows with lights on. But any hope of
spotting him at the window was squelched by curtains or shades
blocking every clear view. I honked twice anyway. Maybe he
would hear.

He didn't. No problem, then, except finding a parking space.

I circled his block and the next one twice, which produced no
result except to annoy the hell out of normal-speed drivers.
There are people who were probably always courteous about
hitching their horse and wagon in a previous life and who now
have good parking karma. I am not one of them. God knows
what parking sins I committed in past lives, because in this one
I am condemned to spot a space opening up one half second after someone else has executed a wild U-turn in order to cover it.

I almost always have to stifle an urge to solidly ram the good-
karma cars in their parking spots, which should earn me an even
worse parking karma in the next life.

For the third time I made my way toward the shingled house,
creeping down the street, certain that if I were very attentive,
something would open up at the last minute. I glided along, then
slid, as softly and slowly as if on ice skates, into the vicinity of
Bartholomew Dennison the Fifth's apartment. I'd have to double park and run up. One foot on the brake, I reached over and
relocated a bouquet from the passenger seat to the ledge in the
back that is only jokingly called a seat.

I had dithered over a gift. I'd thought of a book, but realized
that Woody had been operated on both hands and couldn't use
them for a while. I didn't want to provide unnecessary frustration. I would never presume to pick music for a teen, and so

flowers it was. Flowers for the young man hiding inside the glowering hostile student—a young man who just might be delighted—secretly—by being given something beautiful and perfumed.

I turned off the radio, doused the lights, put my hand on the car keys—and felt the door beside me yank open. Cold metal pressed on the side of my forehead.

"Get out," a voice growled. "Get out and leave the keys."

My hand froze. I couldn't believe it. I was in a university neighborhood, in front of a friend's house.

"Move it!" he shouted. "You want to be killed?"

Killed? What was wrong with him? What was wrong with me? I was paralyzed, sure there was something I should be doing— look at him so I could ID him, maybe? I turned my head, and screamed. A gorilla aimed a gun at my head.

The mask was terrifying, gorilla mouth half open, full of teeth. "I said *move it!*" he snarled.

Oh, and I should, I knew I should. *That* was what you were supposed to do—go along, don't annoy, don't build the tension. Wasn't that it? But instead of moving, which I couldn't, I screamed again. "You can't!" I heard myself insist stupidly. "This is *my* car!" sounding like a two-year-old fighting over toys. And then I remembered the H word. "Help!" I screamed. "Help! Help!" And my muscles regained their strength and I turned the key and tried to grab the gear shift and remembered that I hadn't released the brake so I reached with that hand, too—

That was close to the last thing I remember. That and the sound of my own voice, the feel of a large, gloved hand slapping mine away from the brake release, yanking my hair, pulling me sideways and hitting me—all in a split second while my scream was still in the air, hitting me again on the side of my head while my car sputtered and I felt the shock of the earth by the curb— hard on my shoulder and arm, even the tufts of grass—and then he hit me again.

And that was that. No flashing lights like in the comic books, no tweeting birds. Nothing, except deathlike darkness.

Twenty-Two

THE hand was on me again. On my shoulder. Behind me.
I screamed for help.

"I *am* help. Mandy, are you all right?"

I wasn't sure how to answer. What was I doing in a patch of weedy dirt by a curb, my head against a tree, my feet in the street?—and I felt damp, even wet, and terrified what that might mean. Blood? I took a deep breath and put my fingers to my cheeks, then looked at them. It was dark—how much time had passed? Then I heard thunder and noticed that the pavement was wet, that rain was falling, and felt a little calmer. I was hurt, confused, and wet, but not necessarily bloody.

Was that the same as being all right?

"I was afraid to move you, or leave you, but I'm going to go away for a second now and call nine-one-one. Okay? You understand what I'm saying?"

I tested my neck's ability to rotate, half expecting my head to fall off as a result. Something wasn't right with me. However, it wasn't my neck, which creaked and groaned but worked. Now I could see to whom the voice belonged. "Five!" I said. "What are you doing here?"

"I live here. You were picking me up, don't you remember? We were going to visit Woody in the hospital."

"What happened?"

"I hoped you could answer that. I heard honking, then somebody screaming, and when I came out to check, you were on the curb and you wouldn't answer me. Listen, I really should call the ambulance, so don't move and—"

"No." I was surprised at how sure I felt of this. I was positive that if I were seriously damaged, I'd have a sense of it at the core, know that my wiring was down, a feeling like that. But I felt only achy and bruised, superficially bashed, and I couldn't bear the idea of being handled by paramedics, being strapped on a gurney, any of it. "I'm fine," I said. "I don't feel up to visiting Woody, though. I think I'll just go home and take a warm bath." I was filthy, in addition to achy. The earth around me was slowly mixing itself to mud, and I was a smeared mess.

"You're not fine at all. You're bruised and you've been unconscious. Of course you can't visit the boy. You'd scare him to death. You obviously don't remember what happened."

I remembered all-encompassing, near-paralytic fear. I remembered hurting, and falling.

"That kind of amnesia means a concussion," he said. "And your face is scraped and about to turn the color of spoiled beef. I can't let you drive in this condition."

I understood his logic. But his words also produced a sharp-edged sliver of hazily remembered fear. "I drove here," I said. "They fixed my car." I listened to my own words, knowing they

222

were important, worth another experiment with head and neck motion. I felt a little more able to move this time, but the results were dismaying. *"My car!"* I cried out, understanding. "Where is it?"

He shrugged. "I thought maybe you'd parked it somewhere I couldn't see."

"They *took* it! They *stole* it!"

"Who are *they*?"

I shook my head. It wasn't a great idea. I was suddenly very aware of the shape of my eye sockets, and of a rare variety of headache—socketache—rimming them. "A gorilla took it!"

Five said nothing. I could practically feel his anxiety sky-rocket.

"Somebody in a gorilla mask, I mean."

His relief was audible, exhaled breath and something near a chuckle of released tension.

"I was coming to get you," I said, "and I opened the car door to get out and somebody—maybe several somebodies—hit me, and that's what I remember."

"You were carjacked."

Carjacked is such a modern-sounding, almost romantic con-cept. Echoes of the frontier, masked bandits—not gorilla masks, either—Wells Fargo bags of gold, stagecoaches, hooves pounding in the night.

Being jacked sounded a whole lot better than being robbed. My car had been jacked. Had I also been jacked? Was that what these bruises were called? Why *Jack*? Who was he?

Something dreadful had happened, and I was mulling seman-tics. Maybe I had suffered brain injury, after all.

"I'll drive you to the police," Five said. "After we visit the emergency room, and if they say it's okay."

I sputtered a protest. "I want to go home. Please. Now."

"Go home? Can you?"

I stared at him blankly, which probably didn't help the case for my mental okayhood. "Is this an existential surprise quiz? Or like Thomas Wolfe? As in I can't go home again? I'm too tired for literary—"

"Do you have a house key?" he asked in the long-suffering voice of a wet and tired good Samaritan.

"Sure. Why?" They had thrown my pocketbook out after me, and it lay in the dirt a few inches away. I groped for it, moving my head and body as little as possible. But before my fingertips made contact with the leather, I stopped trying. They'd taken my car, with the key still in the ignition. The key that was on a ring of all my keys, including the one to my front door. I felt still further violated. Robbed, jacked, battered, and locked out—while they, whoever they were, could get in and out of my home at will.

"Should I call a locksmith? Or a friend who has a spare?"

"I have a spare in the window box. In a little metal box in the dirt."

He nodded. "Okay, then."

"So I can go home?"

He shook his head. "Let a doctor look at you, take some X rays. I didn't think women played macho games like this—don't be a fool and run a risk like that. What if you're bleeding internally?"

That is how we wound up at our original destination—University Hospital—after all, but in the emergency room, not Woody's. Luckily, this was a different hospital and emergency room than I'd visited yesterday, although I was questioned about my scratched cheek and peculiar eyelashes. The E.R. doctor, a cute Malaysian with a great deal of energy and an indecipherable accent, cleaned my cuts and bumps, scanned and probed and looked through my skull via my eyes, her eyes, and a great sci-fi scanning machine. I tried not to think what portion of this high- and low-tech attention my insurance might pay because I already had several continguous headaches and I didn't need any more.

"She was unconscious," Five said.

The diminutive doctor nodded. "Finned hullbet."

What relevance had halibut, or any fish for that matter?

"Fainted!" Five finally said, his voice filled with the excitement of discovery. "Is that what you said? That she fainted?"

The doctor nodded vigorously. "Hull real bet. Scare."

Scared. I'd fainted when I was hurt real bad. Got it.

"Bet!" she said again, looking sternly at Five. "Real bet! Cheek bet, too."

"No," I said. "Like I said, the cheek happened . . . another time."

"Too much times!" She glared at him.

It took me a while to get it. "He had nothing to do with this!" I said. "He *rescued* me."

"Good," she said. Or maybe it was, "Like I really believe that. Another fool defending her abuser." But she declared that I was only superficially damaged and I could go home. Or that's what I think she said. Either that or she warned me that I only had a few minutes left to live and I might as well enjoy them in familiar surroundings. In either case, she let me leave, and she gave me a prescription for an enormous amount of painkillers. She was either setting me up as a drug dealer or assuming I was going to be around, feeling rotten, for a long time. Both options translated into having a future.

"You should get a second opinion," Five said when we were back in his car. "They shouldn't let doctors who can't speak English deal with the public. Injured people need to know what's going on. And who knows in what godforsaken rice paddy she was trained?"

"I got the message. I'm alive and likely to stay that way," I said. "That came over loud and clear. And she had to pass her boards here, didn't she?"

"I still don't think she knew what she was doing," he said huffily.

"Is that the sound of sexist horror? As in what could a girldoc possibly know?" I asked. Maybe it was ungrateful of me, given his TLC, but my knees—and their ability to jerk at the sound of a putdown—hadn't been injured at all. And the rest of me was too weak to stop them.

He gritted his teeth and drove on. Right to the police station.

"Now this is silly," I said. "Can't I call this one in? Don't they come to your house, like in the movies?"

225

"Old movies, I think," he said. "Besides, we're here. Get it over with. The sooner they know, the faster they can find it."

"It's a collector's car," I said sadly. "One of the most stolen models. I'll never see it again. And I just paid the body shop. In cash." But I nonetheless followed him in.

"Carjacked," Five said from behind me. "Assaulted, too. You can see."

"License number?" the policeman asked.

Oh, boy. I had always meant to learn it. I remembered a Z, and maybe a four. But I wasn't really sure of either. Words make sense. Numbers and isolated letters don't, didn't stick even in my preconcussed brain. I've thought of getting a vanity plate just so I could remember the thing, but I haven't gotten around to it yet. Much to my mortification, I had to dig through my wallet. I pulled out my driver's license, which didn't tell me what I wanted, and finally found my owner's registration card. "There," I said, pointing to my license number.

"You've had the car for how long?" Five asked as the cop filled in the form.

I tried to remember. It had been my brother-in-law's in an early phase of his devolution from an interesting young man to a staid suburban lawyer. So how long ago was that? My injured head resorted to my mother's no-numbers calculations. Had Sam sold it to me before my niece was born? Yes, because my sister was still working at Bloomingdale's, getting her employee's discount, and I bought a leather skirt through her just before I bought the car, which I remember, because of a guy I was dating then who . . . "Eight years, give or take a few," I finally said. "A while."

Five's rugged cowboy jaw dropped. "I told you that doctor was incompetent. You have brain damage. I don't mean to alarm you, but you need more tests."

"Scary when they lose parts of their minds," the cop said with a pink-cheeked joyful expression.

Sure, and his brain was probably clogged with the stats for every team throughout its history, the obscure sports records that flash across the screen. He'd know which left-handed player had the most four-yard gains since the Nixon Administration. And he'd think that was a proper—*normal*—use of intellectual storage space, and that he had every right to look at me as if I'd been administered a lobotomy by my muggers. But this didn't seem the time to say that I consider numerical jock-glop a serious collective aberration.

I thanked both of them for their concern—but I was not woman enough to admit the truth of what I had never known and how little I cared about not knowing it.

I wanted to go home, to rest on my frayed couch, do ordinary pleasurable things like hear the cat purr and harass him by kissing that place between his ears. To hold the intact parts of Mackenzie and he mine, and for both of us to be glad we were still alive and even had some working parts left. And to figure out what I was going to do about transportation from now on.

The merry policeman, so gleefully worried about my reduced mental capacities, didn't seem concerned about ever finding my car again. "Probably moving it out of state even as we speak," he said. "They'll change the serial number and advertise it as privately owned, and those babies move fast."

Melancholy filled me at the thought of never seeing my beloved wheels again. I needed whatever was left. My place, my belongings, my life.

The men, in some misguided show of chivalry, drilled me on whether I remembered my phone number (yes), my Social Security number (no), my birth date (yes), and my Philly Prep employee number (no! Why fill brain cells with things you can look up and check out?)—at which point I whimpered and said how much my cheekbones ached and how very, very tired I was.

They seemed to understand the irony of worrying about my brain's decline while the rest of me expired around it.

Five drove me home and found a parking space about a block away. I said I could make it on my own from here on, but he'd been schooled in Western gallantry and escorted me.

My unprepossessing rented sliver of a shelter looked wonderfully inviting, although when I rang, nobody answered. Not that anybody was expected to, but it would have been a comforting

227

surprise if the somebody had been back there by now. Even after I'd dug in the planter box—twice, because I'd forgotten which side was the hiding place—and found the spare key box and used it, not only was Mackenzie nowhere in sight, but he hadn't even remembered to leave a light on. I felt abandoned, and grateful for Five's presence. I flicked the switch next to the entry.

"Will anybody be with you, in case?" Five asked.

He hadn't given up on finding out my living arrangements. I was still mildly flattered by his interest. "The cat," I said, letting the game continue.

He stood in the doorway, about a foot away from me, looking unsure of himself. "Are you all set? Not apt to do anything crazy, like take a run or something? Have everything you need?"

"Yes," I said. "Stay a moment. I'll make tea. But please close the door. The cat occasionally bolts if he sees an opening." When I'd found Macavity, years back, he'd been dazed and mangled by an encounter with a fender, but he always acted as if given another round, the car would be the one to limp off.

It seemed that Mackenzie had been here, and had left a souvenir of his stay, or a trap—because I nearly fell over his crutches, propped against the side of the sofa with a note attached. How touching to be remembered. "Free at last," the note said. "Great God Almighty—give these to Tiny Tim! See you soon. Got news."

No mention of when *soon* might be. Was he actually going to work an entire shift his first day back? More likely he was out hanging with his homeboys, catching up on missed murders. I'd better get used to uncertainty as to his where and whenabouts.

"Maybe I'd be in the way," Five said, with a none-too-subtle glance at the crutches and then at his watch.

"Don't you want tea?" My painkillers had kicked in to the point where the throbbing was like distant, annoying drums and the pain an arm's length away. Also, my mouth was incredibly dry. As soon as it was back to normal, I'd find the words to properly thank Five. "Or something stronger? I'd better not, because of the pills."

"I'll pass." He checked his watch again. "I have to leave in a few minutes." He carefully stepped around the crutches—but not before he'd read the note—and settled in on the sofa after offering to make me the tea. I needed to prove my competence, or at least my ability to boil water. Macavity, who'd been warily observing from the middle of the staircase, descended and tentatively approached the visitor.

It was almost the domestic scene I'd envisioned, just with an understudy playing a key role. But that's how it often would be from now on with Mackenzie, whether or not I liked it.

And deciding whether or not I liked it took too much effort for this particular night.

The kettle puttered its way to the boil, the cat seemed to be giving me a grace period before begging for more food, and the answering machine light blinked. Three more messages. Mom was back on-line.

"Do you mind if I play this back?" I asked. "My mother was told that I'd been taken hostage, and we've been playing telephone tag. She's in Florida and will be going to sleep soon, so in case I have to return—"

"Of course, go ahead." Five and the cat were sizing each other up.

"I'm not going to mention tonight's episode if I do call her," I said. "Hope you don't consider that lying." I pushed the replay button.

It wasn't my mother, it was the elusive C. K. Mackenzie, trying to be less elusive. "Where are you?" he asked, although he must have realized I'd have to be right there, in the kitchen, in order to hear his question. Once again I experienced the odd Mackenzie-Five tension. Should I slam off the machine? What would that suggest? Or was leaving it on the ruder option? Meantime, I would love to know if and when Mackenzie was coming over.

"I'm celebratin' my regained mobility with some of the guys—one nonguy, too," his voice said. "Thought I'd catch you at home first and bring you along, but you aren't back, obviously, so listen, I don't know when we'll be finished here." I could hear loud laughter in the background, the chunk of glasses and distant music, too.

"So don't count on my showing up tonight, okay?"

There was my answer. I saw Five make note of that as well. I put down the teacup I was holding and leaned over, but by then Mackenzie's tone had changed. The message wasn't done.

"Mandy," he said, "here's the thing. Don't be angry, but yesterday, I asked the guys to see what they could find out about Mr. Slick."

Who? I couldn't connect. Look, my head had been pummeled earlier tonight, and its wiring was still a little loose, flopping around and heavily coated with drugs. But that was enough of this, anyway. Too long a message, not what I'd expected, and too much like eavesdropping on the part of Five, who had stood up and was looking mildly amused.

"Excuse me. Not my mother, and I'm being rude," I said. "Let me just—" I leaned toward the machine.

"No." Five smiled oddly and slowly shook his head. "I want to hear."

I filled with a slow-motion, dreamlike horror. "What do you mean? Why? What—"

"—and the short answer is," Mackenzie's voice said, "I was right. He's bad news. Extremely dangerous. Stay away from him, okay?"

"Enough," I said. I reached out to stop Mackenzie's voice, but Five's hand landed on mine.

"Let the man finish," he said in a soft but chilling voice.

"He's your basic right-wing, hate-monger proselytizer for nutcase neo-Nazis accused of already bombin' a synagogue—killed two people—an' burnin' a black preacher's house," Mackenzie said. "They have a paramilitary camp in central P.A., train kids to shoot—that kind of thing. He's the Johnny Appleseed of hate. Can't make anything stick so far, but he's been watched awhile now, since—"

"Please," I said. "Let's—"

Five smiled.

"—before he left Idaho."

I looked into the frigid eyes of the man across from me. "Surprise, surprise," he said with no emotion. "Surprise, surprise."

Twenty-Three

Outside, the rumbles and crackles of the storm moved closer, and the front window's curtains were briefly lit from behind.

Inside, the atmosphere was even more electrical and tense.

My visitor, a distracted and sickly smile pulling at his mouth, kept his hand clamped on mine, attentively listening to Mackenzie describe him as a pathologically crazed hate monger and killer. Talk about an awkward social situation.

And Mackenzie spoke on. "Woody's conscious again, an' it looks like what happened to him involves Slick, through his disciples. Obviously all set up before we conveniently provided alibis by bein' with him.

"Woody tried to quit them, and this was his punishment. Do not talk about any of this to anybody at school. Do not swap theories. Hope you get back from wherever you are—soon. Stay safe."

The call had come at eight P.M., when I was in the emergency room. A second call, again from Mackenzie, had come in at nine, just about when I was reporting the theft of my car to the police. "Where are you?" he asked again. "I'm gettin' worried." And a third call. "Me again. Hope you're havin' fun, wherever, whatever, but . . ." He left his sentence and the idea dangling at 9:37. Fourteen minutes ago.

And that was that. Except for the rangy man on the other side of the kitchen room divider, his hand clamped on mine. He seemed to notice what he was doing, and he surprised me by letting go.

"I'm sure there's some mistake," I said. "Some logical explanation. Besides, lots of people come from Idaho . . ."

Five sighed and shook his head. "I'm really sorry this had to happen to you."

"What?" I asked, not really wanting to hear his answer. The phrasing of his words reverberated inside me. I had heard it as an expression of sympathy before, in the letters my class wrote to Woody. More specifically, Tony's and Guy's letters. Woody's closest friends. Or maybe Woody's watch guards and Woody's centurions? Had they actually done that to him? Thought it *had* to happen to him?

"Sorry you had to hear that," Five said. "That your friend feels that way about my mission. He's wrong, you know. He twists things around to make us sound awful, but we're nothing more than patriots, good solid Americans, trying to make this a better place for him, too. Like it or not, this country was founded by revolutionaries, and revolutionaries will save it."

"Save it from what?"

"From pollution—disintegration—mongrelization. A complete

loss of identity. Look at us—look what we're becoming! We are murdering ourself, just the way John Adams said. He said there never was a democracy yet that didn't commit suicide."

"That's disgusting." How could the second president of the U.S. be so cynical? "That's wrong. We haven't."

"We *are*. That's what I'm trying to prevent."

"How are you saving anything? By doing—that—to Woody? How could that make anything better for anybody?"

"He needed a lesson."

"A final lesson? A fatal lesson?"

He shrugged. "Perhaps the lesson would be for the others. They needed an example of what happens to defectors. A chain is only as strong as its weakest link. Woody should never have gotten involved with that girl—I warned him. Her people—"

This was what Mackenzie had sensed last night. This was why he felt Five's questions were a sham. The concern hadn't been for the Truongs, but for himself, for Bartholomew Dennison the Fifth. Five had needed to find out what April's family knew about her disappearance and whether it included him, or Woody's affiliation. Her abduction had not been a part of his plan, not something he'd orchestrated, and what it meant or could mean must have driven him crazy. That was why he asked all the questions.

And Five had, of course, also been establishing an alibi by spending those hours—the Truongs, the drink, and if I'd been willing, something extra after the drink—with us while his boys did his dirty work.

"The boy was exceptionally promising." Five took long strides to the front window, then with another few steps returned to the divider. He punctuated his words by punching the palm of his right hand as he spoke. The cat watched him swivel and pace, back and forth, as if he were a one-man match at Wimbledon.

"He had a great future, a role in the big picture." Two punches by the left hand into the right. "He could have made a real difference." Five rigid paces to the window. Military about-face. "He *loved* me—I was his true father. I met him months ago, when I subbed at his school. He needed me. I guided him, explained the world to him. His friends loved him—they saved his life by eliminating Vo Van. He had it all—but she corrupted him, made him quit his *family*, made him betray his friends by leaving. I couldn't let that happen."

I felt as ill as if the venom in him were killing me. He looked at me with something like pity. I tried to readjust my vision of him. So handsome, clean-cut, charming, glib, and educated. So unlike my vision of foaming at the mouth, tattooed skinhead fanatics—and therefore much more terrifying and dangerous.

Lowell had been right. The face of evil didn't have to be grotesque. I had some prejudices of my own to get past. If I lived long enough to do so. About categorizing chinless whiners like Lowell and handsome charmers like Five.

"I wish you hadn't gotten yourself involved with what need not have concerned you," he said. "I know that nothing in that message was news to you. It's been obvious for a long time that you've been prying and assuming and meddling. Baiting me with suspicions about something going on in school. Asking if you could sit in on the noon group."

"But that was about *drugs*. Aldis thought the boys were using you—dealing drugs while you read or whatever."

"Drugs? My boys? I would never tolerate such a thing. My boys have to stay clean!"

"Crucifying somebody isn't clean."

He brushed my words away. "The point is, you've been playing games with me all along. Quizzing Woody, conspiring with the black woman."

"I wasn't—not any of those—Flora? Why did you do those things to her?"

"She brought it on herself. Who does she think she is? Wrote a letter to the paper and couldn't shut up in class about what she thought was going on. She was polluting them, lying to them."

"She was upset about the vandalism at the Jewish cemetery—then that was you, too, wasn't it?"

"Why do you care, Miss Pepper? Any ancestors buried there?"

"And my note. How did you get those copies of the school paper?"

"Come now. They aren't exactly kept in a vault."

"The church—the eighty-eight—that was you, too, wasn't it? Or not you, but your long arms, your disciples, doing your dirty work. And my car—the spray paint."

He smiled and stopped pacing.

"What sense does any of it make?"

He took on the demeanor of an earnest teacher, sharing a necessary lesson. "We are in terrible need of a cleansing. But change will only be the result of accumulated passion," he explained in a patient voice. "Placidity, contentment, leads nowhere, so it's necessary to stir things up, alert the populace, galvanize and generate emotions, create chaos, a vacuum into which order can then be brought. Which is not to be taken as an admission of any felonious act."

I could only shake my head with disgusted amazement. And then I looked at him with new fear. "You—the mugging tonight, the gorilla mask—did you . . . ?"

"Could anyone rational assume I had anything to do with it?"

What did rationality have to do with any of this? Still, he'd *rescued* me. Taken me to the hospital, to the police. But I had also been kept from getting to Woody, who could have told me who had nailed him to the backboard and why. So yes, his hands were again clean—healer's hands, in fact, but I was sure he'd had everything to do with it, through his boys. The octopus's tentacles, working for him. Very slick indeed. Hurt me, saved me—and now?

"What—What are you going to do now?" I forced myself to ask. "To . . . me?"

"What I've intended to do all evening. Leave you. Is the phone call worrying you? Don't. His delusions and even yours make no difference. Your bruises and wounds have been taken care of. We've reported the stolen car, so I'll be going now."

"You're leaving? Like that?"

"Is this an invitation to stay? I hardly think you're up to it tonight, and I was under the impression you aren't overly fond of me. And don't you already have one lover, Amanda?"

Why had he said that leaving was what he'd intended all evening? Why that peculiar phrasing?

"I have to go," he said softly.

I knew too much—and he knew that I knew. And he didn't seem to care a bit. I wasn't to be disciplined, or to become a lesson in his warped curriculum.

Then I thought I understood. If the police were already investigating him, he wouldn't want to hurt me—it'd be too obvious. I breathed a little more easily.

But not for long. It still didn't make sense to let me go on working with him, let me try and stop him from further noon sessions with his *boys*, to have him really face the American way—in prison, behind bars.

Unless he was going to run again. Tonight.

In which case he might as well do away with me.

The teakettle shrieked. I reached over and turned off the flame. My muscles, sore or not, twitched. I was geared for a fight or flight response, but he prompted neither. I was in a new kind of response—the flail.

I knew I was trapped, but I couldn't understand how, or which way was out.

"Goodbye," he said. He went to the door, opened it, and was halfway out within a second. Not one for long leave-takings. Then he turned back, his hand still on the knob. "I want you to know I am truly sorry all of this had to happen, because I thought I was going to like you a great deal."

"All of *what*? What had to happen?" By now even my eyebrows were tense, on hyperalert. He was faking it, he had to be—wasn't leaving at all. He wanted me to drop my guard and then he'd lunge, do something hideous. I slid open the kitchen drawer as quietly as I could and pulled out my most serious knife, holding it low, so he couldn't see it behind the divider, clutching its handle, hoping I could use it effectively on something besides chicken parts.

"It never needed to happen," he said, almost wearily. "If only you'd have . . ." He stood in the half-open door, the rain hissing

237

and pounding behind him, his big frame and handsome face romantically wistful, a film noir picture of a reluctant leave taker.

Behind him lightning cracked and thunder boomed with deafening proximity. The doorway turned white with electrical light—and in that instant I saw not only the dark outline of Bartholomew Dennison taking his leave, but of my cat—leaping in fright at the blast of noise and light, and in a directionless frenzy of feline fear, or simple lack of smarts, bolting out the door.

"No!" I shouted. "Macavity!" Still brandishing the knife, I ran after the cat—but Five stepped forward to stop me.

"*You can't!*" He reached for me. I swung the knife and felt it make contact. He grunted and swerved sideways, jumped out of the knife's arc, hitting one of the crutches. It thudded and clattered against the wall, knocking the other one loose, which flipped onto Five, who pitched forward head first onto and through the coffee table. The no-longer glass-topped coffee table, which shattered with amazing loudness as I raced out to my front steps.

"Macavity!" I shouted into the dark rain. Where was a bolt of lightning when I needed it? "Macavity!" I stood on the top step for a second, looking in both directions, and was granted my wish. The sky turned phosphorescent and I thought I saw a skinny, drowned thing across the street, running toward the far corner.

"Macavity!" I screamed, taking off in his direction.

And then into a blur of light and noise—from above and in front. I saw the headlights and heard the honk, but too late. Something gargantuan bumped my hip and I went down—again—onto the cobblestones. Cobblestones are even less welcoming than a grassy patch.

This was definitely not my night for cars. Or much else. The painkillers kept their troops where they were, so that I had a moment to fully experience this new insult to my body. And then—what was this? Somebody again calling to me? *Five?* How had he extricated himself from the broken glass and wrought iron and crutches and his own blood? *What did he want with me?* I raised my arm—it was one of my few still-functioning parts—and waved it, punched, did whatever one exhausted, abused arm could do.

"Manda f'Go'sake—Manda!"

I let my arm flop down. Five's voice box did not produce that musical mush.

He was hyperventilating. "Than' God goin' slow—saw this *thing* bolt from your—with a *knife*—whatsa *knife*—" The carving knife had landed on the opposite sidewalk. All I could think of for a moment was my mother's strict advice to never leave it wet because it would rust. And there it was on the street in the rain.

"Macavity!" I said. "He ran out! The door was open—Five—your message, C.K.—he heard it, and—but I have to—"

"Whoa! First of all, can you stand up?"

Ah, yes, there was that. Again. I could. I creaked, I inhaled sharply, I leaned on him a lot—the lame leading the dinged—but I could stand. This time it truly amazed me. I was going to have one sore rear end, I already knew, but maybe once again nothing had been broken. I could make money on the side doing testimonials for calcium pills.

"Your face!" he said, finally, through his anxiety and concern and the pouring dark rain, noticing the gauze square, the strips of tape. "M'God, what—" And he tailed off into complete incomprehensibility.

"Later," I said. "Macavity is—" And yet another helpfully timed bolt of lightning scared me to death, but illuminated my entire street, quaint cobblestones, hitching posts, neatly pointed bricks—and a wet slip of a cat cowering in the wrong doorway down the block. I hobbled in his direction and Mackenzie followed, caneless and limping seriously. "Please, puss," I said when we neared. I put my arms out. "Come on home, you silly creature." He mewled and looked at me—I thought with gratitude—but then he opted to be saved by the cop. Mackenzie shrugged and picked him up.

Then all of us—Mackenzie, the cat, and I—jumped at yet another deafening boom—but of a distinctive timbre, a different feel this time. Nothing celestial about it.

I could not bring myself to turn around and face its source. I heard Mackenzie's sharp intake of air. I saw him grapple with the cat, who once again wanted to bolt—and I couldn't blame him. The world was going mad. The only wrong thinking on the cat's part was that it was possible to escape.

"Mandy," Mackenzie said softly. "Your—my God, if you hadn't—Jesus, exploded—it's—"

Now, I didn't need to turn around, but I finally did.

My house was in flames. When a bolt of lightning lit the street, I could see glass on the sidewalk, what looked like window framing, remnants of a planter box full of petunias.

"Five," I said, too softly, perhaps, for Mackenzie to hear. In any case, he didn't react to the name, but instead nearly tossed the cat at me and pounded on the doorway near us, ringing the bell. "Call nine-one-one!" he shouted. "Fire!" He rang the bell next door as well, and then ran, limping, favoring his good leg, but quickly enough, to ring a third bell. Somebody was going to call in my fire. Meantime, C.K. had lurched across the street and was alerting my two neighbors to their personal danger.

I clutched Macavity and gaped. My little house. My all that I had ever accumulated. My all that was left. For a moment I felt I could not go on, and would not.

Five! I realized, envisioning his hitting the coffee table, lying there stunned while the house blew up around him. I'd killed him.

And then, with a great wave of nausea, I belatedly understood what had *had* to happen to me, why he'd needed so urgently to get out of my house—why he'd checked his watch so many times—and why he'd wanted me to stay there.

It would have worked so tidily, too, and again he'd be away from the scene and his hands clean. Except that he hadn't listened to me about keeping the door shut, and then he'd tried to stop me from going after my cat.

"You saved me," I whispered to Macavity, who was now under my wet shirt, sopping wet himself, but at least with the illusion of protection. That's all any of us needs, or gets.

But how—*when?*—had Five had the time or opportunity to

plant a bomb or whatever it had been? He'd been in my sight, in my living room, the whole time.

Of course. He'd told me how and when. He'd been playing a game when he asked me if I could go home again. Car thieves hadn't stolen my car. His *boys* had. They'd killed for him, crucified for him, so what was the big deal about roughing me up and taking the car? And my keys—all my keys. And while my good Samaritan showered attention on me, giving him the perfect alibi, his remote control arms and legs could unlock my front door and plant whatever they liked, and set a timer.

The fire company arrived with amazing alacrity. I heard the comforting whine of the siren and watched while Mackenzie limped double time to move his car and clear room.

It was too late to save anything. My house was gone. It was so small to start with, and now it was nothing. In one night I'd become homeless, carless, and hurt.

I wanted to weep for all the losses, but even more, for the ugliness and the ruination and the pure destructive stupidity of it. And for the knowledge that the end of Bartholomew Dennison the Fifth did not in any way mean the end of the epidemic of hate.

Then, amazingly, from beneath my blouse I heard, above and through the siren and the storm, a low, happy motor sound. The cat was contented. The cat was home.

And I realized that I was, too. Anything I had of true value was out here on the street with me and had been saved—life and love of the human and animal variety.

The rest was stuff. Stuff was replaceable.

For a thousand years before I personally learned it—compliments of maniacs blowing up my house—people have commented on the peculiar ways fate works. After fourteen months of thoroughly modern impasses—of dithering, of inventing reasons for and against, of weighing past experience against future probabilities, of resenting the realities of work schedules and even of the housing market, of thinking I'd think about it when I had the time—the issue of whether my relationship with Mackenzie would move on or die was resolved by a suave but insane racist.

"Don' want you livin' out of a shopping cart with newspapers over your head," Mackenzie said as we stood in the rain watching firemen toss a ruined, smoldering sofa and my best beloved suede chair out onto the street. "Let alone draggin' Macavity down with you."

Call it charity on his part, call it pragmatism on mine, call it whatever you like—we call it living together. And so far, I call it fine. Mackenzie—he calls it "fahn." And the groupie ingrate cat thinks the sunny loft is heaven.

We're testing the cop's theory of balancing the scale, adding a little bit of love as a counterweight to the hating all around us. It's not a bad way of making a difference.

My Mustang was found. After all, the thieves weren't pros at car disposal. They were too busy studying hate and bombs and tooling around on a joy ride. The insurance company felt sorry for me and assumed all of the pocks and scrapes were caused by the thieves. Car had a new paint job and has never looked better.

As for those thieves, Five's *boys*—they are on probation, being counseled and doing long stretches of community service, and I have hope for them. Tony, who admitted to shooting Vo Van, is awaiting trial along with his accomplice, Guy. April is still in New Jersey, and Woody in physical therapy. I try to stay in touch with both and not to think how uncomplicated and ordinary their story could have been. It was nothing more than an adolescent lover's triangle that would have been resolved by time, had not hatred and prejudice and wrongheaded theories been added to the equation.

On the home front, my accumulated bumps and cuts and bruises warranted the much-coveted sick leave. Do be careful what you ask for.

My little house didn't require much of a bomb to be totaled, but some of the third floor's contents were saved—my roll book, for example. And Miles's poem.

As for the loft, we're fixing the plumbing and electrical system. The For Sale sign is down, and the rent-a-room folk have retrieved C.K.'s cloying faux-Southwestern furniture. I have insurance money to buy replacements. Or my half of them. We're doing it slowly, picking items together, assigning each piece to one of us, against such a time as we no longer cohabit. But meantime, the purchase of each new pillow feels amazingly like an upholstered form of commitment. So far, neither of us has gagged on the concept.

We still have our own credit cards, our own checking accounts, and our basic conflicts.

We still have our unmatched suitcases at the ready—but on high shelves, difficult to reach.

Last week *Condé Nast Traveler* did a survey of friendly cities. They set up all sorts of tests for the citizenry, and once again the City of Brotherly Love scored highest. Beat out all the sweetness and light sites in the U.S.

So the most hostile city is simultaneously the most friendly. Fate and surveys work in mysterious ways.

About the Author

Gillian Roberts is the *nom de mystère* of novelist Judith Greber. Winner of the Anthony Award for Best First Mystery *(Caught Dead in Philadelphia)*, she is also the author of *Philly Stakes*; *I'd Rather Be in Philadelphia*; *With Friends Like These* ... ; and *How I Spent My Summer Vacation*. A former English teacher in Philadelphia, she now lives in Tiburon, California.